MURDER AT LAND'S END

SALLY RIGBY

Storm

Ebook ISBN: 978-1-80508-143-2
Paperback ISBN: 978-1-80508-145-6

Cover design: Lisa Horton
Cover images: Arcangel, Shutterstock

Published by Storm Publishing.
For further information, visit:
www.stormpublishing.co

ALSO BY SALLY RIGBY

A Cornwall Murder Mystery

The Lost Girls of Penzance

The Hidden Graves of St Ives

Cavendish & Walker Series

Deadly Games

Fatal Justice

Death Track

Lethal Secret

Last Breath

Final Verdict

Ritual Demise

Mortal Remains

Silent Graves

Kill Shot

Dark Secrets

Broken Screams

Death's Shadow

Buried Fear

Detective Sebastian Clifford Series

Web of Lies

Speak No Evil

Never Too Late

Hidden From Sight

Fear the Truth

Wake the Past

ONE

Detective Sergeant Matt Price leant against the edge of the kitchen units, watching his daughter, Dani. The toddler was giggling at some conspiracy with his mother, the pair of them engrossed in the chaos that came with preparing a family picnic. Today, being his day off, they'd decided to take a trip to the Eden Project, an old clay pit which had been converted into thirty acres of gardens. They'd been there many times, and each visit always managed to conjure up a magic that hadn't worn off, especially for Dani. His daughter, not quite three years old, totally adored the place, in particular the new outdoor adventure play area.

'Daddy, are you going to have the same as me in your sandwich?' Dani's innocent query broke his train of thought. She stood on the chair next to her grandma, her petite frame just about reaching the work top, her face masked in an adorably earnest expression.

He cast a dubious glance at the slices of bread covered in a fusion of peanut butter and Marmite. A grimace tugged at his lips as he envisaged the taste. 'Um... no thanks, sweetheart. I think I'll stick with my usual cheese and tomato. I'm not sure how you can eat that,' he said, trying to mask the twinge of nostalgia with a light chuckle as his mind went back to his late wife, Leigh.

It had been nine months since she'd died and yet the wounds felt as fresh as ever. Leigh loved peanut butter and Marmite sandwiches, a bizarre combination he'd never been able to appreciate. She would tease him, saying it was an acquired taste that he had yet to develop. But he couldn't bring himself to try it. When Dani had asked for it once it had taken him aback because he'd never told his daughter about her mum's strange preference. At the time he did mention that Leigh had also liked it, but it hadn't been discussed since.

'It's the best sandwich ever, isn't it, Grandma?' Dani's words, full of conviction, dragged him back to the present. His daughter's face was lit up with anticipation.

'Definitely, love. But not for me, either,' his mother replied, her voice seasoned with indulgence. She turned towards him, her eyes twinkling in amusement. 'Matthew, go and check on your father and make sure he's nearly ready. The last time I saw him, he was knee-deep in his sock drawer, hunting for his favourite pair. Why he has to wear them today, I really can't fathom.' A gentle shake of her head punctuated her remark, an expression of fond exasperation in her eyes.

'I'm on to it. We'll be leaving in fifteen minutes. Is that okay?' He wanted to go early to avoid the traffic.

'We've nearly finished, so yes.'

With a last glance at the organised chaos, Matt left the kitchen. The quaint terraced cottage they lived in was nestled in the heart of Penzance. After his father's retirement, his parents had bought the bolt-hole wanting to make it their base, while they travelled the world. But fate had a cruel way of twisting plans. Leigh's sudden demise in a car accident had changed everything.

In the wake of the tragedy, Matt and Dani had moved down

to join them and his parents were responsible for taking care of their granddaughter while he was at work. He was lucky that a job with the Devon and Cornwall Police, based in Penzance, had come available. He enjoyed his job and it stopped him from dwelling too much on the past. The smaller, less busy station of Penzance was a blessing in disguise, offering him pockets of precious time with Dani, moments that he guarded fiercely. Although, having said that, they'd had several difficult and demanding cases to deal with since his arrival.

His foot was poised on the first step of the stairs when the shrill ring of his phone sliced through the silence. Fishing it out of his pocket, his brow furrowed when he saw the caller ID. It was his boss, Detective Inspector Lauren Pengelly. What could she possibly want on his day off?

A rhetorical question.

He feared the worst.

Lauren was a workaholic and expected one hundred percent commitment from her team. Having said that, she knew his situation and was mindful of his need to spend as much time with Dani as he could.

'Good morning, ma'am,' he greeted, attempting to sound more cheerful than he felt.

'Are you up, Matt?' Lauren asked, diving straight into business.

'Of course, ma'am. It's half-past seven, which is practically afternoon when you live with a toddler. We've been preparing for a day out at the Eden Project. My mum and Dani are making enough sandwiches for an army, as we speak.'

There was a pause. 'I'm so sorry to disrupt your plans... but I need you today. A young woman has been found dead on the rocks at Land's End. I want you to meet me there.'

His heart plummeted. What on earth was he going to tell Dani? She'd been talking non-stop about their trip for days.

He let out an exasperated sigh. 'Surely you don't need me

for a drowning, ma'am? It's not like they're uncommon around here.' Matt crossed his fingers, hoping that his boss might rethink her need for having him there.

'I'm really sorry, Matt. I know how you value your time off with Dani, but I need you on this. From what I've heard, this might not be a regular drowning. Days off for everyone have been cancelled – it's not just you,' Lauren said, a slight softening creeping into her tone. 'And… please apologise to Dani for me. Once this case is over, I promise to make it up to her. We'll sort out a time when she can play with Tia and Ben. You can come around to my place and we'll go to the park together.'

Lauren, for all her professional steel, had a soft spot for Dani. The two had shared an affectionate bond ever since Dani was kidnapped. And his daughter totally adored Lauren's Border Collies.

'Dani will hold you to that, ma'am,' Matt responded, an amused grin easing his worried features. 'I'll head out to Land's End as soon as possible.'

With a sigh of resignation, he ended the call and returned to the humming frenzy of the kitchen. He wasn't looking forward to breaking the news to Dani and his mum.

'Did you manage to extract your dad from his sock quest?' his mum asked, glancing up from the sandwich she was diligently wrapping in clingfilm.

'I didn't get that far,' he confessed, raking a hand through his hair. 'Lauren called and—'

'Don't tell me. You've got to go into work?' his mum interrupted, the lines around her eyes tightening. 'I can tell from your face. For goodness' sake, I thought the whole point in moving here was because it wasn't as demanding as your last job.' She shook her head in frustration.

He locked eyes with her over the top of Dani's head. If his mum protested it would only encourage his daughter to do the same.

His mum pulled a face and mouthed sorry. She'd clearly spoken without thinking.

'Daddy, you can't go to work. We're going out!' Dani declared, her tiny features crumpling into a frown. Her bottom lip began to quiver, and tears sparkled dangerously in her eyes, threatening to spill over.

'It's Daddy's job, love,' his mum said, ruffling the youngster's hair. 'But that doesn't mean we won't have fun.'

'I'm really sorry, sweetheart,' Matt said, guilt coursing through him. He walked over to where his daughter was standing. 'Lauren needs my help with a case. She wanted me to tell you she's really sorry and she's promised that once it's all over, we can go out with Tia and Ben. Is that okay?'

Dani took a moment to process this, her face thoughtful. After a few seconds she broke into a small smile. 'When will the case end, Daddy? Can I go to Lauren's tomorrow to play with the dogs?'

'I can't promise when it's going to be, but it's unlikely to be tomorrow,' Matt replied, trying to balance honesty with a comforting tone. 'The good news is, you're all still going to the Eden Project. I want you to take lots of photos on Grandma's phone and show them to me when I get home. Then it will be like I went with you and I won't mind missing out.'

Dani's face brightened at this idea. 'Okay. Grandma, can I have ice cream when we're there?'

'Of course, love. Now, let's get a move on and get this picnic packed. I'll have to tell Grandpa that he's going to be driving us now.' His mother turned to Matt. 'Would you like to take your sandwich with you? In case you don't get a chance to buy anything later.'

Matt chuckled under his breath. Despite everything, his mother's instinct to treat him like he was still her little boy was heartening. He accepted her concern gratefully, acknowledging quietly how instrumental his parents had been to his survival.

Without their love and support, he didn't know how he would've kept his world from spiralling into darkness.

'Don't worry about me, Mum. I'm sure I'll manage to grab a bite during the day,' he said.

He glanced at the pile of cupcakes that were sitting, invitingly, on the counter. They were the product of a lively baking session between Dani and his mother yesterday in preparation of the picnic. Unable to resist the temptation, he reached over and took one.

'Daddy, you're not supposed to eat that now. We made them for later,' Dani protested, pretending to be cross.

'Alright, alright, I'll save it for later.' He pulled a comically forlorn face, feigning disappointment, and reached over for a paper bag and popped it inside. 'Think of poor old me, slaving away at work while you lot are having all the fun.'

His exaggerated sadness prompted laughter from both Dani and his mother, lightening the mood considerably.

'Take a cake for Lauren,' Dani suggested, reaching across the counter to select the cupcake that was decorated with the most sugar sprinkles. She handed it over to Matt, a serious expression on her face as she delegated to him this important task. 'This is my favourite one.'

'I'm sure she'll love it,' he said, placing Dani's selected treat next to his own in the bag.

He reached for his jacket and keys, glanced at the bustling kitchen, and reluctantly walked out of the door. He loved his job, truly he did, but the love he held for his family was on an entirely different level. And as he stepped out into the crisp morning air, guilt washed over him. Leaving them behind on a day meant for shared laughter and memories was a blow that hit harder than he cared to admit.

TWO

As Matt's car drew to a halt in the Land's End car park, he surveyed the scene before him. The cliffs stood defiantly against the crashing waves, their jagged edges shaped by centuries of battling with the Atlantic Ocean and their crevices offering shelter to the variety of sea birds to be found in the area. This ruggedness was offset by an array of colour which was splashed across the cliffside, from the emerald green of hardy shrubs to the vibrant hues of wildflowers that clung to the rocky soil and were dotted along the landscape.

The car park where he'd stopped served as a busy hub for the hotel and small retail outlets and food establishments that operated in the area. Often being considered the southernmost point of the UK, Land's End was a thriving area of tourism, attracting hundreds and thousands of visitors each year.

Matt sighed. It was going to be a logistical nightmare if the scene was to be kept secure and away from prying eyes, twenty-four-seven. He got out of his car and glanced over at the cordoned-off section overlooking the rocks, dreading what he was to be greeted with when he finally got to the scene. A knot of apprehension pulled in his gut. But he pushed his thoughts to the back of his mind, allowing his detective instincts to take over.

Lauren's car drew up beside him and he watched her emerge from her vehicle, the Cornish sea breeze whipping the short tendrils of hair around her face. She absentmindedly tucked some strands behind her ear, all the time the expression on her face remaining serious.

'Sorry about dragging you away from your day out with the family, Matt,' Lauren said once she'd reached him, the apologetic tone implying that she really meant it. He appreciated her concern, even if it wasn't going to change the situation.

'No problem, ma'am. Perks of the job.' He shrugged, giving a dry smile.

'It could simply be a drowning but as we don't know for sure, it's important that you're here with me.'

'I totally understand and Dani was fine when she knew that you'd invited her to play with Ben and Tia soon,' Matt responded, the image of Dani's sparkling eyes as she spoke of her upcoming playdate coming to the forefront of his mind. 'Although I suspect she'll be asking me every day, more than once, when that's going to be. You know first-hand how persistent she can be.'

'I do indeed. That's what makes her so delightful. You can promise her that we'll arrange something as soon as we possibly can.' Lauren's eyes mellowed as she spoke. 'But obviously it depends on what happens here and how the case progresses.'

'Of course. I'll explain it all to her. Oh... I almost forgot. She asked me to give you one of the little cupcakes that she'd baked with her grandma for our trip today. It's in the car, with mine. We can eat them later – or not, if cupcakes covered to within an inch of their lives in sugar sprinkles aren't your thing,' he added, grinning.

'That's incredibly sweet of her. Please tell her thank you from me. I'm sure it will be delicious and I can't wait to eat it.'

Matt smiled to himself at Lauren's reaction. He loved witnessing that side of her. She didn't show it often.

'Well, I can't guarantee what it's going to taste like, but she did send you her favourite out of all of those they'd made. So you're very honoured and clearly popular with her.'

'The feeling's mutual, I can assure you. Now let's get moving so we can see what we're faced with down there.' Lauren pulled a face as she took off in the direction of PC French, who was standing beside the entrance to the cordoned-off area, a tablet in his hand.

Matt followed and soon caught up with her until they were walking side by side.

'Good morning, Rick, what can you tell us?' Matt asked once they'd reached him.

'Sarge. Ma'am,' the constable said, acknowledging their presence. 'The body on the rocks was found by a Lexi Lomax, who works at the hotel, as a receptionist. When she arrived for work, she went for her usual morning walk along the front before her shift started and it was then that she spotted it. She phoned 999 immediately and was told to wait for us to arrive. PC Smith and I were on duty and were here within fifteen minutes. When we got here we spoke to her and then Smith and I climbed down the rocks to take a closer look.' He motioned in the direction of the rocks below.

'Describe what you saw,' Lauren said.

'The body is a young woman with a fishing line coiled tightly around her neck. Something appeared off but I couldn't quite put my finger on it. Smith agreed with me. It just didn't seem like our usual drowning, and we've both seen plenty of those in our time. That's what we said when we phoned it in. But... then again, we could be wrong. You'll have to judge for yourselves.'

As French spoke, Matt felt the edges of his stomach tighten as thoughts of what he might be faced with swirled around his mind. He watched as Lauren moved closer to the edge of the cordon, her sharp eyes scanning the scene below. He should do the same but for the moment he was happy to leave it to his boss.

'I take it the pathologist hasn't arrived yet,' Lauren said, as she took another step closer to the edge and peered down to the rocks, sheltering her eyes with her hand to give her a better view.

'No, ma'am, but I've been informed that he's on his way,' PC French said.

'Good. Now, where's the woman who found the body?' Lauren asked, turning and scanning the area. 'I assume she hasn't gone home?'

'No, ma'am. We wouldn't allow that to happen. But I did let her go into the hotel so she could start work. I explained that you'd want to interview her once you'd arrived. I hope that's okay, ma'am. It seemed pointless having her wait, when she could be inside in the warm rather than freezing out here. Someone should tell the weather that it's meant to be summer.' He glanced up to the sky, as if hoping his words would be heeded.

'That's perfectly fine. Thank you, French. Stay here and make sure no one attempts to get through the cordon. I can see that already people are trying to check out what's going on. Bloody rubberneckers.' Lauren nodded towards a small crowd of people who had gathered outside the ice cream shop and were pointing at them. 'Come on, Matt. We'll climb down and investigate.'

'Yes, ma'am,' Matt said, trying to hide his reticence, which he assumed he'd succeeded in doing considering that Lauren didn't pass comment.

After signing the crime scene log, they carefully made their way down the rocks, managing not to slip, until they were standing adjacent to where the lifeless body of the young woman was lying. Her denim skirt, short-sleeved pink shirt, and long dark hair, which was splayed out on the rock, painted a macabre image that turned his stomach.

Matt swallowed hard and averted his eyes. But not before noticing that the body was blue, probably from cold, and that the woman's eyes were open and staring blankly upwards.

Was he going to vomit?

He sincerely hoped not. Especially not in front of Lauren, even if she was aware of his issues.

'Come on, Matt. There's no blood. What's the problem?' Lauren said, her light chuckle offering a momentary respite from the awful situation they were facing.

Her comment was a surprise because she wasn't usually one for cracking jokes. He smiled back – or was it a grimace? He really wasn't sure.

'I still keep thinking about having some hypnotherapy sessions to cure me of my aversion to dead bodies but... well you know what it's like. When I'm not actually faced with one I tend to forget about it,' he said, voicing his thoughts to Lauren.

'And as I've said in the past, it's definitely something you should consider in the future. But for now you're going to have to deal with it. So best foot forward and all that.' Lauren returned to examining the body. 'PC French was right, for sure. The body doesn't have the same appearance as our usual drownings. It's too...' She broke off for a moment. 'I suppose the best way of explaining it is: it's too staged. See the almost deliberate way the fishing line is wrapped tightly around her neck and nowhere else. And her clothes seem remarkably unruffled. Are these things likely to happen if a body has been floating around in the ocean for any length of time?'

Matt stole a quick look at the body. 'Yes, ma'am. I get what you mean.'

'We'll discuss it with Henry once he arrives. Which should be soon, I hope. If this death is suspicious we need to get cracking on first identifying her and then finding possible culprits.'

Matt glanced up to the edge of the cordon and in the distance caught sight of the pathologist marching along the front, swinging his bag, his heavy gait recognisable.

'We don't have to wait long, ma'am, because I can see him heading in our direction. He shouldn't be long.'

Matt waved at the pathologist and he responded by waving back.

'Good. Let's hope we can identify the girl straight away so we can inform her next of kin. Although there doesn't appear to be a bag with her.'

'She might have a phone in her pocket or something else that will help, like a driving licence,' Matt suggested.

'Fingers crossed. After we've had a chat with Henry and have some initial conclusions from him regarding the death, we'll visit the hotel and interview Lexi Lomax.'

'Will he be prepared to let you know his early thoughts?' Matt asked, remembering how the pathologist at Lenchester, Dr Claire Dexter, was at a crime scene. She kept everything close to her chest and rarely could be drawn on the circumstances leading to a suspicious death.

'Of course, why wouldn't he?' She glanced at him, arching an eyebrow. 'Don't tell me... it wasn't like that in Lenchester.'

'My lips are sealed,' Matt said, giving a shrug.

When he'd first arrived at Penzance, Lauren had given him a hard time for comparing the two forces, even though he hadn't done it often, and he'd been careful not to do so again. At least not out loud. But now he had a better relationship with Lauren, he suspected that her words were said in a more light-hearted way.

'That tells me everything,' Lauren said, giving a small smile as they stood side by side, watching Henry while he slowly clambered down the rocks. 'Although I'm not going to pursue that further. Changing the subject, Lexi Lomax is an interesting name, don't you think? It sounds like someone from a superhero film.'

Matt glanced at her, his eyebrows raised slightly in surprise.

'I didn't know you were into films like that, ma'am,' he said, taken aback by the revelation. The dogs, cycling, and knitting were all he had known about what she did away from work. Then again, they hadn't actually discussed film and telly preferences.

'You don't know everything about me, Sergeant,' she replied with a teasing lilt.

'No, ma'am.'

He liked the fact that she'd shared that with him. She certainly wouldn't have been so open when he'd first arrived. It gave him a sense of belonging. Leigh would no doubt approve of Lauren and her capacity for hard work. Especially now that Lauren seemed to be using a lighter touch with the team, which he believed was in part down to him. Leigh had often told him he should change career and become a mediator. She believed he had an innate talent for the job. But he'd never leave the police. Apart from being with Dani, there was nothing that he enjoyed doing more.

THREE

Lauren stared out at the vast ocean in front of her. The waves were lapping in and spraying over the rocks but fortunately the tide was sufficiently out for it not to have covered the body. She glanced at Matt, who was looking anywhere but at the body, and she smiled to herself. When he'd first arrived, she thought his aversion to anything relating to death to be a nuisance and couldn't believe that a police officer could operate like that, let alone make it to being a sergeant. But now she understood and accepted it as being part of who he was. It wasn't as if he shied away from doing the work, it was simply that he found certain aspects of it hard and she admired him for facing up to it. Plenty of officers she'd worked with in the past would have given up, but Matt wasn't like that at all. He was right that hypnotherapy could be the answer to his issue, not that she'd known anyone who'd had it. She certainly hadn't. Thank goodness. But she knew that it was an effective solution for many issues.

She diverted her thoughts to the present as the pathologist climbed down the rocks towards them.

'Good morning, Henry. How are you?' she asked, heading

over to the older man, who was breathing heavily from the exertion and was bending over slightly.

'Not too bad, thank you,' Henry said, standing upright and acknowledging Lauren. 'Could be better I suppose. Being dragged out so early in the day isn't my idea of fun. I received the call right in the middle of my breakfast. Bacon, sausage and eggs.' He sighed. 'But not to worry. The dog enjoyed it.' He chuckled. 'Anyway, I'm here now. Let's get cracking. What can you tell me?'

For all of his bluffness, Henry was an excellent forensic pathologist. One of the best Lauren had come across. What made him particularly useful was that he wasn't precious about his findings. He was happy to share his conclusions straight away because he was conscious of their need to know as soon as possible.

'Nothing other than the body was found on the rocks. We've been to the scene and already believe the death might be suspicious because there's a fishing line wrapped tightly around her neck.'

'That's not unheard of in a case of drowning. It's easy for a body to get caught up in loose line, of which there is much in the ocean,' Henry said, frowning.

'Yes, but this wasn't haphazard. It was too neatly placed. But obviously you know better than us. See what you think. Our main concern now is to identify the body, so next of kin can be informed and we can start on our investigation. If you can first check to see if there's any identification on her, then we'll leave you to get on with it.'

Henry stepped cautiously from their rock onto the next. He was wearing heavy, thick-soled walking boots to stop himself from slipping. After placing his well-worn bag on the ground he crouched down and, with his gloved hands, began searching the body. He also appeared to be taking stock of what was in front of him.

'Hmmm,' he muttered, glancing up at Lauren and Matt, who were standing close by. 'I can definitely see what you mean about this death being suspicious because of the positioning of the fishing line. Informally, I can tell you that it's not the only glaringly obvious suspicious thing.'

Lauren's heart thumped. This was an exact example of why she approved of Henry. He was direct and to the point, holding nothing back.

'What have you spotted, Henry?' Lauren asked, exchanging a quick glance with Matt, who also appeared excited at the prospect of already learning more.

'Marks on the neck which are incongruent with drowning, and it appears that the body has been moved post mortem because of the lividity.' He turned back to the body and slid his hand into the jacket pocket. 'Here's a small purse. I'll photograph it and then you can take it away.'

Lauren observed Henry taking several photos from different angles. He then handed her the small orange wallet-purse. Inside she found a debit card, coffee shop card with only one stamp to go, a driving licence and some money amounting to sixty-five pounds and thirty-five pence. So obviously robbery wasn't the motive. She pulled out the driving licence and read the details.

'Okay, we've got an identification,' she said turning to Matt. 'The victim's name is Sophie Bethany Yates and she's aged twenty-three.' She held the licence up so she could compare the photo with the dead woman's face. It was definitely the same person. 'Yes, that's her. No mistake.'

'I have her phone here too,' Henry called out. 'It was in the back pocket of her skirt.'

'Thanks, Henry,' Lauren said, taking it from him and putting it into an evidence bag alongside the purse. 'We're going to interview the person who found the body and will wait to hear from you regarding actual cause of death.'

'I doubt it will be before tomorrow. One of the technicians is on holiday and we're a bit backlogged. But I'll make this a priority. The main thing is that I, too, believe the death is suspicious and you can get cracking with that in mind.'

'Thanks, Henry.' She turned to Matt. 'You'll be glad to know we're leaving here. We're going to visit Lexi Lomax to find out exactly what she saw.'

They scrambled up the rocks until they were on firmer land and made their way to the cordon, where PC French was still standing ensuring no one could get past. There were plenty of people hanging around and before Lauren and Matt had time to make their way to the hotel, a reporter who Lauren recognised, but couldn't remember her name, made a beeline for them.

'Another drowning, DI Pengelly?' the reporter asked, holding out her phone for Lauren to comment.

Lauren sucked in a breath. She knew they had a job to do but the media was always such a pain in the arse. Unless they could help them, of course. But that wasn't often.

'You know I can't tell you anything at the moment. Not until we have a better idea from the pathologist and we have identified the victim. Out of respect for their family I'm sure you'll now leave us alone to do our job.' She tried to sound neutral but she couldn't help but let some of her annoyance show.

'As I'm sure you're aware, the public are anxious to know what's going on. And that's my job,' the journalist, a woman in her late twenties who worked for the local paper, said, standing her ground.

The woman wasn't prepared to leave Lauren and Matt alone. Talk about persistent.

'Yes, I appreciate that,' Lauren said, peering down at the journalist, who stood at least six inches shorter than her. 'And you must appreciate that we have work to do. I'm sorry, but we really do have to go. We'll be holding a press conference when we have anything to report and your employer will be informed when it's to take place.'

Lauren marched off with Matt trailing behind and they walked around the hotel, a large, imposing whitewashed stone building that dated back to the late eighteen hundreds, and overlooked the ocean. Once they reached the front entrance, they headed through the double doors, and Lauren was immediately hit by the warmth from the central heating. It seemed ridiculous that heating had to be turned on in June, but that was the nature of Land's End. In fact, Cornwall as a whole.

Sitting at the reception desk was a young woman in her early twenties, with long blonde highlighted hair hanging below her shoulders.

'Are you the police?' the receptionist asked, smiling in their direction.

'Yes, I'm DI Pengelly and this is DS Price,' Lauren said, holding out her warrant card. 'We'd like to speak to Lexi Lomax.'

'That's me. We can talk in the bar area; there's no one in there at the moment,' Lexi said, rising from her chair and walking around the desk to join them.

'Are you able to leave the front desk?' Matt asked.

'Yes. The phone will switch to the answerphone if it isn't answered.'

Lauren and Matt followed Lexi through to the back and into a small area where there were many small round tables, with easy chairs around them. Lexi appeared rather unfazed by having found a body, which puzzled Lauren. Most people when faced with something like that were disturbed. Or was it because she already knew something about it? If she did, she wouldn't be the first person to report the death of someone whom they themselves had killed.

'Have you worked here long?' Lauren asked, once they were seated close to the fireplace.

'I've only been here a few weeks. I'm at uni and this is my summer job. I started here after my exams were over.'

'Judging by your accent you're not from around here,' Lauren said, unable to place exactly where the woman came from, other than somewhere much further north.

'That's right. I'm from Derbyshire and working in Cornwall until mid-September when I go back to Durham Uni.'

'What's your subject?' Matt asked.

'Medicine. I'm in my fourth year.'

'Ahh. That will explain why you don't seem overly concerned by having seen a dead body on the rocks,' Lauren said.

The girl blushed slightly. 'It's not that I wasn't concerned. Of course I was. And obviously it was a shock. But in the past one of my holiday jobs was working at a funeral home and helping to prepare the bodies. I've seen plenty and the sight of them doesn't turn my stomach like it did at first. I'm sort of immune to it.'

Lauren glanced at Matt. Was he wishing he could be the same? She imagined he would be.

'I understand. Please could you walk us through the time leading up to when you found the body.'

Lauren leant back in her chair to help put Lexi at ease. Despite being used to seeing bodies, speaking to the police could be an issue for people, putting them on guard for no reason.

'Before work each morning I like to have a walk along the front to enjoy the view. This morning was no different, except I spotted something on the rocks which I couldn't quite make out. I climbed down a little way and then saw it was a woman who was clearly dead. I immediately phoned 999 and the woman who answered asked me to wait there until the police arrived, which I did. I explained everything to the officers who came and they said I could go to work.'

'Was there anyone else around at the time you found the body?' Lauren asked.

'It was only six-thirty and it doesn't tend to get busy until later. There were only a few people walking, and I remember noticing a couple of cyclists.'

'Was there anyone else looking in the direction of the body? Maybe someone acting suspiciously?' Matt asked.

'No. Should there have been? I just thought the woman had drowned. That perhaps she'd gone out swimming and had been taken away with the current and ended up here. We do get a few drownings around in this area, don't we?'

'We do,' Lauren said, agreeing. 'But we don't know what happened to our victim on the rocks until the pathologist has done his investigation. Did you recognise her?'

'No. She definitely isn't staying at the hotel, nor does she work here. But that's all I can tell you, as I'm not a local.'

'What hours do you work?'

'I'm full time, and for the last two weeks I've been doing the early shift so I start at seven when the reception opens and finish at three. Although that does depend on whether they're short staffed. If they are then I do extra shifts. I can do with the money.'

'You must see a lot of people hanging around here, going to the shops, and doing all the touristy things,' Lauren said.

'Yes, we have hundreds of thousands of visitors each year.'

'Have you noticed anything suspicious around here recently? Anything out of the ordinary?'

Lexi seemed to think for a moment. 'No, sorry. It's been the usual. Busy.'

'Okay, thank you very much for your assistance. I don't think there is anything else that we need at this time but we may wish to speak to you again once our investigation is underway.'

FOUR

Matt followed Lauren into the team office, his mind already churning with the dark undercurrents of the new case. The room was filled with the clatter of keyboards and the low sound of conversation.

They walked to the front and stood next to the whiteboard, its surface stark white, ready for them to start covering it with details of the case which was no doubt going to be the focus of their time for many days.

'Can I have everyone's attention, please,' Lauren asked, cutting through the noise.

Matt scanned the room as one by one the team stopped what they were doing and turned to face her.

'Is it the body at Land's End?' Billy called out, his tone tinged with the kind of excitement that only came from being relatively new on the force and having not been beaten down by the horrors they often faced.

Matt's jaw tightened. This wasn't just another body. This was someone's life that had ended. Someone's daughter, perhaps someone's sister. Maybe someone's partner. The reality of it hit him and he fought to keep his face impassive.

'Yes. How do you know about that? None of you were here when the call came in,' Lauren said, an edge to her voice.

Billy shrugged. 'I was speaking to the sergeant on the front desk and he mentioned that there had been one found. Another drowning, I suppose,' he said, rolling his eyes. 'Honestly, when will they learn that we're not living beside an indoor swimming pool. It's extremely dangerous out there.'

The words were flippant, yet Matt knew Billy was affected by it, too. It was a coping mechanism, a way to distance themselves from the stark horror of their work. But it never truly helped, not for Matt.

'At the moment it appears that the death is suspicious. The body was found on the rocks opposite Land's End Hotel with a fishing line wrapped tightly around her neck.'

Matt's mind went back to the scene. The lonely rocks, the waves crashing as if oblivious to what had happened. The image was haunting, the details clinging to him like a ghost.

'What makes you think it's suspicious? There's loads of fishing line in the ocean so that wouldn't be the reason,' Clem said, with a hint of scepticism.

'It was the way the line had been positioned and other indicators that the pathologist mentioned, including the fact that the body had most likely been placed there post mortem. But we've got to wait for him to get back to us with confirmation, which most likely won't be today. In the meantime, we need to research the victim. We have an identification from her driving licence. She's Sophie Bethany Yates, aged twenty-three. Tamsin, find contact details for her next of kin so we can inform them.'

'Yes, ma'am, I'm onto it,' Tamsin said, smiling.

Matt scanned the room, meeting the eyes of his colleagues, seeing in them a shared determination.

'I'll start checking Sophie's background,' Clem said. 'Maybe there's something there that can lead us to why this has happened to her.'

'Good, we need to act quickly,' Lauren said, her eyes filled with resolve. 'This isn't just another case; this is someone's life that was taken away. We owe it to her and her family to find the truth.'

The room fell into a focused silence, each member of the team lost in their thoughts, absorbing the importance of their new task.

Matt turned to the whiteboard, marker in hand, and wrote Sophie's name. Her life, her story, was now part of their lives and he felt a renewed sense of purpose.

They would find the truth. They had to.

Matt scanned the room, looking in turn at each of his team-mates. Since he'd been there, he'd witnessed a marked change in their attitude towards the DI. They seemed much more tolerant and accepting of her as a person. A sense of unity, however fragile, was building.

No longer was he witnessing the rolled eyes, the furtive glances between Billy and Tamsin when they thought no one could see. It was good because it meant the team was more cohesive, a single unit working toward the same goal. It was a nicer place to work because of it, for all of them, and Matt couldn't help but feel a surge of pride at how far they'd come.

His thoughts were interrupted as Billy's voice pulled him back to the present. 'Shall I start digging into her social media?' he asked, already reaching for his keyboard.

'Yes, please,' Lauren said, her tone efficient. 'I took a photo of the driving licence before sending it to forensics, and I'll forward that to you so that you can see her photograph. The rest of you get on with what else you're working on. Jenna, what do you have on today?'

Jenna straightened in her chair. 'I'm still investigating the washing-line thief in Heamoor. I'm planning to question some of the neighbours and check their house cams if any have them. I want to see if we can spot someone sneaking around. From what I've been told so far, and the times when it happens, I think it's schoolchildren daring each other, but we need to catch them in the act.'

'And that's it, folks. The phantom knicker thief is the worst case we have to deal with at the moment,' Billy said, laughing. His eyes sparkled with mischief, and the others joined in, the laughter a release of tension, a momentary reprieve from the gravity of the other case.

'Unless this death does turn out to be suspicious, which it most likely will,' Jenna reminded them. 'Then we're faced with a murder investigation.'

'Yeah, well, it would still be nice to have something to get our teeth into. Things can get boring round here,' Billy said. 'Although, having said that, we have had more exciting cases since you joined us, Sarge.'

'Don't blame that on me,' Matt said, holding up his hands in mock surrender. 'I didn't bring them with me.'

'I'm not complaining. It's much more interesting than having to deal with graffiti and stolen knickers all the time.'

'Well, Billy, if you want something exciting then I suggest you move to a big city. I'll be more than happy to write your reference,' Lauren said, her eyes twinkling. Her tone was light-hearted, a playful jab that held no real sting.

The others laughed, and Matt found himself smiling as well. The laughter was more because of the good nature of the comment, not the content itself. The camaraderie in the room was palpable, a shared understanding that let them find humour even in the face of joyless work.

'I can certainly tell you all the statistics of murders in the big cities if you want to know,' Clem added, with the serious-ness that had earned him the nickname 'Clemipedia' from Billy.

'No, it's okay. I want to stay here for the moment,' Billy said, his face turning a shade redder and his eyes darting around the room.

'Why have you gone red?' Clem asked, his tone filled with curiosity rather than malice.

'I'll tell you,' Tamsin said, with a conspiratorial smile. 'It's because he's met someone, and now he doesn't want to leave her. So even if he does moan about being here and the type of cases we have, he's staying.'

Billy's blush deepened, and the room erupted into teasing laughter. Matt couldn't help but feel a warmth for his team-mates, a connection that had grown over the time since he'd been working there.

'I told you that in confidence,' Billy said, staring directly at Tamsin.

'No... you told me that when you'd had one too many the other night when we went out for a drink,' Tamsin countered. 'Not once did you tell me it was a secret, or you know I wouldn't have said anything.'

'So, why were you keeping it quiet?' Jenna asked, with amusement. 'Because we'd really like to meet her sometime.'

Matt watched Billy, seeing the embarrassment but also the happiness in his eyes.

'Um... well...' His voice fell away and he glanced down at his desk.

'Okay, team. Leave teasing Billy for now; we need to get on,' Lauren said, her tone firm but not unkind.

'But once the case is over he's fair game,' Tamsin added, smirking. 'It's about time we had the chance of getting our own back.'

'I'll second that,' Clem said.

The room settled and the hilarity faded as they all returned to their work. But the moment lingered in Matt's mind, a snapshot of what the team had now become.

Lauren's phone rang, the sharp trill cutting through the

busy hum of the office. 'Pengelly,' she said, answering it with her usual assertiveness.

Matt watched her closely, noticing the slight tilt of her head as she listened. After a few seconds the expression on her face froze, and her eyes widened a fraction. Whatever was being said by the person on the other end of the phone, it was enough to make his usually unflappable boss falter.

'Okay, I'll be down straight away,' she said, sounding concerned.

Matt's stomach tightened. 'Is everything okay, ma'am?' he asked, unable to hide his worry. Something was off. Her whole manner had shifted. Gone was her relaxed stance. She was as tense as they came.

Lauren seemed to hesitate, her eyes meeting Matt's for a fleeting moment before she looked away. 'Yes, it's fine,' she said, giving a dismissive wave of her hand. 'Nothing to worry about. Right, everyone carry on. Matt, when I get back, you and I will visit the victim's next-of-kin once Tamsin has the details.'

She turned and left through the main office door, her departure so swift that Matt was left staring at the empty doorway. She hadn't even gone back through her office which is what she usually did when she went anywhere, to pick up her phone or her jacket.

Matt glanced around the room. The rest of the team were staring directly at him. It was as if they all sensed that something was wrong but no one dared to speak it aloud. Matt's mind whirred, piecing together the fragments of what he'd just witnessed. Lauren's reaction to the voice on the phone. Her abrupt departure from the office. Her attempt to brush it off as nothing. It was odd and totally out of character, and that was putting it mildly.

'Come on, you lot,' he said to the team. 'Let's get cracking. Whatever's going on with the DI, it's nothing to do with us.'

Okay, so he didn't actually say outright there was something odd going on with the DI but considering they were all thinking it, he didn't think it did any harm pointing it out.

'Okay, Sarge,' Clem said.

'Thank you. Because she won't be happy if she returns and finds us having done nothing in her absence other than debate what had called her away.'

Matt headed back to his desk, pushing aside the nagging feeling that Lauren might be facing something bad. He hoped it wasn't the death of someone close. He knew first-hand how much that changed everything.

But until she came back and she explained what had happened, it was pointless trying to guess. They had a death to deal with and that was more important for everyone involved.

FIVE

'What the hell,' Lauren muttered to herself, a whirlwind of emotion swirling within her as she strode down the corridor, her heels clicking rhythmically against the floor. Her mind raced.

Her aunt, Julia Cave, was in reception asking for her. Why? What did she want?

You could have knocked Lauren over with a feather when the desk sergeant had told her who was visiting. As far as Lauren was aware, none of her family had known she worked in Penzance, and she'd been there for two years.

Lauren had a different surname from the rest of them and over the years had carefully built herself a separate life. One that was so far apart from that of her family that no one would have guessed they'd come from the same gene pool.

Roy, her uncle, and two cousins, Connor and Clint, were serial lawbreakers, who had found themselves on the wrong side of the law time and time again. Prison sentences were nothing new to them, and Lauren had as good as disowned them. In fact, if it hadn't been for her aunt Julia, her mum's sister, then she would have.

All Lauren ever did regarding contact was to send a

Christmas card each year. It was a token gesture, in a way just to let them know she was still alive. She was glad not to have anything to do with them, her uncle in particular. The mere thought of him sent a shiver down her spine, causing unwelcome memories to resurface. Memories she liked to keep hidden.

He'd made her life a misery when she was young. His harsh words and cruel indifference to her feelings had shaped her in ways she was still coming to terms with. When she was sobbing at her parents' funeral, he was nasty, telling her to stop being a baby or she wouldn't be welcome in their house.

So, she'd learnt to hide her emotions, to bury her vulnerability beneath a facade of strength and determination. It was thanks to him, in a twisted way, that she'd developed into the person she was now.

As she neared reception, her heart pounded in her chest. What could her aunt possibly want? Why was she here? What did it mean?

A thousand questions swirled in her mind, but she pushed them aside, steeling herself for what lay ahead. She was DI Lauren Pengelly, a woman who faced challenges head-on, who didn't back down and who didn't let her past define her.

But as she stepped into reception, and she caught sight of her aunt standing by the door, uncertainty coursed through her. Lauren couldn't even remember how many years it had been since they'd met in person.

Julia appeared uncomfortable and out of place in the stark setting of the station. Lauren's insides clenched as she took in how much her aunt's formerly blonde hair had greyed, and deep worry lines now framed her face. But Julia's familiar smile still lit up when she saw Lauren heading towards her.

As Lauren approached her aunt, she smiled back. She might not want to be a part of the family because of her uncle and cousins, but her aunt had always been kind and treated her well. 'Hello, Auntie Julia, what can I do for you?'

'I'm sorry to bother you here at work, duck, but I'm at my wits' end.'

Lauren frowned. What could be so important that it couldn't wait? Whatever it was, the look in her aunt's eyes meant it was serious. The woman was afraid.

'I'm really busy at the moment with work so can only spare five minutes. Shall we talk outside?' Lauren said, firmer than she'd intended and making it sound like an order, not a question.

'Yes, of course. I'm sorry.'

Lauren ushered her aunt out of the police station, and around the back where they couldn't be seen.

'How did you know I was here?' Lauren asked.

'I saw you on the telly ages ago. It was a press conference. But I figured you wouldn't want to see us and that's why I didn't tell anyone or come to see you,' her aunt said, her voice trembling.

'I've been busy,' Lauren responded, wanting to defend herself for not contacting her aunt, yet not sure why.

'It's okay,' Julia said, resting her hand on Lauren's arm. 'I know you can't mix with the likes of us. Not with your job. I wouldn't be here if I hadn't been totally desperate. It's the boys...'

A hollow laugh threatened to escape Lauren's lips. What a surprise. Her cousins, Connor and Clint, were nothing but trouble. But something in her aunt's face made her hold her tongue.

'Yes, I guessed it might be them. What have they done this time?' She gave a frustrated sigh, annoyed that even in their forties, her cousins could still cause such trouble for their mother. 'You do realise that they're adults. You shouldn't have to come to their rescue all of the time. Or they'll never learn.'

Her aunt's eyes filled with tears, and something in Lauren's chest tightened. Was this more than the usual mess they found themselves in? More than a petty crime? She shuddered at the thought.

'They've got themselves in big trouble and need money. And not the sort that I can help them with.' Julia's words were punctuated by desperation and fear.

A surge of conflicting emotions coursed through Lauren. Anger, frustration, worry. She forced herself to take a deep breath, determined to sound neutral. 'You shouldn't have to, Aunt Julia. My advice to you is to let them deal with it themselves. They're grown men, and they have to face the consequences of their actions. It will do them some good. You're not going to be around forever, are you?'

Her words were firm, but inside, doubt gnawed at her. This was different. Her aunt's face was pale and her eyes were filled with a terror that Lauren hadn't seen before.

'Yeah. I get what you're saying. I know I've been too soft on them in the past and that's why they've turned out like they have.'

'No. It's not your fault. Uncle Roy had a lot to do with it. You mustn't blame yourself.'

Lauren said the words to placate her aunt, but in truth she did believe that Julia was in part to blame. She'd let the boys get away with way too much when they were young. If she'd have been stronger they might have turned out differently. Then again, it wasn't Lauren's place to apportion blame.

'This is different, Lauren. It's very serious. They could end up dead.'

Lauren's heart skipped a beat at those words. Dead? A chill crept down her spine as she searched her aunt's eyes, looking for any sign that this might be an exaggeration. But all she saw was fear. Was she surprised? In a way, no.

'Tell me exactly what they've done and I'll see if there's anything that can fix it,' Lauren said, hoping to soothe her aunt.

Aunt Julia wrung her hands anxiously, her eyes darting around the car park as if afraid they were being watched. 'They'd planned to burgle a mansion on the outskirts of St Austell because they'd heard rumours the owners had a stash of cash and coins,' she whispered. 'But the night they went, a gang who work for Bill and Bernie Frame had put together an operation to steal some valuable pieces of art. When the boys broke in they triggered the alarm, and it meant the gang couldn't carry out their raid.' She took in a shaky breath. 'They found out about Connor and Clint and came to them demanding fifty thousand pounds as a down payment, and then after that they wanted regular payments of five thousand a month.' Her voice dropped even lower. 'They threatened to kill them.'

Lauren's stomach dropped. The Frame brothers were notorious criminals who controlled much of the underworld in Devon and Cornwall, despite their legitimate construction business front. If Connor and Clint were on their bad side, they could be in real danger. Her aunt's worry might be well founded.

'So the Frame brothers actually visited Connor and Clint themselves?'

Aunt Julia shook her head quickly. 'No, of course not. They sent their men.'

Lauren's mind raced. 'How do you know the Frames are behind this?'

'It's what the boys told me,' Julia said nervously, wringing her hands even harder now. 'They're really scared, Lauren.'

Lauren stared intently at her aunt. 'Do the boys know you're here asking for help?'

'Of course not,' Aunt Julia exclaimed, her eyes wide. 'I've already told you that.'

'I hope you didn't entertain paying because you know it wouldn't end there.'

'I thought about getting another job but we'd never be able to give them even five thousand, let alone the fifty they want.'

'What did Uncle Roy say?' Lauren asked, her mind spinning at the implication behind this. It wasn't good.

'He thinks they should get the money from somewhere and pay them off. But I said to him: where will they get it from? If they try and borrow it, they'll only end up in trouble for not being able to pay it back. Roy reckons they could steal it.'

Of course he did.

A cold, hard truth settled over Lauren. She had no choice but to help.

'You mustn't let that happen. No money is to change hands. There's got to be another way of dealing with this. Leave it with me, and I'll see if I can come up with something. Stall the boys for now.'

'I'll try... but...' Her aunt's words fell away.

'What?' Lauren asked.

'Whatever you decide,' Aunt Julia said, with trepidation. 'The Frame brothers mustn't know that I've come to the police because otherwise... we'll all be for it.'

'Don't worry, Auntie Julia. I'll make sure that you're safe. Leave it with me, and I'll be in touch. I mean it. We're working on a big case at the moment so it won't be immediate. Were the boys given a deadline?'

'They've got until the end of the month. That's twenty more days. Please, Lauren, if you can help...'

Lauren stared at her aunt, not knowing what to think. The woman had gone through so much with her husband and kids, and yet still was prepared to look after Lauren. That's why Lauren still had a soft spot for her mum's sister because without her she'd have ended up in care after her parents had died in the car accident.

'I'll get back to you when I can. I promise.'

Julia's visit had brought up complicated feelings for Lauren.

As she watched her aunt leave, Lauren's thoughts went to how the past and present had unexpectedly come together. There were clearly problems that needed to be dealt with, but the way forward wasn't obvious.

Lauren wanted to help Julia, both for her aunt's sake and for her own peace of mind. But she'd need to be careful not to make the situation worse. Her mind turned to practical next steps as she headed back into the police station. She had a lot to consider when figuring out how to best provide support for her family while not affecting her own position in the force.

SIX

Lauren shook her head in an attempt to pull herself together before she returned to the team office. But the situation still played on her mind. How could her cousins be so stupid? Actually, she knew exactly how: because they were as dumb as shit. But to get themselves in that sort of trouble was ridiculous even for them. She needed a plan, but for now she had other things to deal with.

She stopped at her office for a few seconds to calm herself down and was about to go back to the main room when she saw Matt heading in her direction. She opened her door and marched forward to meet him.

'Sophie's next of kin are her parents and they live here in Penzance, ma'am,' Matt said grimly. 'I hate this part of the job. They're going to be devastated.'

'Yes, I know. And there's no easy way to deliver the news. We'll go now and take my car.' She glanced at the rest of the team. 'Is everything okay in here?'

'Yes. I've asked Billy to check all CCTV cameras leading to Land's End to see if we can work out the exact time the body was brought to the scene. There might be a vehicle heading there and back that we can spot.'

'Assuming she came by car or van,' Lauren said.

'There are no cameras facing the ocean, so if it was by boat then we've got no chance. Although, surely a boat wouldn't be able to get so close to the rocks,' Matt said, frowning.

'Henry might have something that will help us,' she said.

They left the room together and walked in silence until reaching the car park. Lauren took a sideways glance at Matt, only to see him staring at her, but he quickly averted his eyes.

Was he going to ask her why she'd taken off so quickly and what it was all about?

She hoped not.

Once they were inside her car with their seatbelts buckled, Matt turned to her, appearing worried. 'Is everything alright, ma'am?'

'Yes, why?' Lauren responded, a bit too quickly, her eyes darting away. It was obvious that she was trying to evade the issue. Opening up wasn't an option. Not yet.

'Because something's on your mind and, judging from your demeanour, it happened when you were called to reception. Is there anything you'd like to share with me?' Matt asked, his tone gentle but not insistent.

'It's nothing to do with work,' she said, brushing off his concern with a flip of her hand, her mind a jumble of clashing feelings.

'That wasn't what I was asking. Is there anything I can help you with or anything you want to talk through? You know I'll keep it confidential.' Matt's tone was earnest, his eyes sincere.

Lauren started the engine and drove out of the car park and into the traffic, her hands gripping the steering wheel. Should she trust Matt enough to let him into the secret? Once she'd told him, then he'd know all about her past. But would that really matter? Sometimes it was useful to have someone to share things with... Did it have to be Matt? Would that affect their working relationship?

So many different thoughts were careering through her head but, on balance, she decided maybe she should tell him.

She dragged in a long breath. 'There is something and yes it's personal, and no one knows. So if I hear that it's got out, it could only have come from you.'

Matt's expression was serious and his palms were raised in a calming gesture. 'Ma'am, you know you can always confide in me. No matter what it is, I'm here to listen and support you.' He exuded a quiet confidence. She could rely on him.

'Thanks. The thing is, I have relations in the area who... let's say... skirt on the wrong side of the law. Well, more than skirt. They live on the other side of Cornwall at Bodmin, and I didn't even think they knew I was here. My aunt came to see me because my cousins are in trouble, yet again, and she needs my help. They're messing with the Frame brothers.' She glanced at Matt to see his reaction.

'I don't know anything about these men,' he said, appearing confused.

'You'd certainly know of them if you were from these parts. They're famous... or should that be infamous,' Lauren said wryly.

'Are you going to help your family?'

'I don't know. They want money, which I won't give them. But maybe I can help without breaking the law or jeopardising my job. Not that I've worked out how, yet.'

'Well, if you need anything from me, just say the word.'

Lauren gave him a small, grateful smile. She was glad to have someone like Matt on her side.

'Thanks, I appreciate it.' Her voice broke slightly, but she quickly pulled herself together. 'Right, it's time to put this to the back of our minds because we have to inform Sophie's parents that their daughter is dead. And that never gets any easier no matter how many times you have to do it.'

Her words hung heavily in the car, a sombre reminder of the harsh reality they faced. Lauren realised that she'd made the right decision in confiding in Matt, and she felt a newfound strength as they continued on their journey. They drove in silence the rest of the way, and when they arrived at the parents' detached cottage, she took a moment to collect herself before stepping out of the car.

They walked up the path and rang the bell. The door was opened by a man who looked to be in his late fifties, his eyes curious.

'Hello?'

'Are you Mr Yates?' Lauren asked, forcing herself to sound composed, despite her nerves.

'Yes, why?' he asked warily.

'I'm Detective Inspector Pengelly and this is Detective Sergeant Price. We're from Penzance CID,' Lauren said, softly, holding out her warrant card. 'May we come in, please?'

'What's it about?'

'Is your wife here?' Lauren asked, avoiding answering the man's question.

'Yes, she's working. We both work from home.'

Lauren breathed a sigh of relief. At least both of the parents were there, and they didn't have to call them away from their workplaces.

'We'd like to speak to you both please.'

'What's it about?'

'Please, Mr Yates,' Lauren said, taking a step forward.

He moved to the side, his eyes slightly glazed. 'It's Sophie, isn't it? She didn't come home last night. We thought she might be staying with a friend or her boyfriend, but she didn't, did she?' His voice cracked, a hint of despair creeping in.

He turned and headed into the house, not waiting for

Lauren to reply, and they followed him down the hall into a room, which was set up like an office. A woman sat behind her computer.

'Mrs Yates?' Lauren said.

'It's the police, Eileen,' her husband said.

'What is it?' the woman said, colour draining from her face. She rose from the chair and walked around the desk until she was standing next to them.

'Shall we all sit down?' Lauren asked, pointing to the small coffee table and three chairs that were in the far corner of the room.

The couple did as they were told, their movements slow and mechanical, their faces drawn and anxious.

'Mr and Mrs Yates,' Lauren began gently. 'I'm so very sorry to have to tell you this, but a young woman who we believe to be Sophie was found this morning on the rocks at Land's End.'

'What do you mean found?' Mr Yates asked, the colour draining from his face. 'Is she okay?'

Lauren's insides clenched at having to deliver the tragic news. 'No, I'm afraid she's dead. We are so deeply sorry for your loss.'

Mr Yates stared at Lauren and Matt, disbelief etched on his pale, shocked face.

'Our Sophie? Dead?' he croaked out, tears welling in his eyes. 'How... how could this happen?'

Lauren sucked in a breath. 'We don't know the exact cause yet. But we're treating it as suspicious and investigating fully.'

'No,' Mrs Yates cried. 'Not our baby girl. This can't be real...' She dissolved into gut-wrenching sobs.

Lauren felt tears prick her own eyes. Having to shatter this family's world was the hardest part of her job. She continued explaining the identification process, each word like a knife twisting into the couples already broken hearts.

Mr and Mrs Yates were silent, stunned by the devastating

news they'd received. Their world had been shattered in an instant upon hearing that their daughter had died. Lauren's heart ached for them as they sat there, utterly consumed by grief. She knew the pain of such a tragic loss was unfathomable. Having to relay the terrible news was hard, even though it was part of her duty. It was a stark reminder of how fragile life could be. All she could do now was give Mr and Mrs Yates time and space to begin coping with their immeasurable sorrow.

'I'll arrange for our family liaison officer to stay with you and keep you updated with the investigation,' Lauren said kindly. 'I know this is very difficult, but we need to ask some questions about Sophie, if you're up to it.'

'Yes, that's okay,' Mr Yates said, sounding detached as if he was acting on autopilot, his mind grappling with the incomprehensible. Beside him, Mrs Yates stared blankly ahead, absent-mindedly twisting a tissue between her fingers.

'What was Sophie like?' Lauren asked softly, knowing that no question would be easy for them.

Mr Yates's eyes brimmed with tears. 'She was lovely. So kind. So thoughtful.'

'Everyone liked her,' Mrs Yates said, dabbing at her eyes.

'Where did she work?'

'She was an accounts clerk in Penzance.'

'Did Sophie have a partner?'

'Samuel Finch,' Mrs Yates whispered. 'We thought maybe she was with him when she didn't come home last night...' She brought a trembling hand to her mouth, shaking her head.

'Had she been seeing him long?'

'Quite a while,' Mrs Yates said.

'And what about friends?' Lauren asked.

'Her best friend is Imogen Halford, who works at The Seaside Inn.' Mrs Yates's voice cracked. 'I don't get it. Why would anyone want to harm Sophie. She's a lovely girl.'

Mr Yates rested an arm around his wife's shoulders.

'We'll need to speak to Samuel and Imogen but first, is it possible to see Sophie's room?' Lauren asked.

Mr Yates moved to stand but Lauren held out her hand to stop him. 'You stay here with your wife. Just point us in the right direction.'

Mr Yates sank back down, his shoulders slumped in defeat. 'It's upstairs, the second door on the left,' he murmured tonelessly, staring down at his clasped hands as a tear rolled down his cheek.

Lauren and Matt left the room and headed up the stairs. Stepping into Sophie's bedroom was like intruding into a private sanctuary. Photos and postcards lined the walls, chronicling friendships and travels. A stuffed animal collection was carefully arranged on a chair in the corner.

Lauren opened the wardrobe door, revealing neatly hung tops and dresses, while Matt checked the chest of drawers containing folded jeans and T-shirts, all perfectly organised. A jewellery box stood on the dressing table full of earrings, bracelets, and necklaces. And next to it an open makeup bag, hairbrush and hand mirror. It was as if Sophie had only just got herself ready for a night out.

'What's this?'

Lauren turned to see Matt pulling out a box from under the bed. He took off the lid.

'Bloody hell, look at all this fishing stuff,' he said, holding up the box crammed full of books, hooks and more so Lauren could see inside. 'Why on earth does she have it?'

Lauren frowned thoughtfully. 'We'll have to ask the parents.' Turning away, she spotted a laptop on the floor and picked it up. 'I'll send this to forensics to see if there's anything useful on it. Come on, let's head back downstairs.'

Mr and Mrs Yates sat motionless in the lounge, their faces ashen.

'Did you find anything helpful up there?' Mr Yates asked dully.

'A box full of fishing paraphernalia. Was Sophie keen on angling?'

Mrs Yates appeared baffled. 'Fishing? She was interested years back. Even talked about working in the industry. But we told her it wasn't a proper career. That's why she went and got her qualifications in bookkeeping instead. She eventually wanted to become a chartered accountant and had planned on training through distance learning.'

'I've got Sophie's laptop,' Lauren said, holding up the evidence bag. 'I want to take it to the station to see if there is anything on there that might help us. We'll return it after.'

'Yes, okay,' Mr Yates said.

'Here's my card,' Lauren said, handing it to the man. 'Please contact me if you need anything at all. And let the family liaison officer know when you're ready to come to the morgue to identify Sophie.'

At the mention of having to identify her daughter's body, Mrs Yates let out a broken sob. It was a raw, choked sound of bottomless grief. Mr Yates quickly wrapped his arms around his wife, his own eyes filling with anguish as she wept into his shoulder.

Lauren's heart ached for them. 'We are so very sorry,' she offered, hating that her words sounded like platitudes with nothing behind them, because that wasn't her intent. She genuinely meant it. 'We promise to do everything possible to determine what happened to Sophie.'

Mr and Mrs Yates clung to each other, overcome with pain. Lauren and Matt quietly showed themselves out, the click of the door behind them echoing with finality. As they walked to the car, Lauren was consumed by the couple's sorrow. She wouldn't rest until Sophie's killer was found.

SEVEN

'Ma'am, I've just heard back from Tamsin,' Matt said, looking up from his phone and the text message he'd received. 'Samuel Finch is a plumber, and he works for a company in Penzance.'

Lauren was driving them away from Sophie's parents' house, and up until that moment there had been silence in the car as both of them had sat absorbing the information they'd learnt from Mr and Mrs Yates.

He couldn't help but be reminded of when he'd found out about Leigh's death. It was stamped in his mind as clear as if it had happened yesterday. People talk about things being a blur but that wasn't the case for Matt. He wished they were. Then he wouldn't have to constantly relive it.

'Okay, we'll head right there,' Lauren said, thankfully cutting across his thoughts about his wife. His mind moved on to what his boss had told him.

He was shocked when Lauren told him about her family. But he wasn't surprised that she'd decided to help them even though she'd cut ties. Lauren acted tough on the outside, but he'd learnt since working with her that deep down she cared about injustice and would help if someone was in trouble. He admired that about her. It showed real strength and compassion on her part.

They arrived at the plumbing supplies company that, according to the sign outside, was open to the public and the trade, and left the car directly outside the entrance. The show-room had an entire wall displaying a selection of different showers and in the middle there was a range of toilets and baths. On the far side attached to the wall were bathroom mirrors, and a rack featuring a variety of different taps and mixers.

They marched up to the reception desk, Lauren's warrant card already in her hand. 'We need to speak to Samuel Finch. Immediately,' she demanded.

'He's out on a job,' the man behind the desk droned, barely acknowledging them.

Matt scanned the area. The entrance to the warehouse was behind the desk; and in there were shelves piled high with boxes. Matt also spotted a rear exit, and kept his eye on it in case Finch was really there and not out on a job and decided to do a runner.

'Call him back now. This is urgent police business,' Lauren commanded.

The receptionist sighed theatrically. 'I'll have to check with the manager first.' He stood up and headed out the back where he exchanged words with a tall man with a shaved head. After a few seconds, they both came over to Matt and Lauren.

'I'm the manager. What's this about?' The man's eyes were sharp and assessing.

'We need to speak to Samuel Finch straight away. It's a police matter,' Lauren said, giving nothing more away.

'He might ask why. What can I tell him?' the manager asked.

Matt gave a frustrated sigh. The man was nothing if not persistent. Not that it would make any difference to Lauren.

'You may inform him that it's in relation to one of our inquiries. That's all he needs to know at this stage.'

The manager stared directly at them for a few seconds. 'Okay. No problem. He's working around the corner. I'll call him now.'

'Thank you,' Lauren said curtly.

Matt exchanged a look with Lauren, as they stepped to the side of the desk. Finally they were getting somewhere. As soon as Finch arrived they might get the answers they needed to move this forward.

After several minutes, a figure emerged from the warehouse and headed around the counter. The man appeared to be in his late twenties, at least six feet tall, and well-built. He was dressed in a pair of navy overalls with the name of the company displayed on it.

'I'm Sam Finch,' the man said, looking first at Matt and then at Lauren.

'DI Pengelly from Penzance CID and this is DS Price. Is there somewhere quiet we can speak?' Lauren asked, her voice carrying the authority they needed.

The man glanced over his back towards the way he'd come. 'Umm... yes. I think so. We'll go through to the staff room. There shouldn't be anyone in there at this time of day.'

Matt frowned. Why didn't he ask what it was about? Surely that would be his first question. It was a small detail, but in his experience, small details often led to significant insights. He made a mental note to ask about that shortly if Lauren didn't.

They followed Finch behind the reception desk and into the cavernous warehouse, their footsteps reverberating around the enormous space. Matt observed the handful of workers stacking boxes onto industrial shelving, and made a mental note of each person and what they were doing.

Finch guided them through the labyrinth of floor-to-ceiling storage units to a spacious industrial kitchen tucked away at the back. Stainless-steel units lined the walls while a large wooden table sat in the centre, surrounded by mismatched chairs. The lingering smell of cooked breakfasts caused Matt's stomach to rumble.

As Finch offered them a seat at the table, Matt noticed the fire exit in the far corner and sat next to it, just in case Finch tried anything stupid.

'You didn't ask why we wanted to speak to you,' Lauren said the moment they'd sat down. 'Why's that? It's most unusual.'

Good, Lauren had noticed too. They were clearly on the same wavelength.

'Umm... well... I was waiting for you to tell me. When the boss called I asked him, and he said he didn't know. Just that it was something to do with your enquiries.'

Matt watched Finch's face closely as he spoke, trying to spot any hints of worry or lying. This was standard in every investigation. From where Matt was sitting, he could see all of Finch's facial expressions. He'd notice if Finch's eyes darted around, and could already see the tension in his jaw. Everything the man did would give Matt clues.

'We understand Sophie Yates is your girlfriend,' Lauren said, deliberately using the word *is* because he hadn't yet been told of her death.

'Yeah, she is. Why?' Finch asked, eyes widening worriedly.

Finch wasn't a suspect yet, and they were about to deliver some terrible news, so they had to tread carefully. Show some compassion.

'I'm so sorry to tell you this, but Sophie's body was found on the rocks at Land's End this morning,' Lauren said.

'What? Sophie's... dead?' Finch's face paled with shock, his voice rising in disbelief. Tears welled up in his eyes and his body started shaking.

Matt studied Finch's reactions closely. Either the man was an incredible actor, or he truly had no clue this was coming.

There were subtle signs of real anguish – Finch's hands clenching, the raw pain in his eyes. Yet something still bugged Matt, a faint niggle he couldn't place.

Lauren reached out and put a reassuring hand on Finch's arm. 'We understand this is incredibly distressing news,' she comforted. 'But we do need you to answer a few questions as best you can. Is that okay?'

'Yes.' Finch nodded.

'First, you need to know that we're treating Sophie's death as suspicious.'

'What? You think someone killed her?' Finch said, sounding scared and confused.

'That's what we're investigating. When was the last time you saw Sophie?' Lauren asked, leaning forward slightly.

'A… a couple of nights ago.' Finch stuttered, his face flushed.

'So you weren't out with her last night? Her parents seem to think you might have been.'

'I didn't see her because she was out on the boats.'

'What do you mean?' Lauren pressed.

'It's a secret… I mean…' Finch's voice trailed off, his emotions apparently getting the better of him. 'Sophie was training on the side to work on the fishing boats. But she didn't want her mum and dad to know yet because they wouldn't like it. They're really snobby. They never cared about what she wanted to do. They were happy for her to be stuck in an office and be an accountant, or whatever.' Finch sighed, and a tear rolled down his cheek.

'How often did she go out?' Lauren asked.

'She'd go out with a trawler from Newlyn once or twice a week for about five hours a time. That's where she was last night.'

So that explained all the fishing stuff they'd found in Sophie's room. But something still wasn't sitting right. Was

Finch really upset? Or was he hiding something? Matt's gut told him to keep watching the man's reactions.

'It's an unusual career for a woman. Why did she want to pursue it?' Matt asked.

'That's what I asked her and she said it was the unpredictability of it. The fact that no two shifts were ever the same. She hated the routine of her job. She said fishing was exciting because they never knew what they were going to catch. But...'

'But?' Matt pushed.

'I didn't really get it. It's not a good life for anyone. Well, I don't think so. But Sophie didn't listen to me.'

'How did you feel about that?'

Finch shrugged. 'Not happy but she refused to give it up.'

'How long have you been together?' Lauren asked.

'Um... maybe eighteen months.'

'How did you meet?'

'I was on a friend's stag night and Sophie was in the pub. We got chatting and got on well and she gave me her number. The next day I called and we went out for a drink.'

'Did she tell you about working on the boats?' Lauren asked.

'She wasn't doing it then. But she did say she wanted to learn and then once she got the job she told me.'

'She didn't discuss it first?'

'No. I wasn't happy about it. But she told me that she wasn't going to give it up.'

'Do you know the name of the trawler she was out on and the captain?' Lauren asked.

'The boat's called *The Siren's Call* and the skipper's Jack Trembath. They don't call him captain.'

'What were you doing last night, while Sophie was on the boat?' Lauren asked.

'I was at my flat playing video games,' Finch mumbled, his eyes downcast as he fidgeted nervously.

He wasn't telling them everything.

'Were you alone?' Matt pressed.

'Yeah, alone. I swear,' Finch insisted, his voice cracking slightly.

'Can anyone confirm this?' Matt asked, fixing him with an intense stare, making him squirm in his chair.

'No... I told you, I was by myself.'

'What about the people you were gaming with? Were they strangers, or can they vouch for you?' Matt asked.

'Well, yeah, I was playing online with others. But I don't know them in real life. Just their usernames, not their actual names.'

'What's your username?' Matt asked sharply.

'It's, uh, GamerX23. I was playing with KillerShadow88, DeathBringer, and NinjaMaster.'

'Which game was this?' Matt asked, jotting down the details in his notebook.

'Er, Fortnite,' Finch murmured, avoiding eye contact.

'Right. Thank you,' Matt said briskly.

Finch's body language screamed deception. He was definitely hiding something but whether or not it related to Sophie's death was something they needed to investigate. But at least now that they had the other gamers' details, Tamsin should be able to find out more.

'Did you have any contact at all with Sophie last night?' Lauren asked.

Finch's face crumpled, tears brimming in his eyes. 'She messaged around five to arrange about us meeting up tonight. I can't believe that Sophie's dead. It's just...' Tears ran down his cheeks and he brushed them aside, while staring at Lauren. But his eyes were glassy, as if he wasn't actually seeing her.

'We're very sorry for your loss, Samuel,' Lauren said. 'Thank you for your assistance. We may wish to speak to you again, so please don't go anywhere without first contacting us.'

Matt and Lauren exited the kitchen, leaving Finch slumped

at the table. As they walked in silence through the warehouse, Matt sensed their every move was being watched by the people working there.

Once they were outside, Lauren turned to Matt, her face etched with unease. 'What did you make of that?' she murmured.

Matt scanned their surroundings warily. 'I'm not sure. Finch seemed distraught by the news, but something was off. Did you notice his reticence when asked what he'd been doing all night?'

'Yes, but he provided those gaming contacts who can give him an alibi – providing Tamsin can verify them.'

'Another thing. When you told him about Sophie's death, although his reaction was intense, in his eyes... it was like there was a flicker of something else.'

'Shock, maybe?' Lauren suggested half-heartedly.

'Or guilt.' The word hung ominously between them.

The interrogation had raised more questions than answers. Finch's emotions had appeared raw and powerful. Or were they merely a performance?

'Let's see if we can confirm his alibi and also find that trawler,' Lauren said, her eyes hardened with resolve.

'Agreed,' said Matt grimly. 'Because we need more to go on than we have at present.'

As they headed for the car, Matt sighed loudly. Somewhere, Sophie's killer was on the loose and they needed to be caught fast – in case this wasn't a single murder and there were more to come.

EIGHT

TUESDAY JUNE 11

The next morning Matt arrived at work before anyone else. In fact he'd left home before Dani had got up and she was very often the first to rise. It was going to be a busy day trying to uncover what had happened to Sophie Yates, especially as they hadn't much to go on. The skipper of *The Siren's Call* had been uncontactable yesterday, and they intended to pursue that line of enquiry today.

Matt hung his jacket on the coat stand and walked in the direction of his desk. Glancing up, he noticed Lauren standing at the door of her office, beckoning for him to go over.

Retracing his steps, he made his way to her.

'Morning, Matt. I've decided that we'll drive to Newlyn today to see if we can find the trawler skipper. If Sophie was out with them the night of her murder, then the people on the boat could have been the last to see her alive. I tried the phone number of the skipper again when I arrived at work, but there was still no answer. If they were out again overnight, then I'm not sure what time they'll be back on shore...'

'Why don't we send uniform out to bring the skipper in for

questioning?' Matt suggested, not wanting to waste time going to Newlyn and finding the man not there.

'No. I don't want to alert him or the crew in case they were involved in her death. DCI Mistry is running a press conference later this morning to find out if anyone saw anything, but he's not going to mention the death being suspicious. Not until we hear from the pathologist with official confirmation. Do you know whether the team found anything from the CCTV footage after I left yesterday afternoon?'

'Not that I'm aware of. There are so few cameras... which is ridiculous, when you think of the number of visitors. It's not like in—'

'Lenchester. Yes, I know,' Lauren said rolling her eyes.

Lenchester *was* a much bigger force with more resources but in actual fact, that hadn't been what he was going to say.

'I was going to say in a big city, ma'am. I didn't intend to mention Lenchester because I know your feelings when I do. But now you have brought it up... well yes, there are cameras galore there. Although, as you also know, people still get away with murder.' He smiled and gave a gentle shrug.

'Touché,' Lauren said, returning the smile. 'I'm hoping the rest of the team will arrive early knowing that we're dealing with a murder. We'll have a quick meeting to make sure everyone's up to date.' The phone on her desk rang, and she walked back into her office to answer it. 'Pengelly.' She nodded. 'Right. We'll be there shortly.' She ended the call and replaced the handset. 'Forget my previous words. That was Henry. He wants us over there now. Thank goodness because it will give us more to work with.'

'He's already there?' Matt said, glancing at his watch. 'How come? I know he's not keen on early starts.'

'I suspect it's because he's short staffed. One of his technicians isn't around and the work's piling up. He told us that yesterday. Don't you remember?' Lauren asked, frowning.

'To be honest... no. But I was probably too busy concentrating on keeping the contents of my stomach in place,' Matt said, laughing.

'I see. It appears that Henry did as promised and worked on our case first. Grab your jacket and come back here. I've got an important email to send before we leave.'

The sound of voices caused them both to glance across to the other side of the main office. Jenna and Clem had walked in together and were engaged in an animated conversation.

'I'll let them know where we're going, ma'am,' Matt said.

Lauren returned to her desk and Matt headed over to Clem and Jenna, who were discussing what sounded like a programme on the television last night.

'Morning, Sarge,' they said in unison.

'The DI and I are off to see the pathologist. I want everyone working on Sophie Yates's murder. Everything else can wait. Double-check the CCTV at Land's End and any cameras leading there. Also, continue researching into Samuel Finch and Sophie Yates's backgrounds and anything else you think might assist.'

'Will do,' Jenna said.

'Let us know if Tamsin's able to track down the people Finch was gaming with on Sunday night.'

'She hadn't had any luck when we left for the evening yesterday,' Clem said.

Matt's thoughts immediately turned to DC Ellie Naylor from Lenchester. She'd have been able to locate them in a heartbeat. But he pushed those thoughts aside. They were pointless.

'Let's hope today she does. We shouldn't be gone too long.'

He turned and headed back to Lauren's office to collect his boss.

'We'll go in your car, Matt,' Lauren declared as he entered. 'Mine was acting up this morning and it took several attempts to start. It desperately needs a service, but there never seems to be enough time.'

'No problem, ma'am,' Matt responded, caught off guard by her request because more often than not she drove.

They exited the station, and made their way through the station car park until reaching his car.

'I've been giving more consideration to you having hypnotherapy to cope with bodies,' Lauren said, once they were settled in the vehicle and heading to the hospital. 'It definitely seems a viable option. Perhaps it can be arranged as part of your ongoing professional development. What do you think?'

'Thank you, ma'am,' Matt replied, slightly taken aback by her sudden endorsement, yet grateful for her understanding. And if it were paid for by the force, then it would save him some money which he could put towards a holiday for the family. 'I'll certainly consider it once the case is over.'

'Good.'

After a few minutes' silence, Matt decided to broach the subject of Lauren's latest family problem.

'If you don't mind me asking, ma'am, have you thought further about how to help your cousins with their problem?'

'No, I haven't. This case is my main focus right now. My cousins' situation, or whatever you want to call it, will have to wait.'

'This case might take a long time, though. There's a chance that it might never get solved. Maybe you should think about your cousins some more before it's too late.'

Was he prying too much? He'd become Lauren's confidante, but wasn't sure how far he could push it.

He waited nervously for her response, keeping his eyes fixed on the road ahead.

'You make a fair point, Matt. But, like I've already said, this investigation comes first for me right now,' Lauren replied evenly, no defensiveness in her tone.

Matt felt a wave of relief. He admired Lauren's commit-ment and ability to separate personal and professional matters. Her unwavering focus was something he tried hard to emulate. Not easy when life pulled him in so many different directions.

They lapsed into comfortable silence, but Matt's mind kept churning, thinking about Lauren: her unexpected openness, iron determination, and family issues. He felt a renewed moti-vation not just to work the case, but also to better support his boss however he could.

They arrived at the hospital and Matt parked as near to the morgue entrance as possible. An icy chill crept into his bones as they made their way inside. It wasn't just the sight of the deceased that unnerved him; it was the knowledge that he might encounter some other bodies, with even worse injuries.

They found Henry by a gleaming stainless-steel table, his expression unreadable, and hands planted firmly on his hips.

'Good morning, Henry. I hope you've got something useful to tell us. We need some help with this investigation,' Lauren greeted, her voice betraying a trace of urgency.

'And good morning to you both,' Henry replied, his glance briefly flicking over them before returning to the body. 'I don't have much time either, so let's get straight to it. This isn't your bog-standard drowning, as we initially suspected. First of all, she was drugged. I found evidence of petechiae – that's broken blood vessel capillaries – on the eyes and skin, caused by increased blood pressure. It could be ketamine. Her bloods have gone off to toxicology for confirmation.'

'Did the drugs kill her?' Lauren enquired.

'No, the cause of death was asphyxiation due to strangula-tion,' Henry stated clinically. 'Note the distinct fingerprint bruising pattern encircling the anterior cervical neck. This purple contusion in the shape of the assailant's digits clearly indicates fatal compressive pressure was exerted on the victim's airway.' He pointed to the deeply ingrained purple bruising, an unsettling testament to the violence that had ended Sophie Yates's life.

'Can you tell whether the marks were made by a man or woman?' Lauren asked, peering at the body.

'Not conclusively, but judging by the size they're more likely to be from a male. As a rule, women have smaller hands than men.'

'So that narrows it down a bit, I suppose,' Lauren said, with a shrug.

'Additionally, during examination a small slip of paper was recovered from the victim's mouth,' Henry continued. 'It contained the typed phrase "*Men must work and women must weep.*"'

'What does that mean?' Lauren asked.

Henry handed over a photograph of the note. 'You'll have to work that one out for yourself. The note has been submitted to forensics for testing.'

Matt's eyes remained fixed on Henry, deliberately avoiding the sight of the body. 'Do you recognise those words at all?' he asked.

'Haven't the foggiest, old boy,' Henry said, giving a dismissive wave of his hand. 'Moving on. The victim's last meal was fish, chips, and mushy peas, which I believe concealed the drug. Made a nice mess in her stomach, I can tell you.'

'Was the body moved as you believed?' Matt pressed, trying to focus on the facts rather than the gruesome details.

'Yes, absolutely,' Henry confirmed. 'We know that because of the lividity patterns. I'd have expected to find darkened areas where the blood had pooled to be evenly spread on the back of the body because she was found lying face up. In this instance the darker areas were in the lower limbs, indicating that she was sitting when she died. Furthermore, there were some drag marks on the legs.' Henry pointed to some abrasions running down both calves.

'Any unknown fibres on the body?' Lauren asked.

'I've sent off for testing samples of mud and fibres I found on the body and will let you know when the results come back.'

'What about signs of sexual assault?' Matt asked.

'None,' Henry said, waving his hand as if dismissing the question.

Matt breathed a sigh of relief. If there had been it would have changed the whole dynamics of the case – and not in a good way.

'Time of death?' Lauren asked.

'Between eight pm and midnight.'

'So we have a body with a note in the mouth, placed on the rocks with fishing line wrapped around her neck. What do you think that means?' Lauren asked, a frown creasing her forehead.

'Again, that's for you to work out,' Henry replied, coldly clinical. 'All I'm telling you is how she died. My report will follow, but this should give you sufficient information to work with for now. Now, as much as it's been a pleasure, I have work to do. Please see yourselves out.'

Matt exited the morgue behind Lauren, the stark facts of the case gradually sinking in. The bizarre note and deliberate post-mortem staging raised troubling questions. Why use the fishing line if it wasn't the cause of death? Was it symbolic? And, if so, of what? As for the note... what did it mean, and why place it in the victim's mouth?

He followed Lauren to the car, unable to shake the memory of the vivid bruising around the victim's neck and the violent end it represented. They were dealing with one cold callous murderer, for sure.

As he pulled out of the hospital car park and into a queue of traffic, Matt silently acknowledged his fear that this case wasn't going to be solved easily.

What sort of twisted mind would murder like this? And what were the odds that this wasn't going to be the last?

NINE

Matt followed Lauren into the office, his heart pounding in his chest. The quote that was typed on the piece of paper in Sophie's mouth had sent a chill down his spine, and now Lauren was writing it up on the whiteboard. This was different from anything he'd encountered before.

'Right, we have official confirmation from the pathologist that this is a suspicious death. We're now looking for a murderer. We also know that in the victim's mouth a typed note was discovered, with these words written on it.' Lauren pointed at the board.

Matt stared at the words again, struggling to find any meaning in them.

'"*Men must work and women must weep*",' Jenna read aloud slowly.

'What the hell does that mean?' Billy said, looking at each member of the team in turn as if seeking an answer. 'Clem, you're the expert on everything. Do you know?'

'No idea.' Clem shook his head, appearing almost embarrassed that he couldn't answer the question.

'Well, it's what we need to find out. Because right now, that quote is our only solid lead,' Lauren said crisply. 'Beyond the fact that the victim was deliberately posed on the rocks with fishing line binding her neck. But that wasn't what killed her. Sophie Yates was drugged and then manually strangled, most likely by a man.' Lauren returned her attention to the whiteboard. 'We have to determine why these particular words were chosen and what meaning can be derived from the elaborate post-mortem staging. What message was the killer sending? If we work that out and we have our motive, then we have a chance of catching him before he strikes again.'

'The words and setting must mean something specific to the killer,' Jenna said, as if working it out in her mind. 'The whole thing is too deliberate, too calculated.'

'Or to the victim,' Tamsin added, emphatically. 'Maybe it's something personal, that's just between them.'

Matt considered their words. They were homing in on something, he could sense it.

There was certainly some warped intent behind the killer's actions. If only they could fathom what it was.

'Bloody cryptic, if you ask me. Like those stupid crosswords you do, Clem,' Billy grumbled, his impatience clear. 'It feels like we're chasing shadows.'

Matt understood Billy's frustration but they had to dig deeper, beyond the surface.

'You know what, Billy. You've given me an idea. We should approach this like I do my crosswords. Logically,' Clem said.

'Ha. Billy does it again. Where would you be without me?' the young officer said, a broad smile crossing his face.

'Give it a rest,' Tamsin said, teasing.

'Carry on, Clem,' Lauren said.

'Well, if the body was placed on the rocks strategically we have to consider the tides,' Clem said, sounding measured. 'If it's a spring tide, then that's going to make a difference in respect of when the body could have been left.'

'But it's spring for three months of the year so how is it going to make a difference?' Matt asked, hoping for some clarification.

Could Clem's expertise on tides be the key to unlocking the timeline of the murder? Everything was interconnected, every detail significant.

'A spring tide isn't to do with the actual month.' Clem stared at Matt while tapping his finger on his chin. 'Okay... here's a brief lesson on tides. Tides are caused by the gravitational pull of the moon and the sun. Imagine a slow-moving wave, created far out at sea, that travels gradually towards us, guided by the moon's cycles – though the sun also has a role to play. The moon has about two-thirds of the gravitational pull that affects our tides. It's called gravitational gradient. Despite the sun's strength, the moon, being closer to the earth, exerts more influence over our oceans. Does that make sense?'

Matt sort of understood what the officer was saying. 'I think so. Does that then explain high tides and low tides?'

'Exactly,' Clem said, beaming. 'High tide is when the ocean is full and waves are breaking close to the shore. Think of it as the moon pulling the water close when it's nearest to us. And low tide is when it's farthest away, leaving the beach exposed.'

'And what about this spring tide you mentioned?' Matt asked, intrigued, his mind buzzing with new understanding.

'Spring tides are also known as king tides. It's when there are *high* high tides and *low* low tides. If you're at the beach during a full moon or a new moon, you'll see a big difference between low tide and high tide. That's because the sun and the moon are aligned, creating a very strong gravitational pull,' Clem explained.

'Thanks, Clem. I get it now,' Matt said with genuine appreciation, feeling a sense of relief as the confusing details finally clicked into place. Now he felt like they were getting somewhere. If only they could learn something about the quote.

'My pleasure,' Clem said warmly, a spark in his eyes.

'It's all bloody confusing if you ask me,' Billy said, giving a frustrated sigh. 'It's alright for you locals; you were brought up with all this. I really don't get it. Science was my worst subject at school.'

'I thought you came from Cornwall, Billy,' Matt said.

'I do, but inland, so I don't know this stuff about tides.'

'Well, that aside, now we need someone to check the tides which will then give us an indication of when the body was left,' Lauren said, authoritatively, bringing them back to the task at hand. 'According to the pathologist, the time of death was between eight and midnight. Which also has to be thrown into the mix.'

'Leave it to me, ma'am,' Clem said, volunteering.

'Thanks. As the person who most understands all of this, you're definitely the best placed person to do it,' Lauren said, signalling her appreciation.

'See, being a walking, talking encyclopaedia can come in handy,' Billy said, laughing.

'Shut up, Billy,' Jenna said, light-heartedly.

'Just saying... that's all.'

'Okay, enough,' Lauren said, holding up her hand to silence them. 'We also know that Sophie's last meal was fish, chips, and mushy peas. I want someone to check with all the local fish and chip shops in the area to see if we can identify which one she went to and at what time. Show them her photo.'

'Don't mention food, I forgot to have breakfast this morning,' Billy moaned.

'Why's that, Billy. Were you too busy with—'

Lauren's phone rang, interrupting Tamsin's comment.

'Pengelly,' Lauren said after pulling it out of her pocket and checking the screen. 'I'll be there shortly.' She ended the call and put the phone back into her pocket.

Matt watched her, curious about the call, but knowing she'd tell him if she believed he should know.

'The DCI has asked to see me, so Sergeant Price will wrap things up here.' Lauren turned to Matt. 'When I get back, we'll head to Newlyn. Hopefully we'll be able to talk to Sophie's trawler crew. With any luck, they'll be in port by then and can tell us more about her fishing job.'

'Yes, ma'am,' Matt acknowledged with a tilt of his head.

He felt motivated. Bit by bit, they were figuring stuff out. Every new clue and interview brought them closer to the full story of what happened to Sophie.

He glanced around at his teammates. They were all in this as a group. No one said a word as Lauren left the room.

'Do you know, I was thinking last night how weird it is that she worked on the boats a couple of nights a week yet her parents had no idea. Did she take time off work on the nights she went out? Surely she couldn't do a full day's work after,' Jenna said, thoughtfully.

'Contact her workplace and find out,' Matt said.

'Working on the boats must have been very different from working in an office, for sure,' Jenna said. 'It's a shame that she felt she couldn't tell her parents what she really wanted to do. They must feel bad about that.'

'Bloody parents,' Billy muttered, sounding bitter. 'Mine hated me joining the force.'

Matt's attention snapped to Billy, seeing a rare glimpse of vulnerability in the young officer's eyes.

'Why?' Tamsin asked. 'Mine loved it when I joined. They were so proud when I qualified as a detective, too. We had a big celebration party.'

'You're very lucky then. Let's just say some of my parents'

friends wouldn't have approved,' Billy said, sounding surprisingly reticent.

'Why not?' Tamsin pushed.

'Why do you think, Tams?' Jenna said, shaking her head.

Matt could see the unspoken words in Billy's expression, the family pressures and societal judgments. He wanted to ask more but knew this wasn't the time or place.

'Come on, let's not get diverted. We'll save this conversation for another time,' Matt said, moving them on.

'Thanks, Sarge,' Billy said.

'No problem. Let's make sure we all know what we're doing. Tamsin, keep looking for stuff on Samuel Finch; in particular, we need to locate those gamers he was supposedly playing with. Billy and Jenna, you can visit all the fish and chip shops between Land's End and Newlyn.'

'That's too cruel, considering I'm starving,' Billy said, with a grimace.

'If you want to stop for something to eat on the way, then do so. But don't take all day about it,' Matt said.

'You're the best, Sarge,' Billy said, as he stood.

'If you say so.' Matt laughed. 'Clem, you concentrate on the tides so we can get a better indication of when the body might've been placed there. Also, see if you can find out what those words mean. The language isn't modern, and it's certainly sexist,' Matt said in a commanding tone. He knew they had to stay focused, follow the evidence wherever it led.

Billy and Jenna left and the others started working, the room becoming a hive of activity.

After a few minutes, Lauren returned and she called Matt over to her office.

'Are you ready to go, ma'am?' he asked when he reached her.

'Yes. I explained to DCI Mistry where we were up to with

the investigation and we decided that the press conference should take place this afternoon. Now we know it's a suspicious death he's going to announce Sophie's name. We need to let the FLO know so the parents can be prepared, because no doubt the media will be waiting outside their house for hours on end. The DCI and I discussed the note left in Sophie's mouth and decided not to mention it. We need to keep something quiet, so we can sort out the genuine phone calls from those that come in from the crackpots who always seem to appear at times like these.'

'Good idea, ma'am. It never ceases to amaze me how these people come out of the woodwork. It's like all they want to do is mess with our cases by giving us false leads.'

'It's even worse when there's a reward offered. I always advise against that,' Lauren said, rolling her eyes and throwing her hands up in exasperation.

'Been there, done that... got the T-shirt,' Matt said, shaking his head ruefully. 'By the way, does the DCI need you with him for the press conference?' He hoped not because it would stall the investigation – Lauren would definitely want to interview the skipper with him.

'No, not at this stage, thank goodness. We have more important things to be getting on with. After we've been to Newlyn, we'll visit Sophie's friend Imogen at The Seaside Inn. Maybe she can shed some light on what's happened.'

TEN

Matt gripped the steering wheel tightly as he navigated the winding coastal roads from Penzance to Newlyn. Beside him, Lauren peered out of the passenger window, taking in the rugged beauty of the Cornish countryside. Rolling green hills dotted with sheep stretched out to the cliffs that dropped dramatically into the steel-blue sea. The sky overhead was grey, threatening rain even as the morning sun tried to break through thick clouds. As they approached Newlyn, fishing boats bobbed in the harbour while hungry seagulls circled and shrieked overhead, their cries mingling with the scent of the sea, which enveloped them as Matt pulled into the docks.

After parking, Lauren and Matt hurried towards the docks, weaving between weathered fishing vessels. 'Keep an eye out for *The Siren's Call*,' Lauren said, scanning the names painted on sterns and bows.

'I'll ask someone,' Matt said, stopping beside a trawler where a man in oil-stained overalls was coiling thick ropes on the deck. 'Excuse me, where's *The Siren's Call*?'

The man hooked a thumb over his shoulder. 'She's over

there, couple of slips down. But you'll have to wait, the boys are washing her down right now.'

Lauren squinted through the gloom and saw a small crew on the deck of a boat, hoses in hand, spraying her down. 'That's her, let's go,' she said to Matt, having no intention of waiting.

The deck of *The Siren's Call* glistened with water and white suds slid down the hull. Lauren stepped aboard, her shoes sloshing on the slippery planks. It was time to get some answers.

'We'd like to speak to the skipper please,' Lauren said, approaching one of the deckhands, as she held out her warrant card.

'He's over there,' the man said, pointing towards a figure standing on the pier in conversation with someone. His eyes were curious but wary, a typical response in these situations.

'Thank you.' Her tone was polite, but her mind was already moving on to the next step.

She walked with Matt towards the skipper, who looked like an experienced fisherman, with weathered skin and a thick, grey beard. His sharp blue eyes seemed to reflect years scanning the horizon. Lauren guessed he was about sixty, but even so there was a strength and stubbornness radiating off him.

'Who are you?' the skipper asked gruffly before they'd even got close.

'DI Pengelly and DS Price. Are you Jack Trembath, skipper of this trawler?' Lauren asked calmly, hiding the urgency bubbling underneath.

'Yes, why?' The skipper's eyes narrowed, assessing them both.

'We'd like a word with you in private.'

'Can't it wait? I'm in the middle of something.' His tone was dismissive, almost defiant.

The hairs bristled on the back of Lauren's neck. She hated being side-lined, as he was obviously trying to do. This was important, and she wouldn't be brushed off.

'No, it won't,' she said, leaving no room for doubt.

'I'll leave you to it then,' the other man said, nervously, as he walked away.

'This had better be important because you've interrupted a business meeting,' the skipper snapped.

'You were standing on the dock. How can that be an important business meeting?' Matt asked, sceptically.

'It's how we do things around here,' the skipper said, his eyes flashing with stubborn resolve.

The tension in the air was obvious. Lauren knew she had to tread carefully, and handle the skipper's unwillingness while still getting what they needed. Her mind was focused, and her determination strong. They were here for a reason, and she wouldn't be deterred. But at the same time, she was delivering what could be some upsetting news, and she had to be mindful of that.

'I'm sorry to tell you, Sophie Yates, who we know works for you some nights, has been found dead,' Lauren said. Her voice was steady as she delivered the sad news.

'Dead?' His eyes widened and his face lost colour. His previous gruffness was replaced by something raw and vulnerable.

'Yes, and her death is being investigated as suspicious. We understand she worked for you on Sunday night. Is that correct?' Lauren watched the skipper closely, alert to his every reaction.

'No. She didn't show up and didn't message me, either. We left harbour at ten and got back around four-thirty,' the skipper said shakily, his words tumbling out as he appeared to be making sense of the news.

'Was it unusual for Sophie not to turn up for work?' Lauren asked, wanting to be sensitive but get the facts.

'Not really, no. She's usually good about contacting me... Dead? I can't believe it. What happened?' He looked at

Lauren as if desperately seeking answers. But she couldn't give them.

'That's what we're investigating,' Lauren said. 'Did you try calling her before you set off to check why she wasn't there?'

'No. I just thought... well, you know how young people are. I figured something came up and she'd tell me later. It's not like she's paid crew. So I couldn't dock her wages.'

'Do you ever fish during the day?' Matt asked.

The skipper shook his head. 'No, we mainly catch squid, monkfish and megrim, which come out at night.'

'Do you stay out for multiple days at a time?'

'No, we go out each night and get back around four or five in the morning to deliver the catch to the fish market. We're an OTA boat.'

Lauren's forehead creased. 'Which means what?'

'It stands for Outright Track Allocation. We get a quota on how many fish we can catch and anything extra gets released. It's responsible fishing.' The skipper shrugged.

'Do you have a regular crew or do they vary?' Lauren asked, wondering how involved Sophie was with them.

'I've had the same crew for a couple of years now. A couple have been with me even longer.'

'When did Sophie last come out with you?' Lauren asked, moving the questioning along.

'Last week.'

'And did she seem okay to you?'

'Yes. She was the same as usual.' His simple words carried confusion and disbelief. He was clearly deeply affected.

'Did Sophie go out with you on regular nights?'

'No, it varied depending on what else she had on.'

'We know that she had a day job. How did she manage both?' Lauren asked, trying to fit together the pieces of Sophie's life.

'It was fine if she came out at the weekend. Usually she'd do a Friday or Saturday. If it was during the week, she'd head into work after. Young people can handle that. I'd be knackered if it was me.'

'What can you tell us about Sophie?' Lauren asked.

'She was great. Would've made a fantastic female fisherman, which is what she wanted. But her parents didn't want her training for it. I can't believe she's dead...' His voice cracked on the last word.

'Why call her a female fisherman rather than fisherwoman?' Matt asked.

'That's the language used in the industry,' Trembath replied firmly, almost defensively. But Lauren sensed it was more about clinging to the familiar in the midst of the incomprehensible news he'd just been given.

'Was Sophie close to any member of your crew?' Lauren asked, her eyes scanning the bustling scene on the deck. Personal relationships could often provide essential clues in a case like this.

'She was quite friendly with George Bray over there,' Trembath said, pointing at the man who had sent them over. 'He's my second in command. They're a similar age, and got on well.'

Lauren studied the man, taking in his posture, the way he moved... anything that might tell her more about his relationship with the victim.

'Okay, we'll speak to him next. Going back to the last time you saw Sophie, did she say anything that seemed odd? Was she worried about anything or anyone?' Lauren's voice was gentle but insistent. Even seemingly insignificant details could be crucial in a murder investigation.

'She wouldn't confide in me. I'm the boss. All I know is that she was really good at her job, as I've already told you.'

'Thanks for your help. We'll go and speak to George. Oh, and by the way, have you ever heard of the words "Men must work and women must weep"?' Lauren asked, her mind still whirring with possibilities as to what they might signify.

'Yes, that's from a famous poem. Well, famous around here, anyway. It's called "The Three Fishers". I can't remember all of it, but the line goes, "For men must work, and women must weep, And there's little to earn, and many to keep. Though the harbour bar be moaning..."' His words trailed off as if lost in thought.

'Thank you for helping us identify that.'

Lauren and Matt left the skipper and made their way back to the boat. As they walked, Lauren's mind was a flurry of thoughts and connections. The poem, the words, the staging of the body... all of it was starting to form a picture in her mind, though there were still pieces missing.

'Great call asking if he knew the poem, ma'am,' Matt said, his eyes wide with recognition of the lead they'd uncovered. 'Now we've got something to work with. We just need to find out what it means in relation to Sophie.'

'Yes, although by now I expect they know what it is at the office. At least they should do, if it's that famous. Not that I've heard of it. Have you?'

'No, ma'am, but I'm not much for poetry,' Matt admitted, his expression sheepish. 'I don't get it. Never could at school, and still don't.'

They reached the boat and went up to the crew member. 'Excuse me, can we have a word, George,' Lauren called out, signalling for him to come over.

'Yeah, what is it?' Bray said, taking a step towards them.

'We'd rather you come over here,' Lauren said, not wanting to deliver the bad news in such an open area.

'Okay.' Bray shrugged.

They waited until he had reached them. 'According to the skipper, you were friends with Sophie Yates?' Lauren began, keeping her tone neutral.

'Well, not friends exactly, like I am with the others on the boat. But we get on well, and she's a great girl. Why?' Bray's eyes turned sharp and piercing, as if he sensed something was wrong.

'I'm very sorry to have to tell you this, but Sophie's body was found on the rocks at Land's End yesterday.'

'What? She's dead? Did she drown?' Bray paled, disbelief on his face.

'No. We're treating her death as suspicious.'

'You're saying she was murdered?' Bray's voice shook.

'It's what we're investigating,' Lauren confirmed, her eyes fixed on him, watching for any sign that he already knew. 'We'd like to ask you a few questions about Sophie. Did she confide in you? Were there any problems in her life?'

'Sophie was great. We got on well. But... Well I don't know if it means anything. She was very upset last week when she came to work.'

Lauren went on alert, sensing a lead. 'Why? What happened?'

'It was that tosser of a boyfriend. God knows why she stuck with him. They'd had a fight in the pub.'

'Do you know him?' Lauren asked, wondering why he had such a bad opinion of Finch.

'No. Sometimes he'd come with her when she started work. He'd watch her get onto the boat. Then stare at the rest of us as if he thought we'd do something to her,' Bray explained, his face twisted with distaste.

'Did she say what the fight was about?' Lauren pressed.

'He was always jealous of her doing anything on her own. She said he'd gone into one of his possessive rants.'

'Possessive in what way?' Lauren asked.

Bray shrugged. 'Sophie didn't say. I can't believe she's dead. Why haven't we heard about this?' His eyes were filled with confusion and grief.

'It only happened yesterday, and the press conference isn't taking place until this afternoon. Thank you for your help. If you do think of anything, maybe something Sophie told you that at the time didn't seem important, please let us know,' Lauren said, handing him her card.

'Yeah, sure I will. I'm so sorry,' Bray said, his voice choked with emotion.

Lauren and Matt left and headed back to the car.

'We need to look more seriously at Sophie's boyfriend. But first we'll speak to her friend Imogen who works at The Seaside Inn pub in Penzance,' Lauren said, her mind racing with the new information.

The pieces were starting to come together, and Lauren felt a growing sense that they were on the right track. But there were still many questions unanswered, and the clock was ticking.

ELEVEN

Lauren and Matt entered The Seaside Inn, the hum of conversation and clinking glasses filling the air. Behind the bar stood an older man wearing a blue sweatshirt with the name of the pub emblazoned across it.

'Good morning,' he said cheerfully, his face etched with laughter lines. 'How may I help you?'

'My name's DI Pengelly and this is DS Price. We'd like to speak to Imogen Halford, if she's working today,' Lauren said, holding out her warrant card.

The smile on the man's face disappeared, and he became serious. 'She is, but she's in no state to talk to anyone. When she came into work this morning, she learnt about the death of her best friend.' His tone indicated that he clearly cared about his colleague.

'That's what we're here to talk about,' Lauren replied, her tone professional yet sympathetic. 'Where is she now?'

'She's sitting over there with a drink,' the man said gesturing to the far end of the room. 'She wanted to be left alone, so I don't know if you'll get much from her at the moment.'

'Well, this can't wait. Thank you,' Lauren said, acknowledging his cooperation. She turned and walked in the direction he'd indicated, with Matt close behind.

Imogen was sitting in the corner, a glass in front of her on the table, her head lowered, appearing lost in thought.

Lauren approached cautiously, mindful of the delicate situation.

'Imogen?' she enquired softly when they reached the table, not wanting to startle the grieving woman.

'Yes?' Imogen glanced up, her cheeks stained with tears.

'My name is DI Pengelly and this is DS Price. May we sit down?'

'Yes,' Imogen said, her voice barely above a whisper.

Lauren pulled out the chair facing the young woman, and Matt sat next to her.

'We understand that you've recently learnt about what happened to Sophie?' Lauren probed, maintaining a sympathetic tone. 'It must have been devastating for you.'

'Yes, I couldn't believe it. Someone who came in the pub told me this morning.'

'Who was that?' Lauren asked, curious, but not totally surprised that it had already got out.

'A guy who works at the hospital.' She glanced away, as if checking the bar. 'He's not here now.'

'What did he say exactly?' Lauren asked, wanting to know how much Imogen knew.

'He said...' Fresh tears filled Imogen's eyes. 'He said she was found at Land's End. That someone had k-killed her.' She choked out a sob. 'That she was m-murdered.'

Lauren reached out a comforting hand. 'We're investigating what happened.'

'But it's not been in the news or anything. Why?' Imogen's voice shook and she dabbed her eyes with a tissue.

'We'll be announcing it publicly later today. I know this is hard, but can you answer some questions about Sophie?'

Imogen blinked away more tears. She picked up her glass with a shaky hand and took a sip before setting it down. Despite her obvious grief, determination flashed in her tear-filled eyes. 'Yes. What do you want to know?'

As Lauren looked at Imogen, a wave of sympathy washed over her. Facing someone's death at any age was hard, but when it was someone so young, like her friend, that was a different level.

'Can you tell us a bit more about Sophie? What kind of person she was,' Lauren asked.

Imogen sniffed back her tears. 'Sophie was... she was so great. Even when things were hard she was full of life. We always had a laugh together when we went out. But she was more than fun. She was kind and caring, too. Sophie was such a strong person. If she wanted something, she went for it, no matter what got in her way. She never gave up on her dreams.'

'You two were clearly very close. How long had you known each other?' Lauren asked, observing the grief etched across the young woman's features and not wanting to push too hard.

'We grew up together,' Imogen confirmed, her gaze distant as she stared past Lauren, lost in memories. 'We lived next door to each other, and were pretty much inseparable since we were toddlers. She was more like a sister to me than a friend.'

'That must make this even harder for you,' Lauren sympathised.

Imogen bit down on her bottom lip. 'I keep thinking it's a bad dream, and I'll wake up and Sophie will be okay...'

Lauren reached out, placing a reassuring hand on Imogen's arm. 'I understand this is a lot to take in. But you're doing really well. We need to find out what happened to Sophie and your cooperation is very important to us.'

The young woman simply nodded, her focus returning to the half-empty glass in front of her. Lauren sighed inwardly, knowing the road ahead was fraught with many difficult conversations like this one. But for now she had to continue talking to the young woman.

'Can you tell us more about her boyfriend, Samuel Finch?' Lauren asked.

Imogen took a deep breath, her fingers nervously twisting the edge of her cardigan. 'Sam is, well, he's kind of a character, you know? He's charismatic and funny, and can be really charming when he wants to be. He's got this energy that lights up a room, and people really seem to like him.'

'But?' Lauren prompted, sensing the woman's hesitation.

'But the thing is, underneath all that charm, Sam can be... complicated. His moods are all over the place sometimes. One minute he's the life and soul of the party, the next he's sulking in the corner. And he doesn't cope well if he can't get his own way.' Imogen sighed, tucking a strand of hair behind her ear. 'I don't know. It's... it's... not always easy being around him. Sam is... a lot to handle sometimes.' She gave a small, self-conscious laugh. 'I'm not explaining this very well. Does it make any sense?'

'Yes, it does. We've been told that the other day Sophie and Sam were here in the pub and they had a row. Is that what you're referring to?' Lauren asked.

'Yes,' Imogen replied, her nod barely noticeable. 'It was actually the last time I saw Sophie. We'd arranged to see each other later this week to go to the cinema. But—' A sob escaped the woman's lips. 'I'm sorry. It's just... It's too much to take in.'

'We understand. Take a few minutes if you need to.'

Imogen sniffed. 'It's okay. I can carry on. The row happened on Friday night, and it did get a bit nasty.'

'What do you mean by that?' Lauren quickly enquired, going on alert.

'They were shouting, and... well... I suppose it was mainly Sam doing the shouting. He can be aggressive sometimes.'

'Do you know what they were arguing about?' Lauren prodded, her mind churning with possible scenarios.

'Sophie was fed up with him being so possessive. He tried to control her all of the time. She was going to finish with him over the weekend, but I don't know if she did or not. He'd been cheating on her. She'd found proof.'

'Do you know what this proof was?' Lauren asked, piecing together the possible implications of this revelation.

'She saw texts on his phone when he'd left it lying around,' Imogen replied, her face paling at the memory.

'Do you know who he was cheating with?' Matt asked, his pen poised over his notebook.

'Yes. Courtney Inwood. We went to school with her,' Imogen said swiftly. 'But she's not our friend anymore. At least not now.'

Adrenaline coursed through Lauren as they uncovered more about Sophie that could lead to her killer.

'Did Sophie confront Courtney about it?'

Imogen shook her head. 'No. But when I saw Courtney in town on Saturday I gave her a warning.'

'What sort of warning?'

'I told her to back off Sam or she'll be sorry.' Imogen's voice hardened.

'How did she respond to the threat?'

'She didn't say anything, just pushed past me and hurried down the street and into one of the cafés. I didn't follow her.'

'It must have been so hard for Sophie to learn about her friend's betrayal like that.'

Imogen sighed. 'Yes and no. Courtney was always up for a good time with any boy, no matter whose boyfriend they were. She never cared who she hurt.'

They needed to dig deeper into Courtney and this love triangle. It seemed like it had been about to explode.

'What can you tell us about Sophie going fishing on *The*

Siren's Call?' Lauren asked, wanting to explore all aspects of
Sophie's life.

Imogen gave a faint smile. 'She loved it. She really wanted it
to be her career. But Sam...' Her smile faded. 'He hated her
being out there with all those men. He was really jealous
about it.'

Lauren leant forward slightly. 'Did he try to get her to quit?'

'Yes. And that was another reason Sophie wanted to end
things. They constantly argued about it. Sophie said she loved
Sam but couldn't take his constant complaining. Finding out
about Courtney was the last straw.'

There seemed to be a pattern of controlling behaviour
emerging.

'Other than Friday, were there any other rows that you
witnessed?'

'Actually, yes,' Imogen said. 'They had a huge fight on the
Wednesday before. I recorded it on my phone because I wanted
Sophie to see how it appeared to everyone else. She needed to
break up with him – he was toxic.' Imogen paled. 'You don't
think... he couldn't have hurt Sophie, could he?'

'We're investigating everything,' Lauren replied evenly,
though inwardly her mind was racing through the implications.

With shaky hands, Imogen pulled out her phone, scrolling
to the video before handing it to Lauren. 'Here it is. Just hit
play.'

Lauren watched the violent exchange, Sam's hand lifting
threateningly before he stopped himself. She turned to Imogen.

'Did Sophie ever mention physical violence from him?'

Imogen lowered her eyes, shaking her head. 'No, she never
outright said he hit her. But the way he acted...' She trailed off.
'The shouting, the raised hand... it was like watching a storm
brewing. I worried it could get worse. Sophie didn't talk about it
much. She didn't want to admit it, I suppose. But I saw fear in
her eyes that I'd never seen before.' Her voice had dropped to a

pained whisper. 'I wish I'd done something to try and stop him. But what could I do?'

Lauren's heart ached for the scared friend Imogen described, so different from the bold, unbeatable girl she'd portrayed earlier. If only Sophie had confided in her. Maybe things would be different now.

Lauren reached over and placed a comforting hand on Imogen's. 'You can't blame yourself for this,' she reassured her.

'I know, but...' Imogen wavered. 'It was Sam, wasn't it? He must have done this to Sophie.'

'We can't jump to conclusions,' Lauren warned. 'But every piece of information you've given helps us put together a picture of events. You've been extremely helpful.'

Learning what they had about Samuel Finch certainly put a different perspective on things. Had he strangled Sophie and then, realising what he'd done, attempted to make it look like something totally different?

'I know she'll never be coming back.' Imogen sniffed, full of emotion. 'But you have to catch who did this to her.'

'We're doing everything we can,' Lauren assured her, squeezing her hand. 'And you've helped immensely. Could you please forward that recording to me?'

'Of course,' Imogen agreed, accepting her phone back along with the card Lauren extended. She quickly forwarded the video file, her hands shaking slightly. Lauren knew the courage it had taken for Imogen to relive those moments, and she was immensely grateful for her cooperation.

'Were there any other threats against Sophie?' Matt asked, speaking up for the first time in a while. 'Had she received any because of working on the trawler? Or for any other reason?'

Imogen frowned. 'I don't think so, but I can't say for sure. She didn't mention anything to me.'

'But as best friends, she likely would have told you about any, right?' Matt pressed.

'Yes, I'm sure she would have,' Imogen agreed.

'Well, thank you for your time, Imogen. We're very sorry for your loss. Shall we take you home now?' Lauren concluded.

Imogen shook her head. 'I'd rather stay here with my work friends. I don't want to be alone.'

'Of course, I understand,' Lauren said. 'We may need to speak again later.'

Outside, Matt turned to Lauren. 'I'm guessing that we're on the same page about Samuel Finch?'

'Yes, he clearly has a darker, controlling side we weren't previously aware of. We need to question him further.'

'And what about this Courtney Inwood?' Matt asked. 'Might she have had reason to kill Sophie?'

Lauren considered it. 'We should look into her, but it doesn't seem likely from what Imogen said. First, we need to go back to Sophie's family. I want their take on the fishing job and the boyfriend. Their perspective could be crucial.'

Matt fell in step beside Lauren as they headed to the car, both deep in thought. The new information had cast an ominous shadow over the investigation.

TWELVE

Matt glanced at Lauren as they walked to the car, her brow furrowed in thought.

'It seems Sophie's life wasn't as rosy as her parents believed,' he commented.

'Yes,' Lauren agreed. 'And now we have the hard task of enlightening them.'

They pulled away from the kerb, heading for the home of Mr and Mrs Yates, which was on the outskirts of town. Matt shifted in his seat, conflicted about destroying the parents' image of their daughter. But hiding the truth would only hamper the investigation in the long run.

'Do you think the parents were aware of her problems with Finch?' he asked.

Lauren shook her head decisively. 'I don't think so, not from how they spoke about him yesterday. They're in for a shock, I'm afraid.'

Matt sighed, staring at the road ahead. Telling grieving parents that their daughter had kept parts of her life secret from them wasn't going to be easy. But finding out those secrets was likely to be the only way to catch her killer. Even though it would be very painful, they needed to know the truth.

The house came into view, and Matt steeled himself for what was going to be a difficult conversation.

Lauren rang the bell and almost immediately Tracie, the family liaison officer, opened the door.

'Morning, ma'am,' Tracie said, her familiar face a welcome sight.

'Hello,' Lauren replied, smiling. 'How's the family doing?'

Tracie sighed heavily. 'As well as can be expected, I suppose. Pretty typical, really. Mr Yates is in there with a stiff upper lip, acting as if nothing has happened while his wife frequently bursts into floods of tears. They're in the lounge, and also Sophie's older brother, Patrick, is with them. I take it you'd like to speak to them.'

'Yes, we would. Thank you.'

'Would you like a tea or coffee? I'm about to make some for the family,' Tracie asked.

'Not for us, we haven't got time,' Lauren declined swiftly.

'Actually, if you don't mind, I'll have one,' Matt said. He hadn't had anything to drink since breakfast and could really do with a pick-me-up.

Lauren turned and looked at him, her eyebrows slightly raised. 'Okay. In that case, make that two coffees, please, Tracie.'

Their steps echoed in the hallway as they walked into the lounge. Each member of the Yates family appeared to be dealing with their grief in their own way. Mr Yates, stoic by the window, Mrs Yates, tearfully distraught on her chair, and Patrick offering silent support beside his mother.

'Good morning, Mr and Mrs Yates. How are you doing?' Lauren asked, cutting through the silence.

'How do you think they're doing?' the brother snapped, the

anger in his words creating a stark contrast to the otherwise sombre atmosphere.

Clearly Lauren's well intentioned question hadn't gone down well. Instantly Matt's mind went into overdrive, analysing the man's outburst. Grief often manifested itself in anger, but this seemed more than that.

'That's enough, Patrick,' Mr Yates said, his words laden with weariness, and his stoicism slipping for a moment.

It was painful to watch.

'I'm sorry,' Lauren said, handling the man's outburst with grace. 'I didn't mean to sound insensitive. You must be Sophie's brother. I'm Detective Inspector Pengelly, and this is Detective Sergeant Price. We've come to speak to your parents a little more. But, also, we'd like to ask you a few questions, if you're up to it. We're very sorry for your loss.'

'Thank you,' Patrick said gruffly. 'There's not much I can tell you about Sophie. We weren't very close.'

Matt studied Patrick, puzzled by his gruff response. It appeared oddly detached, as if he was speaking about a distant relative. Not a sibling. Was the relationship he had with Sophie strained in some way?

'Patrick,' Mrs Yates said, with an undercurrent of disappointment. 'She's your sister.'

'Yes, I know, and I'm really sorry that she's gone.' The words rolled off Patrick's tongue like a prepared script, or perhaps a well-rehearsed defence. There was a detachment in his voice, in his demeanour, that intrigued Matt. 'I'm just saying that we weren't very close because of the age difference. I'm seven years older and so when I was living at home, she was still young. I left home when I was eighteen to go to university and didn't come back. She was only eleven then. It doesn't mean we didn't get on; we did. I'm just saying we weren't close, and I don't know what she got up to.'

Matt watched Lauren, her eyes sharp, perceptive. She

seemed to have understood something about Patrick, too. She had an uncanny ability to see through the noise and pick up on the subtle undercurrents of human behaviour.

'I understand what you mean,' Lauren began, her tone resolute. 'But what I'd like to ask all of you, well, probably Mr and Mrs Yates, is that we've discovered Sophie was going out on a fishing trawler one or two nights a week because she wanted to train to be a female fisherman.'

'She what?' Patrick erupted, his words slicing through the thick silence like a sharp knife. His facade of aloofness shattered momentarily, revealing a glimpse of surprise, shock... maybe even guilt.

Matt scrutinised the man's face for any signs of something not quite right.

'We didn't know anything about that,' Mr Yates added, the creases on his face deepening, his fingers drumming nervously on the window sill. 'When you showed us all the things under her bed relating to fishing, we were as shocked as you. She said she wanted a career in that industry years ago, but we'd persuaded her not to, as we told you before.'

A knot formed in Matt's stomach. Was Sophie's secret life a factor in her death? It was certainly pointing to that. But quite how, he couldn't fathom.

'Well, she did, and she was training. Are you sure you didn't know anything about it? That nothing in her behaviour gave you any clue about this?' Lauren pressed on, her voice unyielding.

'Nothing.' Mrs Yates's whisper echoed around the room.

'Why on earth did she want to work in that industry?' Patrick finally muttered, the shock in his eyes slowly morphing into confusion. 'She was way too clever to be a fisherwoman... person, or whatever they call them.'

'Female fisherman,' Lauren corrected, her tone even.

'Well, that too. She was really smart. She wanted to be an

accountant.' Patrick was calmer now, a whisper of pride seeping through the hard-edged tone.

Matt couldn't help but feel a pang of sympathy. This man, trying so hard to stand aloof, was clearly hurt by the sudden loss of a sister he supposedly barely knew.

The room fell into a silence. The undercurrent of emotions in the room, raw and palpable. Sophie's life, her dreams, her secrets, were becoming clearer. It was like piecing together a complex jigsaw puzzle. Except there were parts of her story and her feelings that were missing or hidden.

'According to Sophie's friend Imogen, and her boyfriend, Samuel Finch, she didn't want a career in accountancy,' Lauren said, breaking the silence.

'Well, he's a waste of space anyway,' Patrick retorted. His offhand dismissal of Sophie's boyfriend caused Matt to go on alert.

'I thought you didn't know much about your sister's life,' Matt said, staring directly at the brother.

'All I know is that she could have done better,' Patrick said, his arms folded tightly across his chest.

'Why do you say that?' Lauren asked.

His cheeks flushed, and he quickly averted his eyes, a guilty demeanour that didn't go unnoticed by Matt.

'What aren't you telling us, Patrick?' Mr Yates said firmly, with an unspoken warning.

'I saw him out one time in a local bar and he wasn't with Sophie. He was with someone else, and they seemed pretty cosy,' Patrick confessed, glancing uneasily around the room.

'Why didn't you say something?' Mrs Yates said, with a mix of disbelief and hurt.

'I didn't want to. I wasn't actually sure if it was anything, and it was the night before I was going away on holiday. And then, well, honestly, I actually forgot all about it until just now,' Patrick admitted.

'But that's your sister you're talking about. How can you forget?' Mrs Yates asked, the disbelief still lingering.

'Because... Look... I'm sorry. I just forgot,' Patrick mumbled, staring firmly at the floor. Matt could see the guilt etched onto his face, the regret and confusion, as clear as day.

'That's okay,' Lauren said gently, turning to Mr and Mrs Yates. 'What else can you tell us about Sophie's relationship with Samuel Finch?'

'She's been going out with him for about two years, I think. I know it's a bit up and down. Not from what Sophie told me, but sometimes I've heard her on the phone to her friend moaning about him. She didn't confide in me,' Mrs Yates said, with sadness.

'We've heard that he can get jealous, and he didn't like her going out on the fishing boat.'

'Well, who would?' Mr Yates interjected. 'Going out all night on a trawler full of men. I assume it's full of men. I'd be worried for her safety too.'

'It's not like that, Mr Yates,' Matt reassured him, his tone low yet firm. 'I understand your concern, but it was perfectly fine. She wasn't the only woman to go out on the boats.'

'Well, that's as may be. But if I'd found out about it, I'd have put a stop to it,' Mr Yates insisted.

The words hung in the air, a promise too late to be kept, a regret too deep to be soothed. As Matt took in the grief-stricken faces around him, he knew they had to get to the bottom of this.

'We also heard that Sam has been seeing another woman, called Courtney Inwood. Do you know her?' Lauren's question echoed in the room, a thread of suspicion woven into her words.

'A little. She's one of Sophie's friends from school,' Mrs Yates answered. Her voice was small, like she was afraid her words would shatter the fragile silence that had fallen. 'I don't think they see much of each other now.'

'Was she the woman you saw Samuel Finch with?' Matt asked, turning to Patrick.

'I'm not sure. I don't know who this Courtney is. I didn't know any of Sophie's school friends.' Patrick's eyebrows furrowed together, deepening the lines of worry etched onto his forehead.

'I've got a photo of her. I'll fetch it,' Mrs Yates said, standing and heading over to the sideboard. She opened one of the drawers and pulled out a photograph. 'This is the three of them at the school ball. There's Sophie, Imogen and Courtney on the right.' She handed it to Matt, who glanced at it and then passed it to her son.

'I'm not sure,' Patrick said finally. 'Maybe. But I can't be one hundred percent. I'm sorry.' He handed the photo back to Matt, who then returned it to Mrs Yates.

'That's okay,' Lauren said, kindly. 'Thank you for answering our questions. We're leaving now. Speak to Tracie if you need to know anything, and she'll get in touch with us straight away.'

'Thank you,' Mrs Yates said, her frail voice barely audible.

Matt was about to stand when the door opened and Tracie walked in carrying a tray laden with coffees which she gingerly placed on the coffee table in the centre of the room. It gave a much-needed distraction.

'Thanks, Tracie.' Lauren smiled at her, her gratitude softening the strain that hung in the room. 'We were about to leave, but we'll have our coffee first. Mrs Yates, do you know, by any chance, where we can get hold of Courtney Inwood?' Lauren asked as she cradled the warm mug in her hands and lifted it to her lips, taking a small sip.

'I do, actually. She works at Newlyn fish market. I sometimes see her when I buy my fish. We like it fresh.'

Matt shared a knowing glance with Lauren. They'd definitely be speaking to Courtney next, before Finch's second interview, so they could get as much background info as possible. The picture was slowly but surely coming together.

He glanced at his watch. The fishery would be closed at this time, so the conversation with Courtney would have to wait until the morning.

As the scent of freshly brewed coffee filled the room, a strange mix of anticipation and dread coursed through Matt. They were getting closer to the truth, but what that truth would reveal was yet to be seen.

THIRTEEN

WEDNESDAY JUNE 12

The shrill ring of Lauren's mobile phone on the bedside table pierced the stillness, slicing through her sleep and dragging her to reality. As her eyes shot open, the remnants of the weird and chaotic dream she was having clung to her. The vivid imagery of blood and cash flying everywhere, with her cousins at the centre of it all. She blinked several times, attempting to rid herself of the lingering memory.

It was her own fault for spending too much time researching those damned Frame brothers last night. She'd dug deep into their construction firm and she'd bet her life savings on the fact that it was a front for their illegal activities, but proving anything would be difficult to say the least. If not impossible.

Her hand fumbled on the bedside table before finally closing around the vibrating phone. She squinted against the dim morning light. 'Hello?' she said, trying to make it sound like she'd been up for hours. But with little success. She sounded decidedly groggy.

She could almost see the eye-roll of the caller on the other end.

'Sorry to wake you, ma'am,' a female officer replied.

'That's okay,' she replied, trying to remember the name behind the familiar voice but failing.

'It's PC Smith.' The clarification jolted her memory into place.

Of course it was.

'You haven't woken me, Smith,' Lauren replied, making a concerted effort to sound normal, and luckily she succeeded because her voice came out stronger this time.

She glanced at the clock. Crap. It was half-past six. That meant she'd slept through her alarm. That never happened. Her bloody cousins. Even when they weren't there, they were somehow interfering with the smooth running of her life. And...

The dogs. They'd be expecting their morning walk. They went out at this time every morning. She focused her mind back on the call, trying to ignore the thought that their whining was bound to start any minute now.

'There's been a body found at Sennen Cove, ma'am,' Smith said.

Lauren's heart skipped a beat, and she hurriedly pushed herself upright. 'Not another one.'

'Yes, and by all accounts it's exactly the same as the one on Monday, ma'am. I'm on my way out there now, with PC French. We drew the short straw again,' the officer sighed. 'I figured you'd want to be informed straight away, before we left.'

'Good call. Thanks. I'll head out there, now.'

'Is there anything you need us to do before leaving?' Smith asked.

'No, thanks. The main thing is you contacted me. You go there now, because it will probably be another forty-five minutes before I'm there. Make sure to secure the scene. Actually, make sure someone phones the pathologist. We need him out there, pronto.'

'Consider it done, ma'am.'

Lauren ended the call and took a deep breath, momentarily closing her eyes. When they reopened, she was filled with determination. She quickly called Matt.

'Good morning, ma'am.' He sounded crisp, even at such an early hour, although there was a note of concern in there.

'There's been another death, Matt. The same MO as Sophie Yates,' Lauren said quickly, without even remembering to say hello.

'You're kidding,' he answered, his incredulity echoing in her ear.

'I wish that was the case. I'll be at your place in thirty minutes, and we'll head straight to the scene. Is that okay?'

'No problem at all, ma'am,' he replied, the gravity of the situation clear. 'I've been up for ages. Dani couldn't sleep and decided to come in to see me at four-thirty.'

'Is she unwell? Do you need to stay with her?'

'She's totally fine, thanks. She might be tired later but that's all. I'll see you soon. Hang on... I thought your car was playing up.'

'I took it to a garage after work yesterday and it turned out to be nothing much. Just a loose something or other that they sorted out while I waited. Thank goodness.'

'That's great.'

Lauren ended the call and pushed off the covers, making a dash for the bathroom. Every second counted. As the shower's water cascaded down her back, thoughts of the Frame brothers, her dream, and the body at Sennen Cove churned in her mind.

Dressed and downstairs in the kitchen within fifteen minutes, she looked apologetically at her two dogs, their tails wagging.

'Sorry, guys,' she murmured, opening the back door to let them out into the garden. 'Short playtime today and no walk. I promise to make it up to you later. At least I'll try. With possibly now two murders to deal with, life's going to be far from normal for the foreseeable future.'

Lauren pulled up outside Matt's parents' terraced house and took a few deep breaths, gathering herself for another day of grisly work. She turned off the engine and stepped out, adjusting her jacket. She walked down the short path leading to the front door, glancing at the small, neatly kept garden to her right. She smiled to herself at the sight of the area of grass which had small pebbles placed in a large circle, inside of which were a family of grey elephants: Dani's favourite animal. She must have been playing out there.

When Lauren reached the front door, she knocked twice and waited. It opened, but it wasn't Matt as she'd expected, and instead she faced an older woman who she assumed to be his mother. They'd only spoken on the phone and hadn't actually met in person. Next to her stood Dani, her bright eyes shining with curiosity.

'Hello, Lauren,' Dani greeted, smiling up at her.

Lauren bent slightly. 'Hello, Dani. How's my favourite girl today?'

Dani's face lit up. 'Very well thank you,' she replied in what appeared to be a response she'd learnt. Lauren smiled to herself.

'I'm Jean, Matt's mum,' the woman, who was strikingly like her son, said. 'It's nice to finally put a face to a name.'

'It's lovely to meet you, too, Jean. I'm sorry to bother you so early but we have an emergency.'

'It's no trouble. We're always up early with this one.' Jean affectionately ruffled Dani's hair.

'Daddy said we can go to your house to see Ben and Tia. Can we go today, pleeease?'

'Not today but I promise, very soon. Daddy and I have some grown-up work to do,' Lauren said, feeling mean having to disappoint the child. But that was the problem with their job. It always had to come first.

'Dani, what did I say about bothering Lauren so early in the morning?' Matt said, walking up behind his mother and daughter and cutting in before Dani could respond. His face was serious, but his eyes sparkled with amusement.

Dani pouted, and turned to face him, her small arms crossing defiantly. 'I'm not bothering Lauren, Daddy. Am I?' she asked, focusing on Lauren again.

Lauren chuckled. 'Of course you're not, Dani. You can talk to me anytime you like. But Daddy and I do have to go out now. We've got lots to do today.'

'That's okay,' Dani said, her face becoming serious.

Matt turned to Dani and scooped her up in a swift motion. 'Come here, you little monster, and say goodbye,' he teased, pressing a kiss on her forehead.

She wriggled in his grasp, her face feigning indignation. 'I'm not a monster, daddy. I'm a girl.'

Matt laughed. 'I'm only teasing. You're my precious little princess.'

Warmth flooded through Lauren. She'd always said she didn't want children, but witnessing Matt with Dani, and the love between the two of them reminded her of how it was with her parents before the accident.

Stop.

This was neither the time nor the place to dwell on her past.

'Does that mean you have to do what I tell you?' Dani said, bringing Lauren's thoughts back to the present.

'Not today, sweetheart. That's Lauren's job. Now, be good for Grandma, okay, and I'll see you later.'

'Okay, bye, Daddy. Bye, Lauren.'

Lauren and Matt headed to the car and they began the drive to Sennen Cove. She couldn't help comparing the rugged beauty of Cornwall to the harsh nature of their profession and what gruesome sight was waiting for them.

As they got closer to their destination Lauren took a moment to absorb the landscape. The rolling green hills in the distance, with the occasional ancient stone cottage. As they approached the coastline she caught sight of the vast expanse of the Atlantic Ocean shimmering under the morning sun.

'Any more thoughts on your cousins, ma'am, and those two criminals?' Matt asked, breaking the silence, his tone a mix of professional curiosity and concern.

Lauren turned from the landscape to face Matt. 'I spent hours last night digging deeper into the Frame brothers. They're clearly on the radar of the Exeter division, but I'm not sure yet how to use that knowledge. I'm still giving it some thought.'

'It's tricky, but you'll think of something – and if you want to brainstorm anytime, you know I'm here.'

'Thanks, Matt. That's appreciated. But for now we've got one and now most likely two murders which are demanding our attention.'

'Do you know anything yet about the second victim?'

'No. All Smith told me was that another body had been found on the rocks at Sennen Cove and it's identical to what happened at Land's End. I don't even know whether the victim's male or female,' Lauren said, her tone dropping, revealing her unease.

'And here was me thinking that I'd joined a force where nothing much happened. Now I have another body to brace myself for seeing.' He gave a dry smile in her direction.

'I'm surprised that after all the bodies you encountered in Lenchester you weren't desensitised to it,' Lauren said, glancing quickly at him and frowning.

Matt shrugged. 'I managed to keep away from them. DCI Walker knew about my issues and would take someone else with her to a crime scene or to the morgue. Usually Dr

Cavendish the forensic psychologist. She'd leave me to manage the team in her absence.'

'Yes, well. Lucky DCI Walker for having sufficient staff to make that possible. You know that's not going to happen here, don't you?' Lauren smiled, to soften her words. She didn't intend for them to be antagonistic.

'Yes. And that's fine, ma'am. I'll make sure to vomit or pass out quietly.'

'What? How often does that happen?'

She had no idea that he could respond in that way. He hadn't so far.

'Only joking,' he said, grinning. 'Well, there was this one time when we came across a man's body minus various parts of his anatomy, and I did throw up then.'

Her body tensed at the thought. She expected that would've turned the stomach of the hardiest person.

'Okay, that's understandable. There's not many people who could witness something like that without it affecting them.'

'Even you?' Matt teased.

'Yes, even me. Right, we're here,' she said, glancing out of the window. 'Let's hope Henry is, too.'

FOURTEEN

As Matt followed Lauren down the uneven steps towards Sennen Cove's rocky shoreline, a cold knot of dread tightened in his stomach. It wasn't just the chilling wind or the daunting cliffs; it was the sheer number of bodies he'd encountered since his move. Despite his assurances to Lauren that he was going to be fine, he hadn't been prepared for the series of events over the past six months. And, yes, of course Lenchester had been crazier... off the scale even... but he'd been shielded from the gruesome bits.

Focus. Dwelling on this wasn't going to do anyone any good at all. He had another body to deal with.

Each gust of wind felt like a slap against his face, but Matt welcomed it. It was a distraction, a momentary escape. And at least he would be viewing the body outside which was far more palatable than the cold, oppressive atmosphere of the morgue.

'Come on, Matt,' Lauren called out, cutting into his thoughts, her tone teasing. 'It won't get any easier the slower you walk.'

He turned to see her grinning, a hint of mischief in her eyes. A far cry from what she was like when he first joined her team.

Then, she was serious one hundred percent of the time. Flashing a smile in return, he picked up the pace and caught up with her.

As they neared the scene, Henry's figure below on the rocks came into focus, his lumbering posture unmistakable. His hands were rested on his hips, and he was staring intently at the body.

The familiar sight of the cordon marked the boundary between the ordinary and the gruesome and they headed over to the entrance, where PC Smith was standing.

'Morning, ma'am. Morning, Sarge,' the officer greeted them.

'What can you tell us?' Lauren asked.

'Harold Wood, the owner of the café by the cliffs over there, found her,' Smith said, pointing to a large area to the left of them. 'He came to work early and was staring at the ocean and spotted the body, after which he contacted us. We allowed him to go back to the café to get on with his work but said he had to stay there because you'd want to speak to him once you arrived.'

'Thanks,' Lauren said. 'We'll interview him shortly. I can see the pathologist's already here so we'll speak to him first. Sign us in, please.' Lauren motioned to the tablet in the officer's hand.

'Will do, ma'am.'

Matt and Lauren navigated their way down the rocky path, taking hold of the rope railing until reaching the bottom and stepping onto the sand, littered with kelp and seashells. They headed towards the imposing granite boulders where Henry was meticulously capturing the crime scene with his camera. The cold, analytical proceedings seemed at odds with the warm morning sunlight that washed over the scene, bathing it in a serene golden glow.

'Morning, Henry,' Lauren called out once they'd reached him and were standing on a nearby rock. 'We've been informed that this death is identical to the one on Monday, is it?'

Henry stood up and took a step towards them. 'Yes, at first

glance I'm afraid it is.' He gestured to the body. 'The staging is almost identical and there's fishing line wrapped tightly around the neck. There's a note inside the mouth but I haven't checked what's on it. I've left it in situ until the body is taken to the morgue. I've had confirmation that the first victim was drugged with ketamine, as suspected. I'll check if this is the same.'

'Two deaths in three days. Just what we don't need,' Lauren muttered, giving a frustrated sigh.

'One more and we'll be facing a serial killer,' Matt added, more to himself than to those around him, but it was loud enough for both Lauren and Henry to roll their eyes in his direction.

'Thank you for your insight, Sergeant. But let's not get carried away. We don't want a serial killer down here. And most definitely not one who gets me up so early in the morning,' Henry said, with a mix of dark humour and weariness.

'Sorry, Henry. I was just saying,' Matt said, regretting speaking his thoughts out loud. 'What about identification; do we have one, by any chance?' he asked, wanting to move things on.

'Yes, I found a photo ID in the woman's pocket,' Henry said, holding it up in an evidence bag. 'She's Courtney Inwood. Aged twenty-three and lives locally.'

The revelation of the victim's identity left Matt momentarily frozen. 'Bloody hell... that's the name of the woman Samuel Finch was seeing on the side while going out with Sophie.' He turned to Lauren. 'Do you think it's her?'

'It's got to be,' Lauren said, appearing equally taken aback at the revelation. 'I mean, it's not exactly a common name, is it?'

'You know this woman?' Henry asked.

'She's come up in our enquiries,' Lauren said, rubbing the back of her neck tensely. 'And it changes everything. Is there anything else you can tell us, before we leave, Henry?'

'Yes. I believe the body has been moved, exactly like it had with the first victim. There are also fingerprints on the neck which are consistent with strangulation, and appear similar in size and shape to other victim. But until the body's at the morgue and tests have been conducted, I can't confirm that officially. As soon as I have anything to report, you'll be the first to know.'

'Okay, thanks, Henry. The sooner the better. Have you finished with the ID?'

'Yes. Take it. I've got photos.' Henry handed over the evidence bag containing the ID.

'Thanks.'

Lauren held the ID up so they could double-check the face on the picture with the body on the ground.

'It's definitely her,' Matt said quietly, gazing from the ID back to the lifeless woman sprawled across the rocks. He shook his head slowly, trying to comprehend the tragedy.

'Yeah,' Lauren said with a sigh, tucking the ID safely into her pocket.

Lauren gave Matt's shoulder a gentle squeeze, which he took comfort in.

'Nasty business,' Henry said.

'It sure is,' Lauren said. 'Thanks, Henry. We'll speak to you later.' She turned to Matt. 'We'll talk to Harold Wood and then inform the victim's family. I'll message Tamsin and ask her to find out where they live.'

'Okay, ma'am. You know... I can't help wondering... if we'd interviewed Courtney Inwood yesterday, would she still be alive?'

'We'll never know, Matt. It's pointless conjecture.'

Lauren's words echoed around in his mind. She was right. But that didn't stop the guilt gnawing at his insides.

How could it?

'Maybe, but it doesn't stop me dwelling on it.'

Retracing their steps, Lauren and Matt slowly ascended the

steep cliffside path away from the grim scene below. As they neared the café entrance, a light breeze carried the rich aroma of freshly brewed coffee. The mundane, comforting scent seemed jarringly at odds with the tragic events of the morning.

A weathered wooden sign hung crookedly outside the café, the faded letters spelling out *Welcome* in a cheery font. But despite the invitation, the café sat dark and shuttered. Matt rapped his knuckles sharply against the salt-bleached door and they waited, but only silence greeted them.

'Where is he?' Lauren muttered with a frustrated sigh. 'He'd better not have left. Not after he was specifically told to stay put.'

'I'll try again,' Matt said, knocking more insistently this time. The sound echoed around them.

After what seemed like ages, the door finally opened, revealing a small, dishevelled man in his fifties who appeared out of breath. 'Sorry,' the man explained between puffs. 'I was in the cellar sorting out the beer barrels. Are you the police?'

'Yes, I'm DI Pengelly, and this is DS Price from Penzance CID. Are you Mr Wood?' Lauren asked briskly.

'Yes, that's me. Harold. But call me Harry, everyone else does. I phoned in about the body on the rocks this morning. Is this a suspicious death, like that other one found at Land's End?'

'We can't speculate on that, Harry,' Lauren replied. 'But we'd like to speak to you about the events leading up to your discovery this morning.'

Harry gestured for them to enter the dim interior. 'Come on in.'

Stepping inside, Matt was struck by the cosy feel of the place. Round wooden tables draped in red-and-white checked cloths were placed haphazardly around the room, each with a small glass vase of fresh wildflowers in the centre.

Harry gestured for them to sit at a table beside the large

front window. The distant cries of seagulls and the earthy aroma of coffee grounds perfumed the air.

'If you could start from the beginning, please,' Lauren said.

Matt pulled out his notebook, waiting to jot down anything of significance.

'Yeah, sure. Before I start, would you like a coffee?' Harry offered. 'I've just put a fresh pot on.'

'No, thanks. We don't have time.' Lauren's smile appeared patient, although Matt could tell by the tightening of the lines around her eyes that she was anxious to proceed. 'Please continue with what happened.'

'Sorry, right. I got here at six, as usual, to prep for the day. I like to get here early to make sure everything is ready because it can be chaotic at this time of year, and it's hard to find time later. Even though it's not yet school holidays, there are so many tourists, as you know. I bet it makes your job hard, too, and—'

'Harry...' Lauren interrupted.

'Sorry. I'd got a lot done and decided to go outside for a few minutes. It gets hot in here so I wanted a breath of fresh air and the chance to take in the view, which is stunning.' He gestured out the window towards the cliffs and roiling sea. 'That's when I noticed something strange on the rocks. So I headed down the path until I was closer and then saw that it was a body.'

'Did you touch it?' Matt asked sharply, studying the man's face.

'God, no. I didn't get that close. As soon as I realised what it was I called 999. The police officer I spoke to told me to stay put until someone arrived. That's what I did. I was over there, about half-way down.' He pointed to the path that Matt and Lauren had taken to reach the café.

'Did you notice anybody hanging around at the scene?' Matt asked.

Murderers often stayed close to the scene of their crime,

especially when the police were present. It was as if in some perverse way, they thought they could get the better of them.

'There were a few people around, but no one seemed interested in the body. I mean... I only saw it by chance.' He rested his hands on the table. 'You know, I've never seen a dead body before. Can you believe it? At my age?'

'It can be a shock,' Lauren said. 'Have you noticed anyone acting suspiciously around here over the last few days? Anyone or anything, even, that didn't quite seem right.'

'No... I don't think so. Maybe one of my staff might have. I'll ask them when they arrive and let you know. But to be honest, we're too busy to notice most of the time.'

'Well, if you could ask that would help,' Lauren said. 'What about when you were closing up last night, was there anybody loitering?'

'Not that I remember. We were late closing because of a last-minute rush. A coach had broken down and so the passengers came here while waiting for a replacement to arrive.'

'Do you serve fish, chips, and mushy peas?' Matt asked, remembering the last meal that Sophie had consumed. If Courtney had eaten the same, and it was bought from the café, it would help. That's *if* she had, which they wouldn't know until Henry had completed his work.

'Yes, that's on our menu, why?'

'Just curious,' he said, brushing off the comment with a wave of his hand.

Harry glanced at his watch. 'Is there anything else, because I still have a lot to do.'

'No, that's all we need for now. Thanks for your help, Harry,' Lauren said. 'If anything springs to mind, then let us know. Here's my card.'

Matt and Lauren left and headed back to the car.

'This isn't good,' Lauren said. 'Two murders, two days apart, and two young women who knew each other, with one common interest. We need to interview Samuel Finch, but before we do that, we must visit the victim's family. Hopefully Tamsin's got an address for us.'

As they climbed into the car, Matt couldn't help letting out a sigh.

'Who would have thought that in a quiet area like this we're potentially dealing with a serial killer.'

Lauren glanced at him, her expression serious. 'We don't know for sure yet, Matt, as Henry said. So, let's not jump to conclusions. We'll follow the leads and see where they take us.'

'Sorry, you're right. I suppose I've been involved in so many serial killings that I automatically think the worst,' he acknowledged.

'I get it. But we have to remain hopeful that the deaths stop here. If it's linked to Samuel Finch then the motive is most likely something personal and so Sophie and Courtney won't be random victims of a serial killer.'

Matt refrained from mentioning that he'd been involved in cases involving serial killers who knew, and specifically targeted, their victims.

FIFTEEN

Lauren's chest tightened as she pulled into the car park. Informing a family of a tragic death was an immense burden and never got easier. When the victim was young, with a life barely lived, the cruelty seemed to magnify tenfold. It defied the natural order.

Tamsin had briefed her on the family. A single-mother household, and nothing was known about the father. Celia Inwood lived with her daughter, Courtney, in one of the flats converted in the 1970s from an old Edwardian hospital in Penzance.

Lauren steeled herself. 'Let's do this.'

They crossed the bleak car park and entered the building, their footsteps echoing hollowly on the tiled floor.

'Would you like me to break the news, seeing as you spoke to Sophie's parents?' Matt offered.

Lauren studied her sergeant. After his own devastating loss, his willingness to shoulder this burden was a testament to his empathy. But she would take the lead. It was her job.

'No. I'll do it. Make sure to have some tissues handy.'

'Will do, ma'am,' Matt said, sounding relieved.

They took the lift to the fourth floor. Their footsteps reverberated as they walked down the barren concrete corridor to Celia Inwood's flat. Matt pressed the doorbell. Its cheerful chime seemed absurdly out of place in the oppressive silence.

Part of Lauren hoped no one would answer. That they could somehow delay this awful duty, even for a few minutes. But that was foolish. The news had to come from them first.

Finally, they heard shuffling coming from inside the flat before the door opened. A woman in a cream dressing gown stood before them, bleary-eyed.

'Are you Celia Inwood?' Lauren asked.

'Yes, that's me. Who are you?'

Lauren glanced at the sterile walls, the harsh lighting, wishing they didn't have to deliver this life-shattering news in such an unfeeling place. She took a breath. There was no going back now.

'I'm Detective Inspector Pengelly and this is Detective Sergeant Price,' Lauren said, holding out her ID. 'We'd like to speak to you. May we come in?'

Celia glanced at her robe, a momentary flicker of embarrassment crossing her face, 'I'm not dressed as you can see; I was working late last night at the club.'

'It doesn't matter,' Lauren assured her. 'Please, will you let us in? We... have some very difficult news to share with you.'

The woman's eyes widened in dawning dread. Wordlessly, she stepped back, allowing them into the sparse, impersonal hallway. The only warmth came from an old rug thrown on the wooden floor.

The living room wasn't much different, furnished with the basics: a television, a sofa, two chairs, and an array of photos. Lauren's attention was drawn to the pictures. Images of Celia and her daughter, happy and alive. A stark contrast to the devastating news they were about to deliver.

Lauren's heart pounded as she began. 'Celia, I'm so sorry… we have terrible news about Courtney.'

Celia paled, a trembling hand flying to her mouth. 'What? Has she been in an accident? Where is she?'

Lauren steeled herself. 'I'm afraid Courtney's body was found on the rocks at Sennen Cove this morning. We are so very sorry for your loss.'

Celia stared back at them, her mouth open in silent anguish. Then tears spilled down her cheeks as she absorbed the devastating news.

Lauren's own eyes welled up in sympathy, but she blinked back the tears. The grief wasn't hers to share. She reached out a hand, wishing she could somehow ease the pain. But no words would suffice.

Matt rose from his seat. 'I'll make you some tea?'

Celia nodded, seeming to be on autopilot. 'Okay,' she said. 'But you might not be able to find where I keep everything.'

'Don't worry, I'm sure I will,' Matt assured her, leaving the room.

Alone now, Lauren sat with Celia in the heavy silence. The awful truth still sinking in.

'What happened?' Celia finally choked out. She wrapped her arms around her knees, rocking backwards and forwards, as if it was her only anchor now.

Lauren chose her words carefully. 'That's what we're investigating. However, we are treating Courtney's death as suspicious,' Lauren shared, her words carefully measured.

Celia's rocking halted and her eyes locked on Lauren, focused and intent. 'You mean she was murdered?'

Lauren swallowed hard. There was no easy way to say this. 'Yes. That's what we suspect.'

Celia's face crumpled again. 'Like Sophie?' she whispered.

'Yes, there do seem to be many similarities between the two

incidents but we're waiting for confirmation from the pathologist.'

'What actually happened to Courtney?'

'I'm sorry we can't share any details yet. Not until the pathologist has done his tests.' Lauren rested her hand on Celia's arm. 'Is there anyone we can ask to be with you?'

She knew that the worst was yet to come. When the realisation of what had happened properly hit. It would be even worse if the woman had to go through it alone.

'No, I'm on my own here. I don't know where Courtney's dad is. She was a result of a one-night stand. And my mum and dad live in Spain. It's just me.' The finality of her words hung in the air.

'What about a friend? Is there anyone we could ask to come round?' Lauren probed further, hoping there'd be someone.

'My best friend's at work and I don't want to bother her.'

'I'm sure she wouldn't mind,' Lauren said, hoping to persuade her.

'She'd lose money if she came over. She's hourly paid and can't afford it.'

'Okay, I understand. I'm going to ask one of our family liaison officers to come round and stay with you while the investigation is ongoing. I'm not sure who it will be just yet, but they'll keep you up to date with what's happening,' Lauren said, the words sounding more like a lifeline than a statement.

'Thank you,' Celia said, with a distant look in her eyes that suggested she was miles away from the room.

'Celia,' Lauren said softly, waiting until the woman refocused on her. 'I know this is hard, but I do need to ask you a few questions about Courtney. Do you feel up to it? I wouldn't ask if it wasn't important. It might help us discover who did this to her.'

'Yes. What do you want to know?' Celia whispered.

'Thank you. I'll try to keep this brief. First of all, did you know that Courtney had been seeing Samuel Finch, who was Sophie's boyfriend?' Lauren asked, deliberately keeping her tone non-accusatory.

Celia didn't speak for a few seconds, her lips pressed together, as if she was contemplating her response. 'Yes,' she finally said. 'And I wasn't happy. Courtney felt really bad about it, too. Whenever I told her it was wrong and she shouldn't see him, she said that she loved him and couldn't give him up.'

'So she wouldn't listen to your advice,' Lauren confirmed.

'No.' Celia shook her head. 'But what girl of her age would. I told her no good would come of it. B-but when I said that... I didn't mean...' The woman's words fell away, and tears streamed down her cheeks. 'I'm sorry.'

'That's okay. You take your time. Would you like a break?' Lauren offered.

Celia sniffed and sat upright. 'No. I'm okay. Carry on.'

'Were Courtney and Sophie good friends?' Lauren continued, sensing the importance of the relationship between the two young women.

'They were at school, but they drifted apart after leaving. I don't think they'd seen each other recently.'

'Did they have any common friends? Anyone who could have been a source of conflict or tension between them?' Lauren added, her mind contemplating all the possibilities.

'Not that I know of,' Celia said. 'They had their separate social circles that didn't mix.'

'What about Imogen? She would have been at school with Courtney, too.'

'The three of them hung around together when they were young, but not recently, as far as I know. Except...'

'What?' Lauren prodded.

'When Courtney came home from town on Saturday she was upset because Imogen had threatened her.'

'Did she tell you what was said?' Lauren asked, immediately going on alert and wanting to know if it matched with Imogen's account.

'Not the exact words, but Courtney seemed scared. Imogen could always be a bit of a bitch... If you'll excuse my French.'

'It's fine, I've heard a lot worse,' Lauren said, waving her hand dismissively, but inwardly wondering whether there was more to Imogen than just a grieving friend. 'I understand that Courtney worked for a fishery, preparing fish and selling it at the fish market. That's quite a male-dominated job, I believe.'

'Yes, I was surprised when she went into it, but she loved it there. When she left school, she didn't know what she wanted to do, and so she took the first job that was offered to her and it turned out well.'

'Did Courtney ever mention anyone at work who may have had it in for her? Perhaps someone who didn't like her working in that role?'

'No, she only had good things to say of her work mates. Most of them were older and she said they treated her like a kid sister.' Celia's eyes grew distant with the memory.

'Did you know that Sophie was working two nights a week on a trawler because she wanted to train to be a female fisherman?'

'No, I had no idea,' Celia said, appearing genuinely surprised. 'Courtney certainly didn't tell me. I don't even know if their paths crossed. So maybe she didn't know either.'

Before Lauren could ask another question, the door opened, and Matt re-entered the room, cradling a mug of tea. He set it down on the small table beside the sofa. 'I've made it strong, with sugar. I hope that's okay. It's good for shock.'

'Thank you,' Celia said with a weak smile before her face turned solemn again. 'Do you have any idea of who might have done this to my Courtney?' Her voice came out in a hushed whisper, her eyes pleading with Lauren in a way that deeply moved her.

'Not yet, but it's early days,' Lauren said, trying to instil more confidence in the success of the investigation than she currently felt. 'Would it be possible for us to take a quick peep at Courtney's bedroom, in case there's anything in there that might help?'

'Yes,' Celia said, standing. 'It's this way.'

They followed her out of the lounge and into a tiny room on the right. It was only large enough for a single bed, wardrobe and dressing table which was situated under the window.

After pulling on some disposable gloves, Lauren and Matt quickly searched the room, while Celia stood at the doorway watching.

'Does Courtney have a laptop?' Lauren asked, after searching and not finding any devices in there.

'No. She did everything on her phone.'

Lauren frowned. No phone had been found on the body or the scene by Henry.

'Did she have it when you last saw her?' Lauren asked, wanting to confirm that it hadn't been left at home.

'She never goes anywhere without it. Even when she's in bed it's next to her on the side.'

'Okay, I think we've seen enough,' Lauren said as they headed out of the bedroom and stood in the tiny hallway.

'What happens now?' Celia asked.

'We need you to formally identify Courtney but it doesn't have to be today,' Lauren replied, resting her hand on the woman's shoulder.

'Oh... um... okay.' Celia audibly sucked in a shaky breath as if the thought of it was more than she could bear.

How could they leave the woman alone like this?

'Would it be okay if we asked one of your neighbours to keep you company until the family liaison officer arrives?' Lauren suggested tentatively. 'We really don't want to leave you alone at a time like this.'

Celia's eyes hardened with resolve. 'No, I want to be on my own. I'll be fine.'

Exchanging a worried glance with Matt, Lauren felt a twinge of apprehension in her gut. It went against every instinct to leave the grieving woman but what else could she do? They had a job to do and time was critical.

'Okay, if you're sure. But remember, if you need anything call me. The family liaison officer will be here shortly.'

The flat's door clicked shut behind them, closing off a world of unfathomable grief. As they descended in the creaky lift, Lauren pulled out her phone to call for a family liaison officer. With theirs already occupied at the home of Mr and Mrs Yates, she had to request one from a station up the coast.

Finally off the phone, she turned to Matt. 'Right, we need to interview Samuel Finch again. But first, let's stop by the pub and have another chat with Imogen. Hopefully she's working today.'

When they arrived at The Seaside Inn, Lauren pounded on the locked door.

'We're not open,' a man called out after a couple of minutes.

'Police, open up,' Lauren ordered.

The door swung open to reveal the man they'd met previously. 'Oh, you again. Are you here about Imogen?'

'Yes, is she working?'

'I gave her the rest of the week off. Poor thing's a total wreck. Do you want to come in?'

Lauren glanced at Matt, then shook her head. 'No, thanks. Do you have her address?'

'Yeah, but she's not there. She said she was going to stay with a friend upcountry. But I've no idea where.'

Lauren sighed, another lead at a dead end. 'Okay. Thanks for your help.'

Back at the car, Matt turned to her. 'What now, ma'am?'

'Nothing on Imogen for now. She threatened Courtney, yes, but these murders are too similar for her to only be involved in one.' Lauren started the engine. 'We'll go back to the station and set up an interview with Samuel Finch. He knew both girls, and could definitely provide some insight.'

SIXTEEN

'Right,' Lauren announced, drawing all eyes to her as they stepped back into the bustling office. Matt could feel the anticipation in the room, like electricity in the air before a storm: everyone realising that the case they were navigating was about to step up a level. 'We now have a second body, staged in exactly the same way as the first. Our link between the two is Samuel Finch.'

Matt watched as Lauren wrote up the name Courtney Inwood on the whiteboard, next to Sophie's. She connected them with a double-ended arrow, placing Finch's name firmly in the centre below them both. Matt's gut churned. He'd seen more than his fair share of crime scenes and suspects, but something about this case seemed particularly sinister.

'He was dating Sophie and seeing Courtney on the side,' Lauren continued, her voice matter-of-fact. 'And, according to her best friend Imogen, Sophie discovered about Finch's cheating when going through his phone.'

Billy snorted, rolling his eyes. 'Seriously, what is it with people not deleting messages to stop themselves from being caught?' He shook his head, disbelief evident.

'Because that's what you'd do, isn't it?' Tamsin said, playfully.

'I don't cheat, if that's what you're implying,' Billy said, appearing genuinely offended.

'It was a joke, Billy,' Tamsin said. 'Chill.'

Matt stared at the officer. Had something happened in the past that put him on edge when infidelity was discussed?

'In this age of technology, secrets are harder to keep. But it does make you wonder why some people don't take more care,' Matt said, agreeing.

'Do you think that Finch killed them both, ma'am?' Billy asked, his brow furrowed.

'We don't know,' Lauren responded. 'But as he's the person linking the two victims, that's what we need to investigate. According to the pathologist, there's a note in Courtney's mouth. But he hasn't yet examined it, so we don't know if the words are the same. Clem, get on to uniform and ask them to bring Finch in for questioning.'

'Yes, ma'am.' Clem responded promptly, his face set in a mask of determination.

'It's the poem that puzzles me the most,' Lauren continued. 'We know it's "The Three Fishers" because Jack Trembath, the trawler skipper, recognised it. It's obviously one that people in the industry are familiar with. Does anyone know who wrote it?'

'It was Charles Kingsley,' Tamsin said. 'We'd already found the poem. It wasn't hard to come across.'

Matt recognised the poet's name from somewhere, but couldn't think where. 'What else do we know about the poem... like what's it about? English wasn't my strong subject at school, so no way would I be able to decipher it,' he admitted with a self-deprecating grin. 'I can tell you that from the few words that we've already seen.'

Billy shrugged, glancing around and seeming equally

confused. 'Same for me, so I have no idea what it's about either,' he murmured.

'Me, too,' Jenna said. 'Clearly we're a bunch of illiterates.'

'Do we have a copy of the poem?' Matt asked.

'Yes, Sarge. I'll put it up on the screen,' Tamsin said.

Her fingers danced over the keyboard, and the screen beside the whiteboard came to life, flickering momentarily before the poem took centre stage. The room was blanketed in silence, broken only by the quiet rustle of papers and the occasional shift of a chair as everyone intently read through it.

A few moments passed before Matt broke the hush, his voice carrying a hint of frustration. 'Is anybody any the wiser about the meaning?' He scanned the room, hoping for a revelation, but was met with a sea of equally puzzled expressions. 'In that case, if it's okay with you, ma'am, while we wait for Finch to come in, I'll contact a local academic. There's got to be someone who can help us. Once we discover the poem's meaning, it might help us understand what's going on here.'

'That's a good idea, Matt,' Lauren said. 'Everyone else, continue with what you're doing. Let me know as soon as Finch has arrived.'

As the hum of activity continued in the main room, Lauren retreated to her office, but left her door slightly ajar.

Matt returned to his desk, powered up his computer and began to search universities in the area. He found an Aiden Rush who was Professor of English at Exeter University and who lectured in poetry. He hoped Rush might be able to provide some much-needed insight.

He called the university, and asked to be connected to the man.

'Professor Rush speaking,' Rush answered after only a couple of rings.

'Good morning, Professor. I'm Sergeant Matt Price from

Penzance CID and I wondered if you had a moment to answer a couple of questions for me.'

'What's happened?' Rush replied, sounding panicked.

'Sorry, I should have explained. I'm after your professional expertise, that's all.'

The professor gave a loud sigh which echoed down the phone. 'Thank goodness. Of course I can help; what would you like to know?'

'In one of our investigations we've come across a poem and we wondered if you could help us understand it. It's called "The Three Fishers" by Charles Kingsley. Do you know of it?'

'Oh yes, of course, I do,' the professor said. 'Kingsley is one of my favourites. His work is quite profound. How can I assist exactly?'

'Well, we're trying to understand its overall meaning and how it relates to our investigation. Although, I'm not at liberty to discuss the case as such. Could you provide some insight?'

The professor cleared his throat. 'Certainly. "The Three Fishers" is a poignant reflection on the dangers faced by fishermen and the heartache of those they leave behind. The poem illustrates the tragic uncertainty of life at sea, capturing the despair and worry of the women waiting onshore. It particularly underscores the bleakness and unpredictability of the fisherman's life.' He was silent for a few seconds. 'If my memory serves me correctly, it goes: "Men must work, and women must weep, Though storms be sudden, and waters deep." It's a commentary on gender roles in society and the inevitability of grief in such a harsh environment. The sea is a relentless force, taking away husbands and fathers, leaving behind widows and orphans. Kingsley's poem is an intimate glimpse into the everyday tragedies faced by fishing communities, the never-ending cycle of hope and heartbreak.'

Ah ha. Now Matt got it.

'I see. Thank you very much,' Matt said, having hurriedly jotted down some notes.

'It's a powerful social commentary, and in the context of your investigation, even though you can't tell me what it is, it might allude to the unpredictability of events or the profound consequence of a person's actions.'

Matt's mind raced as he processed the professor's words. 'Can you be more explicit?'

'Of course. Take the words "And the harbour bar be moaning". According to legend, a moaning sound over the sandbar when the tide goes out points to there being a disaster.'

'So it's like an omen.'

'Exactly.'

'Thank you for your time, Professor. You've been most helpful and have given us a lot to consider.'

Matt ended the call, reread his notes to make sure he understood everything and hurried over to Lauren's office. He had an idea and wanted to share it with everyone.

He tapped on the door and she glanced up.

'Is Finch here already?' Lauren asked.

'No, ma'am. I know more about the poem and thought you'd want to listen while I feed back to the team.'

'Definitely,' Lauren said, pushing back her chair and standing.

She followed him to the front of the room where they stood by the whiteboard.

'Listen up, everyone,' Matt said, so loud that it carried over the hustle and bustle of the team working. He waited until they'd all given him their attention. 'I've spoken to a poetry professor at Exeter University and he explained that the poem is a reflection on the perils of fishing. He called it a profound social commentary. Interestingly, he emphasised how the poem refers to a bad omen. Basically, if there's a noise when the tide goes over the sandbar, it's not good.'

'But how does it help our case?' Billy asked.

'Well,' Matt continued. 'I reckon that this poem has been used specifically to relate to some event? A tragedy of some description.'

Jenna leant forward. 'But how does it relate to Sophie and Courtney, Sarge?'

Matt collected his thoughts. 'Our victims were part of the fishing world. This poem, with its ominous tone and emphasis on tragedy, might not be a simple coincidence. The reference to the sandbar and tide might symbolise an event – a tragedy that perhaps both victims knew about or were involved in. I don't know. It's just an idea that I've got.'

'So you're thinking this isn't really to do with their personal lives but to do with women in fishing generally,' Clem said. 'It's a wider net... no pun intended.'

Matt shot him a quick smile before becoming serious again. 'Exactly. I think it's imperative that we dig into any recent fishing tragedies or accidents. We need to understand the broader context and see if this provides a motive or connection.'

'It's a lead worth chasing,' Lauren said, her eyes sharp. 'Let's pull up any relevant incidents from the past year. Matt, I think you might have cracked the motive. Well done.'

SEVENTEEN

Lauren sat at her desk, deeply engrossed in some budgets requiring her comments, when a faint knock interrupted her thoughts. She saw Matt's frame silhouetted against the frosted glass of her office door and motioned for him to enter.

'Finch's here, ma'am,' Matt reported, his voice carrying a sense of urgency.

Lauren straightened her papers and drew in a breath. 'Okay, thanks. Let's not keep him waiting.'

They strode out of the office together, their steps echoing in the quiet corridor. Lauren's mind raced, preparing herself mentally for the confrontation. She entered the interview room, her sharp eyes immediately landing on Finch. He was sitting with his arms folded tightly across his chest and a scowl marring his features.

'Why am I here?' Finch demanded, his tone icy and defiant.

Taking her seat opposite him, Lauren kept her expression neutral. 'We have some more questions for you.'

'Couldn't you have phoned and asked me to come in? Instead of hauling me out of work like that. How do you think it made me look?'

Finch's irritation was evident but rather than addressing his complaints, Lauren shifted the focus back to the task at hand. 'We'll be recording this interview.'

Before Finch could react, Matt leant over and pressed the record button on the equipment. The red light blinked to life. 'Interview on Wednesday, June the twelfth. Those present are DI Pengelly, DS Price, and...' He stared at Finch.

Finch let out a begrudging sigh. 'Samuel Finch.'

'Mr Finch,' Lauren began. 'We've been informed that your relationship with Sophie Yates was tumultuous, to say the least. Would you agree?'

Finch stared directly at her. 'I don't know what you're talking about.'

With a slight, controlled movement, Lauren accessed the recording Imogen had sent on her phone. She slid the device across the smooth surface of the table towards him. 'Watch this. Then you might understand what I'm *talking about.*'

There was a charged silence as he watched, the colour slowly draining from his face. When the video ended, he seemed almost at a loss for words. 'It was just an argument,' he finally muttered, seeming to downplay its intensity. 'All couples have them.'

'From what we've gathered, such *arguments* were quite frequent between the two of you. It's been suggested that you were extremely jealous and possessive towards Sophie and that this emotion sometimes manifested itself aggressively. Is that true?'

Finch visibly grappled with his emotions. 'Okay, I admit to being jealous sometimes,' he snapped, his mask slipping a bit. 'But being aggressive? That's different. That recording doesn't show everything.' He jabbed a finger in the direction of Lauren's phone. 'Just because I lifted my hand doesn't mean I was going to hurt Sophie. I didn't do anything as you can see. It was a split-second instinct – a reaction. Nothing else.'

Lauren absorbed his words, keeping her expression neutral. She wanted to see his reaction to her next line of questioning. Her gaze never wavered from Finch's eyes, as she tried to discern any hints of deception.

'Moving on. We need to talk about Courtney Inwood. Mr Finch, it seems you weren't just involved with Sophie. You had an affair with Courtney while you were still with Sophie. Is that correct?'

Finch appeared visibly uncomfortable, his fingers drumming on the table. He looked down, as if trying to avoid Lauren's penetrating stare. 'You don't understand,' he started, his voice a blend of frustration and desperation. 'Courtney and I... we go way back. It was just a fling, a slip-up. I loved Sophie. Only Sophie.'

Lauren paused for a beat, before revealing what happened. 'Courtney was found dead this morning.'

His eyes widened, the news clearly blindsiding him. 'Courtney's dead, too?'

Lauren continued watching him intently. His reaction seemed genuine enough, but she'd been in this line of work long enough to know that appearances could be deceptive. Was this just a rehearsed facade? He'd certainly had time to practise it and he'd have known that sooner or later the connection would have been made.

Regardless, she pressed on. 'Yes, Mr Finch. And at this stage in our investigation, you're the common link between these two women.'

For a moment, it seemed like he might crack as myriad expressions crossed his face. 'I didn't do anything,' he finally asserted, his voice laced with panic. 'Sophie was everything to me. And as for Courtney, yes, I'm sorry she's gone, devastated even. But what we had... it didn't mean anything. Nothing. Just a stupid meaningless fling.'

Lauren leant back, noting his response, preparing for the

next set of questions. Every revelation, every reaction, would help lead them to the truth.

'Have you ever come across the poem "The Three Fishers"?' she asked.

Lauren observed the man's reaction closely, searching from any micro-expression that might show his knowledge of it.

Finch smirked, his lips curling with a hint of disdain. 'Do I seem like a poetry nerd to you? Why are you even asking me that?'

'It's significant to our case. It could provide insight into what happened to both Sophie and Courtney,' Lauren said.

A shadow of bewilderment crossed Finch's face. 'Well, I've never heard of it,' he retorted dismissively. 'And I don't think Sophie or Courtney liked poetry.'

'What are your thoughts on women working in the fishing industry, Mr Finch?' Matt asked. 'Some people have quite strong opinions about it.'

Finch's eyes hardened. 'I'm not a fan,' he said, his words edged with contempt. 'It's a man's job. Always has been. The fact that Sophie went out on that trawler, doing the heavy lifting... it never sat right with me. Women shouldn't be involved in such physically demanding work.'

'That's quite an outdated view don't you think?' Lauren said, shaking her head. 'For someone as young as you. You do realise that it's 2023, not the 1950s.'

'It's my opinion, isn't it? I don't care how it comes across,' Finch sneered, his eyes flickering with defiance.

Lauren exchanged a brief glance with Matt. It was clear that beneath Finch's bravado lay a deeply ingrained prejudice, and they needed to unravel more.

'Do you know anyone in the fishing industry, Mr Finch?' Matt asked.

Finch's lips tightened for a moment before he replied, 'Yes. My dad's been a fisherman all his life.'

'Interesting,' Matt said, clearly sensing an opportunity to push further. 'Is his view on women taking part in the industry the same as yours?'

'He's old-school,' Finch replied, a hint of resignation in his eyes. 'Women have their particular roles and, according to him, it's not out on the boats. He thinks things should stay traditional, without any change.'

'Which is exactly what you think, according to what you've just told us,' Matt said.

'I didn't say that,' Finch said, banging his hand on the table.

'Yeah, I think you did. Your exact words were: "Women shouldn't be involved in such physically demanding work." I can play back the recording if you think I've got it wrong.'

'Well, so what if I did say that? It's hardly relevant.'

'Would you say your father played a large part in shaping your views about women in the fishing industry?' Matt asked, leaning in slightly.

Finch didn't reply immediately, as if he was considering how much to divulge. 'I grew up hearing it all the time. Maybe it did influence me, I don't know,' he said, quieter and more introspective.

Lauren observed the exchange closely. While Finch's words revealed bits about his upbringing and influences, it was his hesitation and the subtle shift in demeanour that spoke volumes more.

'You claimed that on the evening Sophie vanished, you were at home, gaming with some online friends. Yet, our investigations revealed that no one can confirm your alibi. We've tried finding your gaming friends, but to no avail,' Lauren said, keeping her voice deliberately even to maintain control over the conversation.

Finch's demeanour shifted, his posture slightly defensive. 'Well... I mean... I wasn't technically alone,' he faltered.

Lauren seized on this moment of vulnerability and pressed on, 'You were with Courtney, weren't you?'

A wash of red spread across Finch's cheeks, betraying his embarrassment. 'Yes, she was there. Sophie was out, and Courtney and I were at my place,' he admitted, eyes darting away.

Lauren leant in, ratcheting up the tension. 'Let me get this straight. While you were gaming at home, Courtney was with you. So, on the very night Sophie was murdered you were spending time with a woman who, just a night ago, was also killed. Do you see where I'm going with this?'

'No, I don't. I had nothing to do with Sophie's death. How could I if I was with Courtney?'

'That's what you say. We can hardly ask Courtney for an alibi, can we?'

'If you think I had anything to do with either murder... Well, it's just fucking stupid,' Finch said, his words defensive and tinged with panic.

Lauren observed Finch, noting the slight tremor in his hands and the subtle shift of his eyes. He was scared.

'Where were you last night?'

'At... at the pub,' he stammered, his leg bouncing nervously.

'All night?'

'I think so.'

'You think?' Lauren repeated, frowning.

'I was wasted. I don't remember.'

'Did you ask Courtney to go with you?'

'No. I didn't want to see her. Not after what happened to Sophie.' He ran a shaky hand through his hair.

'So you drowned your sorrows alone,' Lauren said, her scepticism obvious. 'Which pub?'

'The, um... The Fisherman's Arms, I think.' Finch rubbed the back of his neck, refusing to make eye contact.

Lauren let the silence hang heavy and Finch fidgeted under her scrutiny, picking at a loose thread on his sweatshirt.

'Do you think the staff will remember you being there?'

Finch hesitated. 'I was a mess. So, yeah, they'd probably remember.'

'That remains to be seen,' Lauren mused, continuing her line of questioning. 'You claim not to remember anything about last night. That's quite a convenient blackout, isn't it?'

He threw his hands up in exasperation. 'I was upset. I was drinking heavily. It's not that unbelievable. And it's not a crime.'

Lauren pinned him with a penetrating stare. 'In this hazy, inebriated state, is it possible that you met up with Courtney? A conveniently forgotten rendezvous, maybe?'

'I don't know,' he said, his voice shaking, and what seemed like desperation seeping in. 'All I remember is waking up this morning, feeling like shit. Why would I hurt Sophie and Courtney?'

'Perhaps there were things they knew. Secrets that could expose a side of you you'd rather keep hidden,' Lauren speculated, watching his reaction closely.

Finch's face reddened, his eyes blazing with anger. 'This is stupid. I have nothing to hide, and I've done nothing wrong. I want out of here.'

'And you're sure you don't know anything about the poem "The Three Fishers"?' Lauren asked, hoping to catch him off guard by returning to it. 'What about the line in the poem: "For men must work, and women must weep." What do you make of that?'

Finch fidgeted in his seat, his eyes darting from Lauren to Matt and back. 'I've already told you. I know fuck all about poetry. It sounds to me like some old thinking where men do the tough jobs and women... I don't know, sit at home and cry? Seems ridiculous to me.'

Matt shifted slightly in his chair, making notes. He glanced up. 'Yet, you seem to carry the same old-school thinking when it comes to women working in the fishing industry, don't you?'

Finch's face flushed, and he appeared cornered. 'It's not the same thing.'

Lauren tilted her head. 'It doesn't have to be. What's said in the poem fits exactly with some of your views. Doesn't it?'

Finch exhaled loudly, his clenched fist banging against his chin. 'It's not like that. I just—' His words fell away and he looked down at the table.

Lauren exchanged a glance with Matt. 'We'll verify your whereabouts and speak to the staff at The Fisherman's Arms. You'll remain here during that time. You're not under arrest, but if you do try to leave then you will be. Do you understand?'

'Yes,' Finch muttered.

'If your memory's as hazy as you claim, then maybe your neighbours could be crucial witnesses,' Matt added. 'The question is, will their account support or contradict yours?'

'I'm telling the truth,' Finch said, the uncertainty clear in his eyes. 'Someone will have seen me. You'll see.'

EIGHTEEN

'The DCI has asked for an update on the cases. You go back to the team and let them know about the interview with Finch and ask someone to check his alibi,' Lauren said, as they left the interview room and headed up the stairs.

'No problem, ma'am.'

When Matt arrived back at the office he stood at the front by the whiteboard. 'Okay, everyone. We've finished interviewing Samuel Finch and his alibis are shaky, to say the least. We know that he can be aggressive, but if it is him, we need to consider his motive. Why would he want to murder both women?'

'Well,' Jenna said, drumming her fingers on the table. 'If the two victims had an issue with Finch, maybe they confronted him together? Perhaps he felt cornered and decided to get rid of them?'

'But, if he did feel threatened by whatever they might've known, why the theatrical death scenes? Why not make it appear like an accident?' Clem added, glancing first at Jenna and then Matt.

'I agree, it's puzzling.' Matt pointed at the board and the

photographs of both scenes. 'The way the bodies were left isn't random. It's a message. The killer's trying to communicate something with that particular line from the poem and also the way in which they were killed. We know that Finch has very traditional views about women's roles, which would fit.'

'Are you saying that you believe Finch is the murderer?' Jenna asked.

'I'm not sure. He's not very bright. Staging the deaths as they were, with the notes in the mouth, shows a degree of fore-thought and intelligence. Okay, so he lied about being alone on the night Sophie died, and claimed that he was in the pub all evening and got so drunk he can't remember going home on the night Courtney died. But that's it. We certainly can't eliminate him at this stage, but equally we're not going to focus our investigation solely on him.'

'What if there's someone else involved who manipulated Finch... used him in some way?' Billy suggested.

'That's an angle,' Matt agreed. 'We need to dig deeper into both victims' pasts. Find out if they had any common acquaintances other than Finch. Any shared experiences or places. We need more information if we're to draw any conclusions. I need someone to check The Fisherman's Arms to see if they remember Finch being there and the state he was in.'

'I'll visit the pub,' Billy said. 'They might have some CCTV to corroborate it, too.'

'Thanks,' Matt said. 'Tamsin, dig into the victims' social media circles, check their friends, work colleagues, and any clubs or groups they might've been part of. Jenna, you visit Finch's neighbours to see if they saw him at all and—'

'Sarge,' Tamsin interrupted. 'You know you asked us to dig into tragedies on the ocean?'

'What have you found?' Matt asked.

'About six months ago the trawler *Little Sunshine* capsized in heavy winds. One of the crew died and two others were seriously injured, including the skipper, who's now disabled.'

'Was anyone on the boat female, by any chance?' Matt enquired, unable to contain the urgency.

'Yes, sarge. The skipper was Tanya Chenoweth.'

Matt's eyes widened, his mind racing. 'If Chenoweth was in charge of the boat at the time of the accident and someone believes it only happened because she was a woman, then we have a motive.'

'But why kill women totally unrelated to the tragedy? Why not just target Chenoweth?' Jenny asked, frowning. 'It doesn't add up. And how does this relate to Finch?'

'It might not, if Finch is innocent. That's what we'll find out.' Matt began pacing, adrenaline coursing through him. 'We need to speak with Chenoweth immediately. She may be able to identify who harbours resentment over the incident and we might be able to link it back to the victims.'

'She's now living in Falmouth,' Tamsin said. 'From what I can tell she moved there sometime after the accident.'

'Do you have the name of the person who died?' Jenna asked.

Tamsin checked her notes, 'Yes, a man named Reginald Kerr. The community was devastated. According to the media a lot of people blamed the skipper for the accident because she decided to take the boat out that night.'

'The killer could view this accident as proof that women shouldn't be involved in fishing. Combine that with the emotions of losing a loved one, and you've got a potent mix for revenge,' Clem said, thoughtfully.

'You're right,' Matt agreed. 'If our murderer was affected in some way by that accident and blamed the skipper, then maybe he's been targeting women involved in fishing to make a point.'

'But why particularly Sophie and Courtney? They're not

the only women working in the industry, are they?' Jenna said. 'It's not sitting right.'

'You're right, but until we investigate we won't know. Dig deeper into the relationship between Sophie, Courtney, and this skipper. Also, see if there's any connection with Finch. And look into Reginald Kerr's family and friends. I'll speak to the DI when she returns.'

'You do know that if this is all related to that accident, and our killer is seeking some sort of revenge, then the skipper might be in danger too,' Billy said.

Matt met Billy's eyes, understanding the gravity of the situation. 'You're right. While we investigate, we should consider offering protection to the skipper. If our theory's correct, she could be the next target.'

'But why wasn't she the first?' Jenna asked. 'Surely if the killer specifically blamed her for something she would be top of the list. See... Another anomaly.'

'I'll see if there's any record of threats or incidents involving her since the accident,' Tamsin said. 'In case she's already been targeted.'

'Good idea,' Matt said. 'And—'

The door opened and Lauren walked in.

'How's it going?' she asked.

'We haven't yet checked Finch's alibi, but we have identified an incident that could provide a motive for the murders. A trawler skippered by a woman capsized in bad weather, killing one person and injuring two more. The skipper is now living in Falmouth. We should head out there to interview her.'

'Okay, let's go now,' Lauren said. 'She could be in danger.'

'Yes, Billy suggested that, too. Tamsin, did you find any reported threats or suspicious activities against the female skipper since the accident?' Matt asked.

Tamsin shook her head. 'Nothing's been reported, but that

doesn't necessarily mean they haven't occurred. Some threats might have been deemed unimportant or were ignored.'

'Absolutely,' Matt agreed. 'We need to understand the full scope of what she's faced since the accident. And if she knows or has interacted with our victims.'

'I appreciate everyone's work on this,' Lauren said. 'It feels like we're finally getting somewhere. Matt, gather what we need, and let's head to Falmouth. The rest of you, keep digging.'

'I'm off to the pub, ma'am, to check on Finch's alibi,' Billy said.

'You still believe he's in the frame?' Lauren asked, looking directly at Matt.

'We certainly haven't eliminated him. He could be involved, but I do have my doubts as to whether he instigated it. Simply because I don't believe he has the brains for it.'

'Yes, that makes sense.'

'Rather than checking with Finch's neighbours, shall I ask uniform to do that, leaving me free to see if Reginald Kerr, the man who died, had any close friends or family who might hold strong opinions against the skipper or women in the fishing industry generally?' Jenna suggested.

'Yes, that's a better use of your time for now,' Lauren said. 'Good work, everyone. Let's keep it up. We need to find this killer before they strike again.'

NINETEEN

The little detached bungalow sat nestled between two taller houses, its whitewashed walls gleaming against the afternoon sun. It was a typical quaint Cornish dwelling, from the vintage garden gnomes along the path to the red door with the shiny brass knocker that seemed like it had been polished every day for years.

Taking a deep breath, Matt tapped lightly. The conversation with Tanya Chenoweth was going to be both delicate and crucial, after what she'd been through.

There was silence until he could hear the sound of shuffling feet, joined by the distinct click-clack of walking sticks. The door opened and Matt immediately focused his attention on the woman who appeared. She looked younger than he'd expected but her eyes, a deep shade of hazel, were wary.

'Yes?' Her tone was soft but firm, like someone used to taking charge.

'Good morning. I'm Detective Inspector Pengelly and this is Detective Sergeant Price. You must be Tanya Chenoweth?'

'Yes, that's me. Why are you here?' Tanya replied, staring directly at Lauren.

'We were hoping to talk to you about the *Little Sunshine* incident,' Lauren said, her voice a balance between professional and empathic. 'It might be relevant to a case we're working on.'

Tanya's face transformed instantly. 'Oh... that,' she whispered. Her hands trembled as she held her walking sticks tighter. 'It's been a nightmare. Every day, every night. It never leaves me.'

'We understand this might be hard,' Lauren said. 'But we could really do with your help. We wouldn't be here if it wasn't important.'

Tanya was silent for a moment, then sighed. 'Okay. Come on in.'

The front door opened directly into the lounge, which had a nautical theme. There were pictures of boats, and landscapes featuring the ocean on the walls. Photographs of people Matt guessed might be family members were dotted around.

As Tanya limped slowly ahead, Matt exchanged a glance with Lauren, her eyes reflecting his determination to get to the bottom of what had happened, sensing that it could be crucial.

'Please, have a seat.' Tanya gestured towards a deep red corded sofa. 'Would you like some tea or coffee?'

'No thanks.' Lauren answered for both of them.

Tanya settled into an armchair opposite them, weariness in her eyes. 'What exactly do you want to know?' she asked, a slight sharpness in her tone.

'We're currently investigating the mysterious deaths of two women,' Lauren began. 'Both of them worked in the fishing industry, like you. We're trying to ascertain if there's a connection, a pattern of some sort linking their work to their deaths. It would be helpful if you could tell us exactly what happened on the night your trawler capsized.'

Tanya took a long time to answer. 'It's a night that still haunts me,' she began, quietly, causing Matt to strain in order to hear. 'Everything seemed normal at first, but you know what the weather's like. It can suddenly do its own thing. The winds became huge, like nothing I've seen before. It was almost like they were possessed. I've been on plenty of rough seas, but that night was different.' She shook her head. 'People pointed their fingers at me as if it was my fault. They said I shouldn't have taken the boat out. But no one could've predicted that storm, at least not its intensity. I made the call to sail based on my years of experience, believing we'd be okay.' A distant pain flickered in her eyes. 'That mistake has cost me everything.'

'It must have been awful.' Matt's heart went out to the poor woman, who appeared to have almost given up on life.

'Can you talk to us about Reginald Kerr, the crew member you lost that night?' Lauren asked.

Tanya's lips tightened. 'I'd worked with Reg for years and respected his opinion. He agreed we should go out that night. If he'd have had any doubts, I'd have listened to him. Reg knew the waters better than anyone. But even his experience couldn't save him from the fury of that storm. Before we could get to the lifeboats, a huge wave took him. He was washed overboard and we couldn't rescue him.'

'I'm so sorry,' Lauren said. 'I can't even begin to imagine how awful it must have been for you.'

'It was indescribable.' Tanya's eyes glassed over as if she was reliving the whole experience. 'But...'

'Carry on,' Lauren said, encouraging the woman to speak.

'It didn't end there. That was only the beginning of how it affected me. Mary, Reg's wife, was inconsolable and furious. She saw me not as a fellow victim but as the person who caused her misery. She said women have no place at sea, that it was ridiculous for a woman to skipper a boat.'

'So, Mary Kerr made her feelings towards you known? How? And did she ever go beyond just words?' Matt asked.

Tanya's eyes darkened. 'At first, it was just whispers, nasty comments made behind my back. But then the phone calls started.' She let out a sigh. 'Late at night, early morning, all times of day and night. Sometimes when I answered, a silence greeted me from the other end. At other times it was filled with her anguish and screams. Mary blamed me for her world falling apart.'

'Do you happen to know where Mary Kerr lives?' Lauren asked.

'Yes. Out in the sticks – in a house a few miles from Lower Drift. You can't miss it because it's one of very few out that way.'

Lauren's brow furrowed in thought. 'Given your history with Mary, do you believe she holds any resentment against other women in the fishing industry?'

Tanya frowned, clearly thinking through Lauren's question. 'I honestly don't know. All I can tell you is that she hates me. You know, fishing might be dominated by men, but that doesn't mean women can't be part of it. I was good at my job and well-regarded by a lot of people. My crew trusted me. What happened that night was unforeseen and totally unpredictable.'

'But didn't you say earlier that, in retrospect, you shouldn't have ventured out that night?' Matt said, reminding the woman of her earlier comment.

A shadow of pain crossed Tanya's face. 'Yes, I did say that. And the guilt eats away at me every single day. My mind spins with endless what-ifs. More so at night when I can't sleep. During the day, I can talk myself down a little, reminding myself that the inquiry exonerated me. They combed through every detail and agreed that no one could have predicted the storm's ferocity.' Her eyes glistened. 'Despite this, Mary Kerr still blames me for what happened that night.' Her voice cracked. 'I think that in a way it helps her cope with the tragedy.'

Matt could understand that. He'd never forgive the lorry

driver who crashed into their car, killing Leigh. Although it was different. The man had been speeding and was totally to blame.

'Are you familiar with the poem "The Three Fishers" by Charles Kingsley?' he asked, pushing aside the piercing thoughts of Leigh's death.

Tanya's eyes glimmered with recognition. 'Of course. It's a well-known poem in these parts among those connected to the sea. Why are you asking?'

Matt leant back, linking his fingers together. 'During our investigation, that poem has surfaced. One line in particular has caught our attention: "For men must work, and women must weep". What are your thoughts on that?'

Tanya's face took on a contemplative, yet bitter, expression. 'That line is so sexist. Men should do the work and take the risks, while women are pushed to the side to simply mourn when tragedy strikes. Considering what happened to my trawler, the irony isn't lost on me. According to that poem, I should have been at home weeping and not skippering a boat during the time it capsized.'

'Do you think you faced more blame because you're a woman skipper? That it would have been different with a man at the helm?' Matt asked, anticipating that she'd say yes.

Tanya sighed heavily, a distant look in her eyes. 'Maybe. Yeah, probably. Old beliefs die hard in close-knit communities like ours.'

'Do you visit Newlyn much these days?' Lauren asked. 'It's quite a distance from here.'

Tanya glanced towards the window, as if the very mention of the town weighed on her heart. 'No,' she admitted, wearily. 'I haven't set foot there since I moved here. It's hard enough living with the memories and guilt. I don't need strangers or former acquaintances hurling insults or giving dirty stares. I carry enough pain with me.' She lifted up one of her walking sticks.

'Do you live here alone?' Matt asked, scanning the room and seeing no evidence of there being anyone else.

'Yeah,' Tanya said resentfully. 'My ex-husband's hundreds of miles away, shacked up with some woman he met on the internet. The accusations and abuse that we received were too much for him to handle. He couldn't get away from here quick enough.'

'I'm sorry to hear that,' Lauren said. 'Can you tell me what you were doing last night?'

'I spent the evening as I usually do, on my own watching the telly. It's one boring night after another,' Tanya said, a resigned expression on her face.

A wave of sympathy washed over Matt. It wasn't much of a life for the woman. 'Is there anyone who can confirm this? Any visitors?'

'Actually, yes. My daughter was here. Just for a few hours though. It was her "*monthly*" visit,' she added cynically, making quote marks with her fingers. 'She sees it as a duty rather than a genuine wish to spend time with me. She took her father's side in everything. Blaming me for the job I chose and the risks I took.'

'Does she still keep in touch with your husband?' Matt asked.

A sharp laugh, devoid of real humour, left Tanya's lips. 'Ex-husband, remember? I don't know whether she sees him or not. She hasn't told me and I haven't asked.'

Lauren rose, offering a sympathetic smile. 'Thank you for sharing with us, Tanya. It's crucial to let us know if you feel threatened or if anyone tries to harm you in future. You don't have to face this on your own.'

'Thanks, but hopefully because I'm here – out of sight and out of mind – I'll be left alone.'

'We'll show ourselves out, so no need to get up,' Lauren said, indicating for Matt to follow.

As the door closed behind them, Matt couldn't help but be moved by Tanya's story. Through no fault of her own, the rest of her life was going to be one of loneliness and, he suspected, shame, because she was always going to blame herself for what had happened.

'I'm struggling to understand what's going on,' Matt said when they reached the car. 'If this killer has an issue specifically with female fishermen, then targeting Sophie makes some kind of twisted sense. But Courtney? She was on land, working in the fishery. How does she fit into this?'

'Maybe this isn't just about fishing,' Lauren said, peering over the top of the vehicle at him. 'Maybe it's the mere presence of women in an industry that traditionally belongs to men. Full stop.'

He considered her words. 'It's hard to believe someone would resort to murder over something like that.'

Lauren sighed. 'Around here, traditional beliefs run deep. Not everyone's keen on change. Some people cling to the old ways, the tried-and-true, and they can react aggressively when they feel their values are being threatened.'

Matt drummed his fingers on the roof of the car as he tried to piece everything together in his mind. 'If that's the case, then the dead man's widow, Mary Kerr, might be the missing link. The person tying everything together. She could either be the killer, or at the very least give us some insight into the mindset of the person who is.'

'Definitely. I think visiting her should be our next move. But let's approach with caution. It's getting dark, and I'd rather not stir up trouble tonight. We'll go first thing tomorrow when we can be more prepared.'

TWENTY

THURSDAY JUNE 13

Lauren's grip tightened on the steering wheel as she drove into traffic, leaving the hospital. Their visit to Mary Kerr had been delayed because Henry called first thing that morning, asking Lauren to come by the morgue for the findings on Courtney's death. The chill of the cold room still clung to Lauren, a stark reminder of the harsh realities of her job.

Courtney's post-mortem results were eerily similar to Sophie's. They showed the same drugs in her system, the identical manner and time of death, and the same last meals: both had eaten fish and chips. Not to mention the notes found on them contained the same message.

Lost in thought over what Henry had shared about the similarities, Lauren and Matt were now on their way to finally speak with Mary Kerr, hoping to make a breakthrough in the investigation.

The previous evening Lauren had allowed Samuel Finch to leave custody. The pub manager had confirmed he was drunk and there until late on the evening of Courtney's death but that didn't totally exonerate him. There was no denying that he was a common thread, involved with both victims, but they didn't have sufficient grounds to hold him. She'd issued a stern warning for him to remain in town, hoping that letting him out wasn't the wrong call.

The hum of the engine, coupled with the murmur of Matt's voice, seemed distant, until his words cut through her thoughts. 'Ma'am, are you listening?'

Blinking back to the present, she glanced over to see Matt's expression, a mix of concern and impatience. 'Sorry, Matt,' she said. 'Henry's findings... it's confirmed what we have always believed. The crime scenes are identical and we could be heading for a serial killer if we don't catch them soon.'

'That's just what I was saying, while you were away with the fairies. This vendetta against women is unmistakable. And as much as Finch is in the picture, you were right in letting him go. He doesn't have the motive, or the smarts to do it.'

'I hope you're right. Because if not I could very well have let a killer loose.'

'We had nothing concrete to hold him on, ma'am. Anyone in your position would have made the same decision.'

'Hmm. Yes, I suppose so.' Lauren was distracted by the desolate landscape as they approached Mary Kerr's home. 'We're here. Living in such an isolated place must be difficult for her, at her age.'

Matt gave her a sidelong glance, raising an eyebrow. 'She's in her mid-fifties, ma'am. That's hardly ancient. Because if it is, then it's downhill all the way for the pair of us.'

'Good point,' Lauren said with a half-smile.

She parked in front of the quaint, pebble-dashed cottage, which was in the shadow of the adjacent garage. Getting out of the car, she shivered slightly as a light breeze rustled the leaves.

Lauren knocked on the door, the sound echoing in the still morning air. After no response, and another unanswered knock, she decided to investigate further. Approaching the window, she cupped her hands to block the light and peered inside. 'It doesn't look like anyone's home. We should check the garage just to be sure, though.'

'We really should have a warrant, ma'am.'

Lauren shot Matt a quick glance. 'If Mary Kerr is potentially in danger, we have the right to ensure her safety and check everywhere.'

'I guess so,' Matt agreed, although he still had a dubious expression on his face.

Lauren and Matt made their way to the garage and entered through a side door. The interior was cluttered and chaotic. Fishing reels and rods littered the space, along with boxes of miscellaneous items. In one corner sat a rust-covered ride-on lawn mower that had clearly seen better days – it would be a miracle if the old machine still worked.

Lauren and Matt paced around the disordered garage, pausing at times to stare curiously at the assortment of objects filling the area.

'I can't believe how much junk she's got. How could she ever find anything. I—' Something caught Lauren's eye. Fishing line, unmistakably similar to the one they'd seen before. She held it up for Matt to inspect. 'Doesn't this look like the fishing line from the crime scene?'

Matt frowned, holding the line closer to his eyes. 'Isn't all fishing line pretty much the same?'

'We'll take it. Better to be safe,' she said, pulling out an evidence bag and dropping it in.

She continued her search, coming upon a box filled with newspaper clippings, each focused on women in the fishing industry. Her pulse quickened.

'Matt, look at this.'

He headed over and scanned the contents. 'It's proof, ma'am.'

'Yes,' Lauren agreed. 'She's obsessed with women working in the industry. We need forensics to comb through this place to search for more evidence. But the bigger question remains: where is Mary Kerr?'

'Here.'

The sudden sound made Lauren's heart jump into her throat. She turned swiftly, coming face-to-face with the unmistakable barrel of a shotgun, wielded by a stern-looking woman. The anger in the woman's eyes was almost as threatening as the weapon itself.

'Who are you?' the woman demanded, her eyes darting between Lauren and Matt.

'We're the police. I'm DI Pengelly, and this is DS Price,' Lauren said, keeping her voice low and calm, not wanting to provoke the woman. 'Please, lower the gun before this escalates further.'

The woman's eyes flickered with suspicion. 'You need a warrant to snoop around my property.'

'We knocked,' Lauren explained. 'The house was silent. We were concerned for your safety and wanted to ensure you were okay.'

'Yeah, right. Of course you were. What do you want?'

'We have questions that need answering. Can you please lower the weapon so we can discuss this civilly?' Lauren took a step forward, but the sudden movement caused the woman to focus the gun squarely at Lauren's chest.

'That's a bad move,' Lauren cautioned. 'Threatening an officer is a serious offence.'

The woman's defiant eyes burnt brighter. 'I'll claim self-defence.'

Lauren, despite the mounting pressure, managed a small, incredulous chuckle. 'How? We're unarmed and you're pointing a shotgun at us. Don't make this situation any worse than it already is. Lower the gun or I'll have to call for backup.'

The woman's eyes flared with annoyance. 'Backup? Why are you really here?'

Lauren gestured to the box of newspaper clippings. 'We couldn't help noticing those articles about women in fishing. Seems like you have some strong opinions on the subject.'

Mary eyed her warily. 'So what if I do? A person can think what they want.'

'Of course, but I have to ask... are these views because of your husband's accident?'

Mary stiffened, her knuckles whitening on the shotgun. 'Reg's gone because of that woman,' she said, her voice tight with anger. 'She shouldn't have been put in charge. She didn't know the waters, didn't respect the conditions. Took them out to sea when they should've stayed on land.'

'But the inquiry found she wasn't to blame.'

'It was a fix.' She drew a shaky breath, blinking back tears. 'Women don't belong on the boats. They don't have the experience, or the instincts. Not like...Not like my Reg did. And now he's dead because of her.'

Lauren nodded sympathetically. 'I understand this is incredibly difficult for you. If you could put down the gun, maybe we could talk this through—'

'I've said all I intend to say. Now get off my property before I remove you myself.'

The shotgun rose a fraction, making her intent clear.

'Mary this isn't—'

Lauren stopped mid-sentence, taken by surprise when Matt lunged at the woman from the side. He'd caught her off guard, his momentum knocking the ground from beneath her feet. The two tumbled to the floor, but it was clear who had the upper hand. With a swift move, Matt had wrestled the gun from Mary's grasp.

Quickly moving to assist, Lauren reached for her handcuffs. Mary's face was a mix of shock, anger, and fear as Lauren pulled her arms behind her back and restrained her. The woman's breathing was ragged. Had she realised the gravity of her situation?

'Mary Kerr, I'm arresting you for the unlawful possession of a weapon and the attempted assault of a police officer. And also on suspicion of murdering Sophie Yates and Courtney Inwood. You do not have to say anything, but it may harm your defence if you do not mention something which you later rely on in court. Anything you do say may be given in evidence. Do you understand?'

'Murder? I don't know anything about that. I swear.' Fear shone from her eyes. 'I've got a licence for the gun. You can check. I was just protecting myself. It's not a crime.'

'Your gun licence will be verified at the station,' Lauren said, wanting to keep the situation from escalating. 'But it's illegal to threaten anyone with a weapon, police or otherwise, when there's no immediate threat to you.'

'I'm telling you, I didn't do anything wrong,' Mary cried, her eyes wild. 'I heard a noise and got scared, so I grabbed the gun. But I wasn't going to hurt anyone. I promise.'

Lauren held up a hand. 'That's enough. We're taking you to the station where you'll be interviewed and charged.'

'I haven't done anything wrong. This is my property. I know my rights!' Mary shouted, backing away. 'You can't do this.'

'I can, and I will,' Lauren said, taking hold of the woman's arm.

Mary Kerr's shoulders slumped, the fight draining out of her. The enormity of the situation was becoming clear. She seemed smaller, vulnerable even, a stark contrast to the fiery woman that had confronted them earlier.

'I'll call for backup,' Matt said, heading outside, having pulled his phone out of his pocket.

'Thanks.'

Lauren waited for a couple of minutes, giving Matt time to call the station, and then guided Mary Kerr towards the door.

As they waited for backup, Lauren's mind raced. If Mary Kerr was guilty then they had to build an airtight case, one that she couldn't wriggle out of. Just because they'd established her hatred for women in fishing, it didn't automatically mean that she had committed murder. They needed more evidence.

Soon she heard a siren and a police vehicle came screeching to a halt. Within a matter of minutes, Mary Kerr was whisked away.

'Forensics will be here shortly, ma'am,' Matt said. 'Do you want to wait for them to arrive?'

'No. Let's get back to the station and start piecing this case together.'

TWENTY-ONE

Matt stepped into the office and the buzz of conversation immediately stopped. A couple of seconds later a wave of enthusiastic cheering and clapping erupted around him. The fluorescent lights above illuminated the wide grins and impressed glances of his team.

'Yay! It's the man of the moment,' Billy shouted, jumping up from his chair, raising his arm and punching the air. 'Our very own Penzance hero. You saved the DI from certain doom. We want to hear every last detail, don't we?' Billy turned to the rest of the team, whose faces appeared eager.

Warmth crept up Matt's cheeks, a mix of embarrassment and pride. 'Let's get this into perspective. It wasn't quite the dramatic scene that you're clearly imagining. We were searching the garage belonging to Mary Kerr and she appeared with a shotgun in her hand which she waved in our direction. I did what I had to do. That's all. Nothing more. Nothing less. It was just a normal day.' Matt gave a nonchalant shrug.

Okay, so it might have been a bit more dramatic than he'd made out, but he didn't want it blown out of all proportion.

'What planet are you from? That's not a *normal day*. At

least not for us here in Cornwall.' Billy raised his eyebrows in mock surprise. 'Though I suppose being from a big city, it probably wasn't out of the ordinary. I wish I'd been there. I bet it was like one of those action movies. It all happened in slow motion... intense music... Sarge diving through the air...'

'With his hair waving dramatically,' Tamsin added, grinning.

'Definitely,' Billy said, pretending to leap.

Matt chuckled. 'You lot watch way too many films. I did what any officer in my position would have: made the place safe by disarming a woman who was threatening us.'

'And saving the DI's life in the process,' Clem said.

'You know it could have been a lot worse without you there, Sarge. If that woman was totally out of it then the DI was in real danger,' Billy said.

'Well, she's safe and that's the end of it,' Matt replied, swatting the air as if brushing the words aside and hoping his voice made light of it, even though he actually agreed with Billy. It could have been a really tricky situation.

As if on cue, the door to the DI's office opened, and Lauren stepped out, her attention immediately falling on Matt. She glanced appreciatively towards him. 'Judging by the hilarity I'm hearing from my office it seems like you're all fully aware of today's *incident*.'

Billy smirked. 'We are, ma'am, and now we're singing the praises of our very own Superman.'

Lauren approached Matt, her professional demeanour melting slightly into a genuine smile. 'It was a brave thing you did, Matt. Your quick-thinking saved us both from Mary Kerr. Well done.'

He shifted uncomfortably. 'Thanks, ma'am, but I was only doing my job.'

'Because it was just another day as you've already told us,' Billy said. 'For you maybe, because when you worked in

Lenchester there was apparently a murder every minute. And of course, you have already had your share of bullets. So, I suppose you're right.' He paused dramatically. 'But as for the rest of us...' Billy laughed. 'Anyway, now that we've cracked the case, are we all going out to celebrate?'

'Good idea,' Jenna said, agreeing with Billy.

'Hold on a minute,' Lauren commanded, raising a hand to silence the room. The chatter ceased, and all eyes turned to her. 'Yes, we've arrested someone, but that doesn't mean we've solved the case. It's not over yet, as you all should know.'

'But, ma'am, we've got Mary Kerr. Surely now it's just a question of admin and stuff,' Billy said.

Lauren fixed him with an uncompromising stare. 'Having her in custody is one thing. Securing a conviction is another. The forensics team is combing her place as we speak. And there are still some unanswered questions. I understand your excitement, but let's dampen it down until everything is wrapped up. When the time's right we will celebrate. I promise.'

'Mary Kerr's a puzzle,' Matt said, agreeing with Lauren's need to calm things down. 'How could a woman of her size move the bodies by herself? I mean, she's hardly the weightlifting type.'

'Exactly,' Lauren said. 'Did she have help? An accomplice? It's not just about securing the one we have. It's about ensuring there's no one else out there that we've missed.'

'Like Finch, ma'am?' Billy asked.

'Maybe. We don't know.'

'And don't forget the drugs used to sedate Sophie and Courtney,' Clem said. 'If it was Kerr, where did she get them? From what we've learnt, she's hardly your regular user.'

'Exactly,' Lauren said.

'Do you want us to deep dive into Mary Kerr?' Billy asked.

'I do,' Lauren replied. 'We also need to backtrack on Sophie and Courtney's movements. What were they up to in the days leading to their deaths? I need eyes on CCTV around their usual spots. There's every possibility that Mary Kerr was tailing one or both of them, and if so I want to know.'

'When do you plan on interrogating Kerr?' Matt asked.

'Not until we have all our ducks in a row. We'll collect as much evidence as we can before questioning her, to make sure she can't wriggle out of it. I've been informed that she's asked for a solicitor, so that gives us a window of time to collect what we can. I'll be in my office if you need me.' Lauren turned and headed across the room, the door to her office clicking shut behind her.

The atmosphere in the incident room was electric. 'Okay, everyone. You heard what the DI wants. Tamsin and Billy, you concentrate on the CCTV,' Matt instructed.

'Okay, Sarge,' the two of them responded.

'The rest of us will focus on Mary Kerr's background.'

Matt headed back to his chair and sank down into it, the pressure of the day catching up with him. The what-ifs played in his mind, each scenario reminding him of the danger they'd faced. He knew they had a potential murderer in custody, but Lauren's warning loomed over him like a storm cloud. The case wasn't closed. Not yet.

'Sarge!' Tamsin's voice pierced through his thoughts. 'We've got footage of Mary Kerr and Sophie Yates outside The Seaside Inn.'

Matt sprang to his feet. 'That was quick. Well done. Put it up for us all to see and I'll grab the DI.'

Heart rate quickening, Matt approached Lauren's office. He knocked sharply and opened it, without even waiting for her to call him in.

'Ma'am, you need to see this. We've got CCTV of Mary Kerr with Sophie Yates.'

Lauren rose swiftly, following him back into the main room.

Tamsin had already loaded the footage, and frozen the screen on the interaction between the two women.

'Shall I hit play?' Tamsin asked.

'Yes, please,' Matt replied.

The figures on the screen came to life.

'Right there, see?' Tamsin said. 'Mary Kerr seems really angry. She looks like she's threatening Sophie.'

'It's a shame there's no audio,' Lauren said, sighing. 'Where does this footage come from?'

'The pub's security feed. That's why we have such a perfect spot to view them. I phoned them and they sent it immediately. We were lucky that someone was there at the time to do it,' Tamsin said.

'When did this meeting take place?' Lauren asked.

'The same night Sophie got into an argument with Finch.'

'So what do you think... Kerr and Finch working together?' Billy asked.

Matt stroked his chin, considering it. 'It's a definite possibility. The combination makes sense: her strategy and his strength.'

'See? I'm not just a pretty face.' Billy smirked.

'Not *even* you mean,' Tamsin said, rolling her eyes.

'This is great, Tamsin,' Lauren said. 'Let's dig deeper. See if you can find evidence of Finch and Kerr together. Did you see Kerr with Courtney at all?'

'Not yet, ma'am.'

'Keep looking, and also I'd like anything you can find on Mary Kerr's relationship with Courtney Inwood. Where are we on the fish and chips?'

'No luck with any of the shops recognising Sophie's picture, but maybe they'll recognise Mary,' Jenna said. 'Or Courtney. We haven't yet asked about her.'

'Right. Pay them all another visit, but only show them Mary

Kerr's photo. If she bought those meals, we'll find out. Don't show them Courtney's photo yet. I don't want to confuse them.'

The phone rang on the desk at the front and Lauren picked it up.

'Pengelly.' She listened. 'Thanks. We'll be there shortly.'

'Time to confront Kerr, Matt. Her solicitor's here. I don't want to leave them on their own for too long in case she's advised to "no comment" all of our questions and agrees to do it.'

'Okay, ma'am,' Matt said, grabbing his phone from his desk and slipping it into his pocket.

TWENTY-TWO

Lauren strode into the sterile interview room, with Matt following close behind. Her eyes immediately locked onto Mary Kerr, whose defiant stare met her own. The room was chilly, with a veneer of tension hanging in the air.

'You can't hold me like this. I've done nothing wrong.' A hint of desperation seeped through Kerr's bravado.

Without a word, Lauren took her seat, her mind already preparing for the interview that lay ahead. She gave a slight nod to Matt and he started the recording equipment.

'Interview, Thursday, June thirteenth. Those present are DI Pengelly, DS Price and...' Matt gestured for the two opposite to introduce themselves.

'Mary Mabel Kerr,' came the woman's reply.

'And Jared Rose, representing Mrs Kerr,' the man added crisply, never taking his eyes off Lauren.

Lauren stared directly ahead, focusing on the woman in front of her. 'Mrs Kerr, you've been arrested on the suspicion of the murders of Sophie Yates and Courtney Inwood.'

Kerr sat upright in her chair, crossing her arms defensively. 'I don't even know them,' she said flippantly with a shake of her head. 'So why would I want them dead? I thought this was about the gun.' She locked eyes with Lauren.

'We'll get to that. First I want to discuss Sophie and Courtney. They both worked in the fishing industry,' Lauren responded, unwavering.

A shadow crossed Kerr's face. 'Well, they shouldn't have.'

'That's what we're trying to understand,' Matt said, in a gentle prodding tone. 'We sympathise about your husband, but why hold a grudge against *all* women in the industry?' He leant forward and steepled his fingers, resting his arms on the table.

'Because it cost me my Reg. Women should keep well away from fishing. If it wasn't for that woman, my husband would still be here. I've already told you this when you broke into my house.'

'We didn't break in, as you well know,' Lauren corrected. 'The loss of your husband was tragic. But Tanya Chenoweth wasn't to blame for that unexpected storm.'

'She shouldn't have taken the boat out.' Kerr's voice rose, a mixture of anger and sorrow.

'What happened was unforeseeable,' Lauren countered.

Kerr slammed her fist on the table. 'You're just repeating what was said in the inquiry. But I don't believe it. Someone's palms were greased.' She glared accusingly at Lauren and Matt.

'Why do you believe that?' Lauren asked delicately, her head tilting to the side.

Kerr's lower lip quivered and she averted her attention to the table. 'The company who employed her would lose too much if she was found to blame,' she said quietly. 'This way it was no one's fault and I'm left alone with pennies to my name.' She wrapped her arms around herself, as if trying to hold in her emotions.

Lauren and Matt exchanged a sympathetic look. 'So you wanted to get your own back on everyone?' Lauren prodded delicately after a moment.

Kerr shook her head, a tear rolling down her cheek. 'No, I just...' She put her head in her hands, shoulders shaking with silent sobs.

'I think this is enough,' the solicitor said firmly. 'My client is clearly upset and she has already denied doing anything to these women.' He stared challengingly at Lauren and Matt. 'End the interview now, unless you can provide some solid evidence against her.' His tone was calm, but demanding. He maintained unwavering eye contact, conveying his authority and experience in dealing with police interrogations. His posture was poised and confident as he waited for their response. No doubt prepared to shoot down any dubious accusations against his client.

'The interview will be over when I say it is,' Lauren asserted, not at all intimidated by Rose despite his manner. She was way too long in the tooth for that. 'Mrs Kerr, can you account for your whereabouts on Sunday, June the ninth between the hours of eight pm and midnight?' Lauren asked, referring to the time of death Henry had given for Sophie.

'I was at home. Where else would you expect me to be at that time?' the woman responded, with irritation.

'What were you doing?' Lauren pressed.

Kerr's eyes flitted away for a moment. 'Watching the telly. Reading. I can't remember. Why does it matter?'

'Can anyone vouch for you being there?' Lauren continued, not prepared to answer the question.

'No. I live alone,' Kerr said, her voice dripping with bitterness. 'There's no one to vouch for me. Not now.'

'And on Tuesday evening, during the same hours?' Lauren asked.

'What do you think? At home, of course. Again.'

Lauren's eyes searched Kerr's. 'If you're innocent, then cooperating will help clear your name. But if you're trying to hide something...'

Kerr's eyes flashed defiantly. 'I didn't murder anyone. If you think you can blame this on me... well, forget it.'

Lauren sat back, mentally noting the reactions, the evasions. The woman was hiding something. Lauren was determined to find out what it was.

'Are you familiar with "The Three Fishers", Mrs Kerr?' Lauren asked, sounding devoid of emotion.

Kerr shifted in her chair, eyeing Lauren warily. 'Of course. Everyone round these parts knows that poem. It's like a fisherman's... anthem or something.'

'I take it you believe what Kingsley wrote?' Matt added. 'That while men work, women should weep? Mourn, perhaps? Like what happened to you.'

A fire ignited in Kerr's eyes. 'Stop trying to trap me. You're using my own husband's death against me. Do *you* think I should be weeping in the corner? Keeping quiet?'

Lauren tapped a finger on the table, drawing Kerr's attention back to her. 'When you weren't happy at the result of the inquiry, you turned to threats. Is that right? Directed specifically at Tanya Chenoweth? Phone calls. Day and night. Sending threatening letters. Don't think we're ignorant of that because we're not. Intimidation is a criminal offence.'

Kerr's defiance wavered. Her cheeks reddened as she looked away. 'She needed to know the pain she caused. To feel it. Like I did.'

'Yet your vendetta didn't stop at Tanya,' Lauren pressed on. 'We have footage of you confronting Sophie Yates. What did you say to her?'

Kerr's jaw tightened and she glanced at her solicitor, who shook his head. But she turned back to face Lauren. 'When I said women shouldn't work on the boats she told me I was stuck in the past. She laughed in my face.'

'And in your rage, you decided to permanently silence her,' Matt said, his voice cutting.

'No.' Kerr's eyes glistened with the onset of tears. 'I was angry, yes, but I'd never... I only met her that one time.'

'But you just told us you didn't know her,' Lauren said, her stare intense. 'You thought that if Sophie was out of the picture, she'd no longer be a part of that industry. No longer a constant reminder of what took your husband.'

'You're wrong. I didn't kill her. It wasn't me,' Kerr whispered.

'I believe that's enough, DI Pengelly,' Rose interjected, placing a steadying hand on Mary Kerr's arm as she grew visibly distressed.

Lauren locked eyes with him. 'We're trying to establish the facts, Mr Rose.'

'Yet you seem to be attempting to lead the witness into incriminating herself,' Rose countered sharply.

Lauren ignored the solicitor. 'Courtney Inwood. How well did you know her, Mrs Kerr? And don't say not at all.'

'Okay. I've seen her at the fish market,' Kerr said, staring back at Lauren. 'She's handed me my order a couple of times.'

'You're presuming quite a lot, DI. The link you're attempting to draw is tenuous at best,' Rose said.

'Did you happen to tell her your sentiments about women in the industry?' Lauren asked, forcing back the urge to slap the solicitor, and instead keeping focused on Kerr.

'Maybe. I can't remember everything I say to everyone,' Kerr said, giving a tiny shrug.

Matt jumped in. 'Mary, you can't deny your interactions with Sophie and Courtney or your feelings about their roles in the industry. And your... collaboration... with Samuel Finch, how did that come about?'

'Who? I don't know what you're talking about,' Kerr spluttered, her face red with frustration.

'Detective, this line of questioning is not only inappropriate but seems prejudiced,' Rose said, sighing.

'When you drugged Sophie and Courtney, how did you do it?' Matt continued. 'Did you buy the fish and chips and invite them to your house? Or did it happen somewhere else? How did you put the drugs into their meals without them seeing? And—'

'I keep telling you, that wasn't me!' Kerr screamed at them. 'I don't know what you're talking about.'

Lauren shifted in her seat, her eyes locked on Kerr's. 'All the evidence we have points to you. I'm curious, though. Where did you get the ketamine from? Was it from Samuel Finch?'

'No comment.'

Matt frowned. 'Something else I'd like you to explain. If you're innocent, as you claim, then why did you wave a gun in our faces when you saw us in your garage? And by the way, forensics won't just be going through your garage. They'll go through your car and your home. We'll find our evidence. Be sure of that.'

'I was protecting my property, that's all. I've already told you that. I wasn't going to use the gun,' Kerr muttered.

'How were we expected to know that?'

Rose held up a hand. 'That's enough. My client has explained everything she can and answered your questions. This is just a fishing expedition.'

'Come on, Mary. Tell us what you know. It's for the best,' Lauren persisted, ignoring the solicitor.

'I keep saying, it wasn't me. I'm not saying anything else because you're trying to twist my words.'

Matt sighed. 'But you've already admitted to knowing the dead women and also having conversations with them.'

'No comment,' Kerr said, her voice teetering between frustration and defeat.

'You ought to do yourself a favour, Mary. Plead guilty. Tell us everything. We might be able to talk to the Crown Prosecution Service, and claim that you did it under duress because of the death of your husband,' Lauren said, softer, cajoling almost.

'I'm not going to say I did something I didn't. And that's final,' Kerr said.

'I repeat,' Rose interjected. 'This interview should be over.'

Lauren exchanged a glance with Matt to indicate her agreement. He stopped the recording, stood up, opened the door to the interview room and signalled to the officer standing outside. 'Please escort Mrs Kerr back to her cell.'

As Kerr and Rose's receding footsteps echoed down the corridor, Lauren turned to Matt.

'She knows more. I'm sure of it. She might not be the killer, but she's definitely involved somehow. Maybe with Finch.'

Matt rubbed the back of his neck, visibly frustrated. 'I agree. But she's denying even knowing him. That needs to be investigated further, to see if we can find a connection between the two of them.'

TWENTY-THREE

Matt pushed open the door to the office. The fluorescent lighting buzzed overhead, casting a pale glow over the team who were seated at their desks. The room smelled of stale coffee – a familiar scent that often made Matt feel at home amidst the chaos of his job.

'Okay,' he said, running a hand through his hair, which was slightly damp with sweat from the tension of the last interview. 'The DI has gone to see the DCI, and I want to report back from our interview with Mary Kerr.'

'I hope you nailed her,' Billy said, his eyes alight with hope.

'Not exactly. She denied it, which was to be expected... Although she did confirm that she'd spoken to Sophie Yates, which we already knew from the CCTV, and also that she'd spoken to Courtney Inwood at her workplace.'

Billy grinned. 'Slam dunk then, Sarge,' he replied, doing a fist pump.

Matt shook his head slowly. 'You should know by now that it's never that easy, Billy. But we do know that she's extremely resentful about the fact that after the inquiry into the accident, Tanya Chenoweth, the trawler skipper, was exonerated. The incident was blamed on a weather event that no one could have predicted.'

From the corner, Clem let out a huff. 'That's nothing new then. Over the last twenty years there have been a few accidents and only one was blamed on human error. Now I'm not saying that isn't the case, but statistically speaking—'

'Thanks, Clem,' Matt interrupted, not wanting them to go down one of the officer's rabbit holes.

'Saved from the Clemipedia,' Billy said, smirking. 'Thanks, Sarge.'

The others laughed, including Clem.

'Okay, I know sometimes I can go deep, but it's useful stuff,' Clem said, sheepishly.

'Some of the time,' Billy quipped.

'Enough,' Matt said, holding up his hands. 'If Mary Kerr is our killer then why start now? Has something else happened to convince her to take it out on these women? Could it have been the result of the inquiry? Tamsin, can you find out when the official inquiry took place?'

'I've already done that, Sarge. The report officially came out ten days ago,' Tamsin replied, without missing a beat.

'Ah ha. So, that's our reason why it's happening now,' Jenna said. 'Obviously, there was planning involved and it took her this amount of time to put it in place.'

Matt leant against the table, working through everything in his mind. Something still wasn't sitting right.

'Yes, but what we still haven't addressed is how she managed to lift the women and place them on the rocks. She must've had help,' Matt said, his voice tinged with frustration. 'We put it to her that it was Samuel Finch, but she denied even knowing him.'

Billy snorted. 'Of course she would.'

'We need to check CCTV footage for any time they were together. But if it's not Finch then who else could it be?' Matt asked, scanning the room for answers. 'What have we found out about her family?'

'She has a son, but he works in Leeds, so way too far away,' Tamsin said, her eyes focused intently on her computer screen.

'Was he present at the inquiry?' Matt asked.

'I don't know,' Tamsin said. 'I'll see if I can find out. I know someone who works in the coroner's office who might be able to tell me.'

'Sarge!' Jenna exclaimed, before Matt had time to respond. 'I've received an email from forensics regarding Sophie's laptop. They sent over some files. It looks like Sophie was keeping records of something, but it doesn't make much sense. I'll transfer it onto the big screen so we can all see.'

Jenna clicked her mouse and a spreadsheet appeared on the screen, titled simply *Patrick's Meals*. Two columns were labelled '*Date*' and '*Time*', with a series of entries over the past few months.

'Can we assume Patrick refers to her brother?' Clem said.

'It seems likely,' Matt agreed.

'Do you think it's the times she's met her brother for something to eat?' Billy asked, scratching his head in confusion.

Clem shook his head slowly. 'No, it's definitely more cryptic than that. She was keeping a record of something she didn't want others to know about. It might have nothing to do with her brother.'

The door opened and Lauren walked in. She headed over to where Matt was standing.

'What's this?' Lauren asked, staring at the screen.

'This was found on Sophie's laptop, ma'am,' Matt said, pointing at the wall. 'We were discussing what it might be about. There's only one name on here, which is Sophie's brother, Patrick. But that might just be a front. She's titled it *Patrick's Meals*, but we can't see that she'd record times he went out for a meal. Or had simply eaten, for that matter. Also, was she with him at these times? The latest entry was only a few days before she died.'

'It's certainly odd,' Lauren said. 'We need to speak to the brother to find out what he knows about it. We met him at his parents' house. He might still be there.'

A thought flashed across Matt's mind. 'No, he's not. When Tracie the FLO called in she mentioned that he'd left soon after we did because he had to return to work.'

'Wow, not a very nice son if he couldn't even stay with his mum and dad after they learnt about their daughter's death,' Jenna said.

'We don't know the circumstances... but yeah...' Matt said, agreeing.

'Okay, do we know where he works?' Lauren asked.

'I can find out for you, ma'am,' Tamsin offered, her fingers already dancing across the keyboard.

'Thanks. How far have you got with feeding back on Kerr's interview, Matt?'

'We were discussing her answers and the fact she needed help to commit the crimes,' he responded.

'Ma'am, I've got the work details for Patrick Yates,' Tamsin called out. 'He's a contracts manager for a property development company in Truro. I'll forward the address to you.'

'Thanks,' Lauren said, as she surveyed the room. 'Let's see what this is all about, and if it can be tied to the murders in any way. He wasn't very forthcoming when we met him at the parents' house. In fact, if anything, he was verging on rudeness, which there was no need for. Matt, you can drive. The rest of you, carry on with your research into Mary Kerr and any links we can find, especially with Finch. We've got to make this case airtight.'

Matt followed Lauren out of the office and they walked together to the car park. The scent of rain filled the air. Surely not another storm. It was meant to be summer.

Sliding into his car, Matt glanced over at Lauren, her profile outlined against the car's dim interior lighting. The engine roared to life and he turned left out of the car park and joined the oncoming traffic.

'Do you really think Patrick Yates could be involved in all this?' Matt asked, gripping the steering wheel. The cool leather felt reassuring under his hands.

'His behaviour was strange when we met him, to say the least. Maybe he was grieving, but I got the sense he was hiding something. Don't you agree?'

Matt recalled their first interaction with Patrick. 'His reactions were definitely off. Defensive, even. And now with this record of dates and timings on Sophie's laptop... even if it's nothing to do with her death, it's still weird. Assuming it was about him. Which we don't yet know.'

'We'll soon find out when we question him. He might turn out to know more about this whole situation than we realised.'

'It wouldn't be the first time a family member was involved in murder. He might have had some vested interest or a shared motive with Mary Kerr? If he did, that would certainly answer our question regarding how the bodies were moved,' Matt said, his focus not wavering from the road, as the rain began coming down in torrents and the wipers had to work overtime to clear it.

'Yes, you're right. It's our job to find out. For Sophie's sake.'

TWENTY-FOUR

The sound of construction work filled the air as Lauren stepped out of Matt's car. They'd been to Yates's workplace in Truro and had been informed that he was on site in Redruth today.

The air was filled with dust, the scent of fresh cement lingering with the tangy mix of metal and sweat. Fortunately, the rain had stopped and she adjusted her lightweight jacket and scrutinised the building site. Everywhere, there were signs of progress: buildings taking shape, workers in hard hats and high-vis jackets moving about purposefully.

The distant rumble of heavy machinery served as a reminder of the rapid change and development that places like this were experiencing.

According to the sign at the entrance of the development, they were building eighteen two and three-bedroom semi-detached and detached properties.

They headed towards a wrought-iron hut, with a sign reading *Office* on it. The man inside, engrossed in his work, only looked up once they'd opened the door and stepped inside.

'We'd like to speak to Patrick Yates,' Lauren said, holding out her warrant card, her words an order and not up for debate.

The man rose from his chair and walked around the desk until he was standing next to them. 'Oh... well, the last time I saw him, he was doing a site inspection on one of the properties over there,' he explained, pointing towards a window that overlooked the skeletal beginnings of what would soon be someone's home.

'Can you call him back? We don't want to start climbing over there. Even if health and safety regulations would allow us, which I suspect they wouldn't.'

The man's eyes flitted between Lauren and Matt, uncertainty playing on his features. 'Yes, I suppose so. Do I tell him what it's about?'

'No, please just give him a call and ask him to get back here straight away. Tell him it's urgent, but don't mention us being with the police.' Lauren's eyes never left the man's, ensuring he understood the gravity of their request.

The man shrugged, then pulled a walkie-talkie from the desk and held it up to his mouth. 'Patrick, you're needed at the office.' The man's almost casual demeanour while contacting Yates made Lauren's skin prickle with annoyance. He might as well have been calling him in for a cup of tea. Then again, she had ordered him to not say what it was about or who they were.

'Can it wait?' the distant voice crackled in response. 'I'm in the middle of something.' The slight tone of impatience hinted at a man used to being in control, not wanting disruptions.

'No. There's someone here to see you. It's urgent.'

Lauren scowled at the man, giving a silent reprimand. She hadn't wanted Yates to know he had visitors. She wanted to lessen the risk of him deciding to do a runner rather than speak to them. But it was too late. She had to hope that he hadn't sussed out who they were.

They left the office to wait outside, but slightly around the corner so they couldn't be immediately spotted. After a couple of minutes there was the unmistakable thud of boots crunching on the gravel. Patrick Yates headed towards them dressed from head to toe in protective gear, the bright yellow of his hard hat making him less easy to identify, but Lauren recognised him nonetheless.

He headed straight to the office. However, just before he got there, Lauren and Matt stepped out in front of him.

'Mr Yates,' Lauren began, watching as a range of emotions played across his face. The initial panic, the brief glimmer of recognition, and then a rapid restoration of composure. It was fascinating and telling. In that brief moment, Lauren felt like she'd gleaned more about Patrick Yates than any report could offer.

'Yes?' His voice carried a hint of defiance, maybe even annoyance.

'We'd like to have a word with you about Sophie,' she said, unwavering. The gravity in her tone hung in the air between them, thick with implication.

'Okay,' Yates replied cautiously, his eyes darting around the vast construction site. 'Let's find a quiet place.'

Was his suggestion of somewhere out of the way a tactical move?

'We'll go over there,' Lauren said, gesturing to the edge of the site.

Her eyes moved from Yates to the suggested spot and then instinctively to Matt. While their priority was to gather information, there was still the nagging worry Yates might attempt to escape. At least the vast openness of the land, combined with the heaviness of Yates's attire, made that scenario less likely.

'Okay,' Yates said, agreeing.

They walked over in silence, the tension rising with every step. The normal background noises were drowned out by the sound of their shoes grinding against the rough ground and dirt.

'I'm surprised you're here, to be honest,' Lauren said once they'd reached the secluded area. Her tone was measured but had a hint of real curiosity. 'With everything going on this week, I'd have thought you'd be with your parents, supporting them.'

'We have a deadline to finish this work, or there are penalties,' Yates said defensively. He sounded frustrated, like he was trying to balance grieving with his job responsibilities.

Lauren watched him closely, noticing his body language and tone. She could tell there was more to the story.

'Fair enough,' she responded, shrugging slightly to show some sympathy. 'We're here because we've had the forensics report back to us regarding the contents of Sophie's laptop.' The mere mention of his sister's name caused Yates's already tense shoulders to hunch a little more, as if he was bracing himself. Did he already know what she was about to say? 'We found a spreadsheet with your name on it that seems to track some dates. It looks like Sophie might have been monitoring you. Do you know why?'

Yates's expressions cycled through confusion, realisation, and a touch of fear. Whatever he might tell them, there was no way that he didn't know anything about it.

'No. Why would my sister have been watching me?' His voice was edged with bewilderment, but it seemed forced.

'You must have some idea,' Lauren probed. She could see the inner turmoil on his face. Yates's eyes darted away guiltily. The reddening of his cheeks gave it away. He definitely knew something.

'Mr Yates,' Lauren said formally, to emphasise the seriousness of the situation. 'I believe you know exactly what this is about. I suggest you tell us now.'

Silence surrounded them, but in the distance, construction noises droned on.

'I... I can't,' Yates stammered, pained. 'It's ridiculous this happened. I'm so sorry. I can hardly face my parents; that's why I came back to work. To escape.' He took a shaky breath. 'I think I caused Sophie's death.'

Lauren and Matt exchanged a loaded glance. This confession changed everything. Had they been on the wrong track the whole time?

'What do you mean you caused Sophie's death?' Lauren asked firmly. 'Are you saying you killed her?'

'No. Of course I didn't!' Yates said fiercely. 'Sophie was my sister. I loved her. I loved her a lot. It's just...' He stared up at the sky as if seeking escape from his guilt.

'Mr Yates – Patrick,' Matt said, kindly. 'We have to find out who murdered Sophie and Courtney. If it wasn't you, then what exactly do you know?'

Yates hesitated, before finally relenting. 'Sophie found out that I'd been using again. I'd been clean for a long time, but... you know how life is... I've got a lot of work on. I needed to keep going. The hours are crazy. She saw me out one night and realised that I was high. Then she started following me and saw me with Jack.'

Lauren's eyes widened as she thought she realised who he meant. She exchanged a glance with Matt. 'What... You mean Jack Trembath, the skipper of the trawler Sophie worked on?'

Yates nodded ashamedly. 'Yes.'

'What's he got to do with it?' Lauren asked, millions of thoughts careering through her head.

'He's my supplier. Sophie worked it out. She told me to stop or she'd go to the police.'

Bloody hell. Was this all about drugs?

'And did you?'

'I tried, but—'

'Did you tell Trembath that Sophie knew?'

'No. Of course I didn't. He must have worked it out for himself. Or maybe she approached him. I don't know. I tried not to think about it.'

'Do you think Trembath murdered Sophie and Courtney?'

'I don't know. If you'd have asked me before all this I'd have said no way. But now... I'm not sure.'

'If you suspected he had something to do with it, then why didn't you come to us? Tell us what you knew?'

Yates lowered his head. 'Because... it wouldn't bring Sophie back, and I didn't want to get in trouble. I hate myself for this... but... I just tried to forget all about it.'

'Did Trembath supply you before you got clean?' Lauren asked.

'No,' Yates said, shaking his head.

'So how did you know about him?'

'A friend connected me with him recently.'

'How often do you buy from him?'

'It's not regular. I text him when I need more. I'm supposed to meet him tomorrow night.' Yates fidgeted nervously with his sleeves.

She pulled out her phone, displaying the incriminating spreadsheet. 'These times and dates, are they all your visits to Trembath? Because that's a lot of visits.'

'Ummm... most of them are, yeah,' Yates said, his tone dropping.

'So, are you dealing, too? Selling to others?'

'I'm not a dealer,' Yates said, defensively. 'I just get enough for my friends, or people I know. I don't make money out of it. Well, not much, anyway. They go through me because I'm the one with the contact.'

'But you said a friend connected you to Trembath?' Lauren said.

'Not a friend exactly. More an acquaintance. I couldn't ask him to buy for me.' Yates hung his head.

'So, who is this *acquaintance*?'

'I'm not sure of his name. I got talking to him in the pub one time,' Yates said, shrugging.

'Well, whatever way you look at it, you're dealing. And

that's what you'll be charged with. But if you can help us nail your sister's murderer, then that will go in your favour.'

'I'll do anything. Tell me what you want,' Yates agreed, eagerly.

Lauren studied him for a moment. 'How much have you ordered for tomorrow?'

'Twenty grams,' he responded, his eyes darting between Lauren and Matt.

Lauren's attention didn't waver. 'What does that cost you?'

Yates stilled, the enormity of the revelation clear on his face. 'Fifteen hundred pounds.'

Lauren exhaled sharply, doing the maths in her head. Such an amount for just twenty grams? 'That's quite steep, even for a high-end product. Demand must vastly outstrip supply if he can charge that much.'

Yates shifted uncomfortably. 'Look, I don't ask questions. I just pay.'

'And you buy this for yourself and friends.'

'Yes. I've already told you that.'

'Where does the exchange take place?' Lauren pressed.

'Different spots,' Yates said. 'Sometimes down by the docks, or behind a building. He tells me on the day exactly where to go.'

'Who is his supplier?' Matt asked.

'I don't know.'

Lauren's eyes narrowed slightly. 'Are you sure?'

'Look, I'm telling the truth. My only contact is Jack.' Yates shifted on his feet, glancing at his watch.

'Did you know that Sophie was working on Trembath's trawler when you first approached him for the drugs?' Lauren asked.

Yates shook his head adamantly. 'No. I had no idea. She'd been working in secret. At least, secret from the family.'

'Did he know at the time that you were her brother?'

'No.' Yates crossed his arms, his body language closed off. 'Not as far as I know.'

Lauren studied his defensive posture. 'When did he find out?' she pressed.

Yates threw his hands up in frustration. 'I don't know.'

He met Lauren's scrutinising stare briefly before looking away, shifting his weight from foot to foot. Lauren glanced at Matt, recognising they were going in circles with Yates's vague answers and evasive body language.

Lauren held out her phone again so he could see a photo of the spreadsheet. 'You said these dates and times weren't all yours. Which ones aren't?'

Yates stared at the screen. 'There are three that aren't mine. On the fifth, fifteenth and twentieth of May.'

'Are you sure?'

'Yes. I was away with work on those days.'

'Do you have any idea what they relate to?'

'No. Sorry.' He glanced at his watch and shifted from foot to foot. 'Look, I'm meant to be working. I have to go before they send someone out to find me.'

'Fine. Don't mention this discussion of ours to anyone. And I mean *anyone*,' Lauren said, firmly.

'I won't. What's going to happen now?'

'We want you to go back to work and act as you would normally. Do you understand?' Lauren said.

'Yes,' Yates said. 'Do you want me to meet Jack tomorrow?'

Lauren glanced at Matt, before finally answering, 'We'll let you know.'

Yates hurried off, his shoulders hunched. Lauren watched him go, chewing her lip thoughtfully. There was more to unravel here.

Matt sighed heavily, rubbing the bridge of his nose. 'What do you think, ma'am? Do you believe that Trembath was involved in Sophie's murder?'

'He might not have done it, but he's got to be a part of it somehow. We just don't know how yet.'

'It's possible that Trembath and Mary Kerr were in this together. With Samuel Finch, too, for all we know,' Matt added.

'Yes, there's a chance that could be the case. What we'll do is monitor Yates's meeting with Trembath and catch the drug deal taking place. Once we have him in custody, we'll question him about Sophie and Courtney. If Trembath knows he's a suspect in their deaths, he might take off. This will be our best shot at catching him,' Lauren said with determination. 'We need to plan this meticulously. Let's head back and put together a strategy. We can't afford any mistakes now.'

TWENTY-FIVE

Lauren's eyes darted around the room as she took in the faces of her team. 'Attention, everyone,' she began, standing by the whiteboard, Matt beside her. She pulled the cap off the marker, writing down the words, *Jack Trembath trawler skipper*, and *drugs* on the board. 'We've just been speaking to Sophie's brother, Patrick, and there's another layer to this case that we didn't see coming. Patrick thinks Sophie's death might have been down to him.'

'What? He killed her?' Billy said, frowning.

'No. It's linked to Jack Trembath, the trawler skipper on the boat where Sophie worked.'

'You think the skipper is the murderer?' Billy said.

'Not necessarily,' Matt said, his tone cautious. 'But he is involved in drug trafficking. We're not exactly sure how he does it, but that's what we need to investigate. We also need to know who else could be implicated and how deep this goes.'

'Bloody hell.' Billy let out a low whistle. 'So, you think that Sophie found out and that's why she's dead?'

'We don't know. It's possible,' Lauren said. 'According to

Patrick Yates, many of the dates on Sophie's spreadsheet coincide with when he bought drugs from Trembath.'

'That's a lot of drugs,' Clem said, rubbing the side of his forehead. 'Does he buy for others too?'

'That's exactly what we asked when questioning him, and you're right. He told us he buys for his close circle of friends. But that doesn't mean he's telling the truth. He could be far more involved. He might be the main link or just a small part of a larger chain. Although it doesn't particularly fit in with his job as a contracts manager, not that I'm one for stereotyping,' Lauren said.

'I agree with you, ma'am,' Jenna said.

'There are several entries in the spreadsheet that he says don't relate to Yates's drug-buying activities, so we need to find out what they represent.'

'Another customer?' Billy suggested.

'Perhaps.'

'And all this still doesn't explain Courtney,' Clem said, his brow furrowed in thought. 'Why would Trembath have a reason to kill her?'

Lauren's fingers grazed the edge of the table she was standing next to. 'The only theory I can come up with is if Sophie had trusted Courtney with information she'd gleaned about the drug operation, and somehow Courtney got involved or was trying to help. Or perhaps she knew too much.'

'That doesn't make sense, ma'am, when you consider that Courtney was in a relationship with Finch. She didn't hang out with Sophie,' Jenna said, shaking her head.

'That's the catch,' Lauren agreed. 'There was no love lost between the two women, and if anything there was anger and distrust.'

'Or maybe Courtney found out about Sophie's investigation and wanted to help so they could repair their friendship?' Clem suggested.

'But if they'd become friends again, wouldn't Courtney have told her mum, if they were so close?' Jenna said. 'Maybe Finch is in the thick of it and Courtney found out and spoke to Sophie. They might have shared what they knew, Finch found out, and that's why they had to go.'

Lauren sighed. 'There's definitely a missing connection here. All of the scenarios suggested could be possible. And let's not forget Mary Kerr.'

'It's like we've now got more leads than hot dinners,' Clem said.

'Yes, but remember we could very well be investigating two separate cases. That's why we need to tread carefully,' Lauren said, unable to hide her frustration.

'Do we have any idea what Sophie was planning to do with the information she had gathered? Or even whether she had already done something with it?' Clem asked.

'She was keeping tabs on her brother, and did threaten to go to the police if he didn't stop using. But we know that she didn't do that. It could have been an idle threat.'

'Or she was stopped before having the chance,' Clem said. 'Could the brother have been involved in the murders?'

'We don't believe so,' Lauren said. 'But we're keeping an open mind. He's agreed to help with the inquiry.'

'How would Trembath even know about Sophie's observations? Do you think that she approached him and threatened to report him if he didn't stop supplying her brother?' Jenna said. 'Honestly, it's not all making sense.'

'I agree,' Lauren conceded. 'But for now, our immediate focus should be on Trembath. Dig into his background, his connections, everything. If he's as shady as we suspect, we'll find a trail. We're going to bring him in on the drugs charges and then question him about the murders.'

'Shall I revisit the fish and chip shops to see if Trembath went to any of them?' Billy asked.

'Yes, good idea,' Lauren said.

'I'm on to it, ma'am. They all know me in there now, I've been so often. With a bit of luck I'll get a free portion of chips,' Billy said, smirking.

Lauren looked around at her team, and smiled. She appreciated the way they worked together. 'Thanks, everyone. Let's hope with the leads we do have, we can now uncover the truth.'

'What are we going to do with Mary Kerr? She's still in custody,' Matt asked.

Lauren turned to him. 'She threatened us with a shotgun, Matt. Regardless of her involvement or not in the murders, which as yet we don't know, she's facing charges and will remain in custody.'

'It's possible that Mary Kerr was collaborating with Trembath,' Tamsin said. 'They could they have plotted this together?'

'It's possible, I suppose, for them to have been in it together. With Kerr targeting female fishermen because of her vendetta and the skipper dealing with the drugs side. Different motives but both of them wanting the same outcome. But let's not get ahead of ourselves, as we don't yet know if Trembath is our murderer,' Lauren said.

'I agree, ma'am,' Jenna said, with a sceptical frown on her face. 'For a start, where's the concrete evidence linking Mary Kerr and the skipper? And, more importantly, if his motive was to protect his drug business from being exposed by Sophie, then Kerr's involvement seems... I don't know... pointless.'

'We can't forget Courtney's death, either. It doesn't fit neatly into this theory,' Matt said. 'Like the DI said, we may have two separate cases going on and we're trying to force them together unnecessarily.'

Lauren nodded in agreement. 'Well, Patrick Yates has a meeting with Trembath tomorrow. We're going to use it to catch the skipper in the act.'

'Can Yates be trusted, ma'am?' Jenna asked, her eyes narrowed in suspicion.

'We think so, but we'll be keeping watch at all times.'

'What's the plan? Someone goes with Yates to meet Trembath? Wouldn't he be suspicious if he's never seen this new face before? Or I suppose Yates could be wired and we'll watch from afar. But then we have to hope the skipper doesn't check,' Jenna said.

'All valid concerns,' Lauren admitted. 'It's important for us to be strategic. The element of surprise is paramount. We need to capture Trembath red-handed with the drugs, so there's no escape route for him. I'm going to see DCI Mistry now to get his permission for the operation and discuss its logistics.'

With that, she strode out of the room, leaving her team in a contemplative silence, aware of the gravity of their next moves.

The rhythmic tapping of Lauren's shoes echoed as she headed down the corridor to her boss's office. She stood still for a moment when she reached it, gathering her thoughts. She then gave a sharp knock.

'Come in,' the DCI commanded.

Pushing the door open, Lauren stepped into the spacious room, which he kept immaculately tidy, and nothing like her own place of work.

'Good afternoon, sir,' Lauren greeted, her posture straight.

'Yes, Lauren?' DCI Mistry responded, gesturing for her to sit on one of the empty chairs in front of his desk.

'We're onto something substantial in the murder investigations,' she began, once she was seated. 'We do have Mary Kerr in custody, as you know, but further evidence has been brought to our attention which might either put her in the clear or add another dimension to the case.'

He raised an eyebrow. 'I see. What's this new evidence and how does it affect your case against the woman?'

'We've been grappling with several unanswered questions. Like how a woman who's not sturdily built managed to move both bodies, and, bearing this in mind, whether or not she had an accomplice. So far, we've found no firm evidence proving that she worked with anyone else, and we also haven't located the ketamine used to sedate the victims. It was the fact that she threatened DS Price and me, together with her hatred for any female working in the fishing industry, that led us to believe she was tied to the murders.'

'What else has come to light?'

'According to Patrick Yates, Sophie had been tailing him after finding out that he was buying drugs from Jack Trembath, the skipper of the trawler she worked on once or twice a week. If the skipper discovered what she knew, that could give him a motive for killing her.'

The DCI's eyes widened a fraction. 'How does this tie in with the second murder?'

'We're unsure at the moment. We also don't know whether Kerr assisted Trembath in any way, albeit having a different motive.'

'What are your next steps?'

'That's what I'm here about. Yates has a scheduled meeting with the skipper tomorrow night. We're considering wiring him to capture the exchange as it happens, or to watch proceedings from a distance.'

Leaning back in his chair, the DCI considered the proposal. 'It's risky. You're thinking of letting him walk into that situation alone? If the skipper discovers what's going on he could be in danger.'

'Maybe DC Tamsin Kellow, one of my officers, could accompany him, under the guise of being his girlfriend?' Lauren proposed, her mind racing with strategies and contingencies.

The DCI seemed thoughtful for a moment. 'Okay. As long as your officer remains secure, and you have eyes on her at all times, I'll give my approval.'

Lauren's shoulders relaxed slightly. 'Thank you, sir. We'll make sure everything's in place for tomorrow evening.'

'Keep me updated, Lauren. And be careful. We can't afford any slip-ups.'

'Will do.'

Lauren exited, responsibility pressing down on her, but it was equally matched by her determination to see the case through.

TWENTY-SIX

Matt was writing on the whiteboard when Lauren walked in, her presence immediately commanding the room's attention.

'Perfect timing, ma'am,' Matt said, a knowing glint in his eye.

Lauren raised an eyebrow, pausing for a beat while she absorbed the atmosphere. 'What's got you all excited?' she enquired, her attention shifting from Matt to the rest of the team.

'You won't believe what we've found,' Billy said, barely containing himself. 'I phoned the fish and chip shops on the off chance that they knew Trembath by name, because he's a local, and it seems he made stops at the Blue Lobster chippy on the days both of the victims were killed. The only thing is,' Billy continued, building the suspense, 'he bought the food super early. Way before a normal dinnertime. The chips would've been a cold mush by the evening.'

'Maybe he has a microwave on the boat so the food can be reheated?' Clem said, logical as ever.

'True. But reheated fish and chips? Yuck,' Billy said, shaking his head and turning up the corner of his mouth in disdain.

The officer's comment drew a few chuckles from around the room, briefly breaking the tension.

'Nothing beats the crispy fish from the chippy, right?' Jenna added, playfully.

Billy grinned. 'You got that right. But let's be honest, Trembath probably wasn't picking up his supper for the taste. More to lace it with ketamine.'

'Well, depending on how hungry you are after a day's fishing, even cold chips might seem tempting,' Matt said, causing the others to chuckle. 'Joking aside, though. This is a major break. We have him placed at an incriminating place on the key dates.'

'Yes, well done, Billy,' Lauren said, adding her approval.

Billy flushed and rubbed his neck. 'Thanks, ma'am.'

Lauren's posture shifted as she leant against the edge of a desk, beside the board, all eyes, including Matt's, now firmly on her. 'There's something else,' she began, drawing the team in. 'When I was with the DCI, an idea struck me, something we hadn't considered before. Tamsin, rather than merely wiring Patrick, I'm thinking of getting you involved.' Lauren looked directly at the officer. 'If you're comfortable with it, I'd like you to be wired as well and pose as Patrick Yates's girlfriend. You'd be our insider, keeping eyes and ears on Trembath in case he tries anything unexpected. Patrick Yates, too, for that matter.'

A hush fell over the room. They all understood the gravity of this bold strategy and knew that undercover work carried risks, like what had happened when Jenna went undercover several months previously.

Tamsin's eyes reflected the gravity of the decision and after a moment of contemplation, she straightened up. 'I'm in. If it gets us closer to cracking this case, then it has to be done.'

'We've got your back, Tamsin. Always. So you don't need to worry about that,' Matt assured her.

'Why does it have to be her?' Billy protested, not sounding

convinced. 'Why not let me go? I can be his friend. I am perfectly capable of doing it. And I can run faster than Tamsin if either of them attempt to scarper.'

'Says who?' Tamsin said. 'I was county champion at fifteen-hundred metres, I'll have you know. I'll beat you in a race any day.'

'Okay, you're on.'

'We're getting off track here,' Matt said, holding up his hand to silence them. 'If you absolutely insist, once this case is solved we'll run the race and establish a winner. In the meantime, Tamsin, don't worry.'

'It will be fine, Billy,' Tamsin added, as if to reassure her colleague.

Billy's protectiveness towards Tamsin was no secret to the rest of the team. Lauren suspected that was why he wanted to take her place.

'I just think I could pull it off,' he insisted, his stance rigid. 'Maybe even better... even if you do turn out to be a faster runner. No offence to you, Tamsin.'

'Billy, I know you want in,' Lauren said with a mix of authority and understanding. 'And it's not about questioning your capability or commitment. Or speed, for that matter. I've chosen Tamsin for a specific reason. Our aim is to catch Trembath off guard. Your presence might well put him on alert.'

'Undercover work is all about playing the right cards at the right time,' Matt added. 'It's not a question of who's more skilled, but rather who's the best fit for this particular scenario.'

Lauren met Billy's eye, offering a reassuring glance. 'Matt's right. We value you, Billy. This is just strategy.'

'Besides, Billy, you'd look awful trying to pass as Yates's girl-friend,' Clem joked.

A chuckle rippled through the room, dispelling the tense atmosphere. Even Billy managed a half-smile, although he was still clearly frustrated. 'Okay.' He sighed, rolling his eyes playfully. 'But you'd better let me go undercover next time.'

'We'll see,' Lauren said.

'I'll take that as a yes then, ma'am,' Billy said, the corner of his mouth turning up slightly in a lopsided grin, his eyes shining with mischief.

'Do we have anything else on Trembath?' Lauren asked, turning her attention back to the team.

'Yes,' Matt said, turning to her. 'While you were with the DCI, we've learnt a couple of things that could be relevant.'

'Which are?' Lauren asked, giving him her full attention.

'First of all, he's married and his wife is going through cancer treatment right now,' Matt said with a sigh. 'From what we understand, he hasn't taken any time off to be with her during the whole ordeal. She's been struggling through the therapies on her own. All of his money, every last penny has been spent on some treatment that isn't covered by the national health service. She's been going to a private clinic.'

'Interesting,' Lauren said. 'Anything else?'

'Yes,' Matt added. 'His fishing business is going under and he's drowning in debt. So, if we're looking for a motive for him selling drugs, then we've got one... And possibly one for murdering Sophie, too, if she found out and was threatening to spill the beans.'

The room grew still as the implications sank in.

Tamsin's brow furrowed, the earlier resolve in her eyes replaced by uncertainty. 'So, in his mind he's justified. For his wife and his business.'

'Desperation can make people do terrible things,' Clem said, his arms crossed. 'But it can also make someone dangerous. We need to remember that.'

Lauren pursed her lips, deep in thought. 'It does make our job more complicated. Personal motivations can be strong drivers. But we need to remember, regardless of his reasons, he's still involved in illegal activities and we have two murdered women.'

'And we have a job to do,' Matt said firmly, arms crossed.

Lauren sighed, tapping her fingers on the table. 'You're right. It's always challenging when personal tragedies intersect with our professional responsibilities. But we can't let this cloud our judgment.'

'It's a tragic situation. No one should have to choose between going out to work and being with their loved ones. But we can't use that as an excuse for drug dealing, or possibly murder,' Jenna said, resolutely.

'I agree,' Clem added. 'Although knowing what he's going through does give us a clearer picture of his state of mind. If we understand what's driving him, it can help us predict his next move.'

Lauren massaged her temples. 'Yes, but a cornered, desperate person is also unpredictable and dangerous, as Clem mentioned.'

'And we don't even know if he's the killer yet,' Matt reminded them.

'Yes, we do, Sarge,' Billy said. 'The chip shop... Remember?'

'True. And while that's our strongest evidence, our primary concern is justice for Sophie and ensuring no one else gets hurt,' Matt said.

Clem raised an eyebrow. 'Could there be other victims we don't know about yet?'

'Possibly,' Lauren said. 'That's what we need to find out.'

'And we mustn't forget Courtney. There's got to be something else that we're missing that ties her into the case. This might be more than Sophie learning about the drugs and her brother,' Jenna said, staring at Lauren intently.

Tamsin fidgeted with her sleeve cuff. 'Yes, how Courtney fits into the picture is important. Are there any specific questions you'd like me to casually ask Trembath to dig into Courtney's involvement? Anything I can do to subtly steer the conversation?'

Billy waved a warning finger at her. 'You're just the girlfriend, remember? No questions. You have to stand there and act like you couldn't care less what's going down.'

'Billy's right,' Lauren agreed. 'We can't risk arousing Trembath's suspicion.'

'Okay, ma'am. I get that my role is to observe. I won't do anything to jeopardise that,' Tamsin promised.

'Good. Now have we found any connection between Mary Kerr and/or Samuel Finch? We shouldn't forget about him.'

'Nothing, ma'am,' Matt said.

Lauren squared her shoulders resolutely. 'Okay. For now Trembath is our focus. If it is drug related, there may be other connections we haven't yet considered.'

Clem's expression hardened. 'Drug operations have complex webs. We must discover the full picture and hold everyone accountable.'

'Exactly. Now let's keep going with our research into Trembath, so we're fully prepared,' Lauren said.

A collective energy surged through the room and Lauren returned to her office confident that they had everything under control.

TWENTY-SEVEN

Matt's phone pinged with a new message. Glancing down, he saw it was from Lauren, and all it said was:

Come to my office.

Matt peered across the room towards Lauren's door. Why didn't she come over to talk to him if it was about the case, seeing as they'd only just been talking about it? Or stand at the door, even, and call him over, like she often did. The text was weirdly formal. Unless there was something else going on that she didn't want the rest of the team to hear.

Feeling a little uneasy, Matt got up from his desk, absent-mindedly adjusting his tie. He headed towards Lauren's office, his footsteps echoing on the floor, and after pausing briefly at the door, he tapped.

'Come in,' Lauren called out, with a small hand gesture motioning for him to enter.

Matt stepped inside and closed the door behind him. He headed over to her desk and sat on the empty chair. 'What's up, ma'am?' he asked, trying to sound casual.

Lauren twirled a silver pen between her fingers as if she was reluctant to speak. It was strange to see her like that. 'Umm... Could we maybe grab a drink tonight? Now we're coming to the end of this case, I'd like to discuss my cousins and what to do next.'

Ahhh. Now it made sense. But why was she acting so unsure about asking him, when he'd already offered to help her in any way he could? Then again, this was Lauren, and she hated having to ask for help. Even from him.

'Of course, and...' His words trailed off as he remembered his evening plans.

'What is it?' Lauren asked.

'Mum's making my favourite dinner tonight and I promised to be home in time, if I could,' Matt confessed guiltily.

Lauren's face fell. 'That's okay, I understand.'

'Why don't we meet up later, if that works for you?' Matt quickly added, not wanting to let her down.

'Thanks, Matt. That would be great. If you're sure. I don't want to upset your dinner plans. You're the only person I trust to talk this through with.'

He smiled. 'Of course I'm sure. I've already offered to help whenever you need it. What time, and place?'

'How about I pick you up at eight?' Lauren proposed. 'Will dinner be over by then?'

'Yes, well and truly. It also gives me time to read Dani her bedtime story. You can imagine how she'll be if I have to miss it.'

'I definitely can,' Lauren said, smiling. 'Thanks, Matt. It means a lot.'

Their eyes met, an unspoken understanding bridging the gap.

'No problem. And, ma'am. Don't worry. We'll sort this problem out for you.' His voice resonated with steadfast conviction. 'Well, for your cousins, anyway,' he added.

Exiting her office, Matt was met with the usual sounds of

keyboards and light chatter from his colleagues. He returned to his desk and reflected on how his working relationship with Lauren had evolved over time. There was now a genuine trust between them and he liked it that way.

The fading daylight created a soft, warm glow in the sitting room and Matt looked over at Dani playing on the floor. She was fully absorbed in an imaginary world with her toys, unaware of anything else around her. He loved seeing her imagination run wild as she acted out stories and adventures with her toys. There was something special about a child's creativity at that age.

'Come on, you,' he said, his words carrying that unmistakable parental firmness. 'Time for bed.'

Dani tilted her head, her bright eyes searching his. 'But, Daddy, I'm not tired.'

Matt chuckled, ruffling her hair. 'You might feel wide awake now, but if you don't go to bed you'll be tired and grumpy in the morning.'

Her face scrunched up in thought. 'Okay. I suppose so. Will you read me a story?'

'Of course. Which one tonight?'

'The princess and the elephant!' she replied without a second's hesitation.

He sighed in playful exasperation. 'Again? We've read it every night this week.'

'It's my favourite,' Dani said, her resolve unwavering.

'What about the story of the children who discover a hidden world? Wouldn't you like me to read that for a change?' Matt tried, even though he knew what the answer would be.

Dani shook her head firmly. 'No. I want the princess and the elephant.'

'Okay,' Matt conceded with mock defeat. 'That one it is. But first, let's say goodnight to Grandma and Grandpa.'

With Dani held securely in his arms, they headed into the kitchen. The comforting sound of washing up and muted chatter filled the air as his parents tackled dinner's pots and pans.

'We've come in to say goodnight,' Matt said, heading over to his parents.

His mum wiped her hands on her apron and leant over, pressing a gentle kiss on Dani's forehead. 'Night, love. See you in the morning.'

'Sleep tight, little one,' Matt's dad said, dropping a kiss on the top of his granddaughter's head.

'Don't forget to brush those teeth,' his mum said, wagging her finger.

Matt rolled his eyes playfully. 'Mum, we've got our bedtime routine sorted. We do it every night.'

His mum smirked. 'Just making sure. What time are you going out tonight?'

Hesitating, aware that Dani was listening and knowing the likely response, Matt replied, 'Lauren's picking me up at eight.'

Dani tugged on his jumper. 'Can I stay up till she gets here? Please, Daddy. Please.'

He sighed, 'You've got nursery tomorrow, sweetheart. You need all the sleep you can get. You can see Lauren another time.'

Her little brow furrowed. 'What about Ben and Tia?'

He kissed her cheek. 'Once this case is done, we'll sort something out with Lauren.'

Her eyes shone with hope. 'Is it nearly over?'

'Almost,' Matt said. 'Now, come on. Let's get you ready for bed and story time. I don't want to make Lauren cross by not being ready when she arrives.'

Dani giggled, nestling closer, as stories of princesses and elephants loomed in her near future.

Matt stared out of the window after hearing a car horn. It was Lauren. He quickly slipped on his jacket and stepped outside, pulling the door shut behind him. The fading daylight created long shadows on the street.

As he slid into the passenger seat, the cooler air inside the car was a pleasant contrast to the mild June evening in Cornwall. 'Eight o'clock on the dot,' he remarked with a smirk. 'Impressively punctual.'

Lauren grinned, her eyes twinkling. 'I was ready a little earlier but figured you'd be knee-deep in bedtime stories with Dani. Speaking of whom, how is she?'

'The same as always. I don't know where she gets all this energy from. And naturally, the moment she found out I was meeting you, she was full of questions about Ben and Tia and when she's going to see them,' Matt replied, a soft chuckle escaping his lips.

Lauren's face lit up with a gentle smile. 'Hopefully we can arrange something soon,' she said, shifting the car into gear and easing it onto the road.

Matt leant back, allowing the familiar streets of their town to rush past. 'So, where are we going for our drink? Somewhere quiet, I assume?'

'Yes, I thought we could try The Three Wise Birds. It's a few miles out of town, but shouldn't be too busy, as it's a week night. Have you been there?'

'No, I haven't,' Matt replied, shaking his head.

'Well, small and quaint is how I'd describe it. I like it,' Lauren said, tossing a glance in his direction before returning her concentration on the road ahead.

'Sounds great.'

Matt watched as the lights of the town centre faded, replaced by the more serene surroundings leading to the outskirts of Penzance, until they arrived at their destination.

Pulling into the gravelled car park, the pub's exterior ambient lighting cast a warm and inviting glow. And stepping inside, Matt felt immediately immersed in a bygone era: low-hanging wooden beams, antique brass fixtures glinting softly, and the unmistakable, nostalgic scent of beer and old timber. He could see exactly what Lauren meant in her description. The gentle murmur of conversations, punctuated by the distinct thud of darts hitting a board, added to the establishment's cosy atmosphere.

After queuing briefly at the bar for their drinks, Lauren motioned towards a dimly lit corner, which offered the privacy they needed.

'Okay, let's get down to it. I need a strategy,' Lauren said, her fingers playing with one of the beer mats on the table. 'Because otherwise my cousins could be toast. And as much as I don't like them, I don't want that to happen. We need something tangible to get the Frame brothers off their backs, but it has to be legal.'

Matt leant in, the amber liquid in his glass catching the dim light. 'We can't stoop to their level. Blackmail's out. But there must be a chink in their armour. Something we can use to our advantage.'

A furrow creased Lauren's brow, her eyes clouded with thought. 'You know, they do have that construction company,' she began cautiously. 'I'd bet a year's salary that it's just a smokescreen for all their shady dealings. What if we dangled a health and safety inspection over their heads?'

'Ummm... I'm not sure that's going to work,' Matt said with a shrug.

Doubt flickered in Lauren's eyes. 'Yeah. You're right, it does sound a tad... weak, doesn't it? Actually a bit pathetic, really,' she added with a touch of self-deprecation, which was most unusual for her. 'We don't even know if they're breaking any safety laws, anyway.'

'True. But how about this? We could imply we've got the tax office on speed dial, ready to dig deep into their finances. Now that might have the desired effect.'

Lauren's eyebrows shot up, intrigued. 'You think we could pull that off?'

Matt shrugged. 'It's not about whether we actually do it. It's the threat – the doubt it plants in their minds. We just need them to second guess themselves. I reckon it could be worth a try, right, ma'am?'

Her eyes softened, the corners of her mouth lifting into an affectionate smile. 'When it's just us, outside of work, Lauren will do. We've already had this discussion, remember?'

He nodded, but the familiarity of the name still felt somewhat strange on his tongue. To him, the formalities at work kept things professional, but here, in the dim warmth of the pub, it blurred the lines between colleague and friend, something he was still navigating.

'Okay, Lauren,' he began, pausing as he shifted gears mentally to address her more informally. 'I think the tax angle could work. It's a universal truth, after all, that no one wants the taxman looking too closely, whoever they are.'

'True,' she agreed. There was an additional glint in her eye, hinting at something more. 'But there's also something else we could use. Bernie Frame's son is on track for Oxford. Despite the Frame brothers'... how shall I put it... extracurricular activities, they seem keen on giving their children the best education money can buy. Private schools and all that.'

Matt raised an eyebrow in surprise. 'How did you stumble upon that little gem?'

'I came across the school's newsletter,' Lauren said with a smug smile. 'The lad's name stood out and so I checked who his parents were. What about if we subtly hint that we're keeping an eye on the admissions process and can ensure that it doesn't go well?'

Matt stiffened. He didn't like that idea. It wasn't fair. 'Isn't that playing too dirty, Lauren? The boy's just trying to further his education. We shouldn't use him as a pawn in our game. He can't help who his dad is.'

Lauren's hand made a dismissive gesture. 'You don't get it. We wouldn't actually be doing anything to affect the boy's chances, even if we can exert any influence, which I doubt. We're simply hinting that we might. Sometimes, the threat of an action is more potent than the action itself. And starting with this angle, rather than jumping straight to the tax issue, makes it more personal for Bernie. More real.'

Matt took a sip of beer as he considered Lauren's words. The bitter taste blended with his racing mind. 'It's a risky move. We'll have to be really careful. But if we do it right, this could give us the advantage we need.'

Lauren's eyes were full of resolve. She raised her glass in a toast. 'To smart strategy, and protecting what matters.'

Matt tapped his glass against hers, the soft clink underscoring their shared determination. 'To family, and making sure they stay safe.'

TWENTY-EIGHT

FRIDAY JUNE 14

Lauren had woken up very early that morning, the pressure of the day's mission weighing heavily on her mind. That feeling hadn't left her throughout the day, during which time she'd played out in her head every possible outcome to the operation until, after asking Matt for the third time whether all details had been checked, he'd sat her down and calmly explained that everything was under control and that Tamsin would be safe with all of them there.

He'd been right, of course, and she'd chastised herself for allowing the intensity of the situation to get to her. That wasn't how she normally acted.

Now, as they sat in the van, parked in the car park close to where Trembath had instructed the meeting was to take place, Lauren stared intently at Tamsin and Patrick Yates, who were sitting beside her. There was still half an hour to go, but she'd wanted to arrive early to ensure it was all set up correctly.

Tamsin, who was dressed more casually than usual, in a pair of denim shorts, cream and pink striped T-shirt and black ankle boots, was tapping her fingers anxiously on her leg, her eyes darting around the dimly lit area. Patrick Yates sat tall but looked uneasy, fidgeting with his polo shirt collar over the hidden wire.

'Is everything okay?' Lauren asked.

Tamsin met Lauren's gaze directly and cleared her throat. 'Yes, ma'am. I'm prepared for my role.' The officer sounded resolute but her eyes revealed her apprehension.

Yates shifted awkwardly, his jaw clenched tight. 'I'm ready, too,' he muttered.

Lauren studied them a moment longer. 'Look, I know you're both nervous but everything should be fine. We'll be nearby in this surveillance van, listening to every word. Watching every move.'

'If things seem off, we'll intervene immediately,' Matt added.

'You say that,' Yates said, his tense body revealing his reluctance. 'But I've always met Jack alone before. Having your officer with me might raise suspicions. He might suspect she's a cop.'

'Look, I know how these operations work,' Tamsin shot back defensively. 'I can blend in. He won't realise who I am. I can handle it.'

'It's okay, Tamsin,' Lauren said, placing a reassuring hand on the younger woman's shoulder. 'I get that you're both concerned. But we've planned this carefully and will be with you the entire time. Stick to your roles and it will be over soon enough.'

Yates still looked unconvinced, but he gave a begrudging nod. 'Okay. I just hope it doesn't go south.'

'It won't. Not if you stay alert and stick to the plan,' Matt said.

'We're in this together, and after we've got what we've come for, we'll ensure you both get out of there safely,' Lauren said, with quiet determination.

'You'd better make sure of that,' Yates said, a slight tremor in his voice.

There was silence for a while, and Lauren's fingers tapped rhythmically on her thigh while she thought through everything. 'Patrick, tell me. Could the entries on Sophie's spreadsheet that we can't identify relate to when Trembath picks up his shipment of drugs? Assuming it comes by boat. Does he do that with the crew on-board?'

Yates threw a brief, anxious glance around the van before shrugging helplessly. 'You're asking me stuff I don't know,' he admitted with frustration.

Tamsin leant in closer to him. 'It's important. Think back to any conversations you've had with him. Is there anything that might help us?'

'All I know is that I'm due to collect my supply today. I've never asked him where it comes from. That sort of thing isn't done.'

'Okay, never mind,' Lauren said, putting an end to the conversation.

They'd be asking Trembath the question when he was in custody.

With final preparations complete, Tamsin and Yates exited the van and headed to the meeting point, while Lauren and Matt remained inside to monitor the situation.

The surveillance van was parked strategically to observe the meeting spot while staying hidden. In addition to their van, a police vehicle with Clem, Jenna and Billy was parked in another section of the car park. Other officers were on standby nearby if needed.

As the first murmurs of conversation came through, Matt adjusted the settings to improve the audio quality.

Through her binoculars, Lauren watched Trembath approach Yates and Tamsin.

'Something feels off today, Yates. You're never early, and

you've never brought a bird along before. What's the game?' Trembath's voice was gravelly and edged with caution.

'No game, Jack. Tina's just... company. Can't a man bring his girlfriend along?'

There was a pause, during which time Lauren could imagine Trembath narrowing his eyes, sizing Yates up. 'Your personal life's your business,' the man finally said. 'But I don't like surprises. No need for any complications now.'

'Just thought I'd see what all the fuss was about. I promise, no trouble from me,' Tamsin said, with a feigned playfulness.

'You know, my old dad used to say, "If something feels off, son, trust your gut." And right now, Yates, something feels very off,' Trembath said, not sounding appeased.

Lauren's heart rate accelerated. She exchanged a glance with Matt, understanding the potential threat in the skipper's words.

Lauren picked up the radio from her lap, wanting to alert the rest of the team. 'Stay sharp, everyone. Trembath might be onto us. Stand by for my signal.'

The conversation outside continued, every word magnifying the undercurrent of suspicion. The stakes had just risen, and Lauren knew they needed to tread with caution.

'You got the cash?' Trembath asked, leaning in closer to Yates, his voice dropping to a near-whisper.

Lauren continued to watch through her binoculars.

'Yes,' Yates said, clearly doing his best to maintain his composure despite Trembath's evident suspicion. He cautiously pulled an envelope from his inside jacket pocket.

Trembath glanced at Tamsin, his distrust clear. 'Why don't you step back a bit, love? This is just between me and your boyfriend.'

'I'm here with him, remember? Just get a move on and we can go,' Tamsin said, holding her ground.

Trembath chuckled darkly, a sound that sent shivers down

Lauren's spine as she listened. He reached into his coat, bringing out a small, unassuming package. 'Alright,' he murmured. 'Here's your twenty grams.'

As Trembath and Yates made the swap, Lauren's finger hovered over the button on the radio. The moment she saw the drugs clearly change hands, she pressed it. 'The exchange has taken place. Move in, now!'

With their boots pounding the tarmac, coming from all directions, officers ran towards where the meeting was taking place.

In a flash, Trembath pivoted and bolted towards a potential exit. The scene erupted into a blur of motion. Calls and shouts echoed as officers gave chase, but Lauren, having anticipated Trembath's move, was already one step ahead.

She darted between parked cars and dodged startled passers-by, keeping her eyes on her prey. She could hear the others hot on her heels.

Trembath rounded a bend and lost his footing. Lauren surged forward, and caught him in a well-timed tackle. They slid across the pavement, the envelope containing the money floating momentarily in the air before descending a few metres away.

Gathering her breath, Lauren swiftly handcuffed the disoriented skipper and pulled him to his feet. Looking into his begrudging eyes, she smirked. 'Thought you could leg it, Trembath?' she quipped with a hint of smug satisfaction. 'Well, not on my watch.'

She marched him back to the meeting place, with Matt walking beside them.

'Should've gone with my gut,' he grumbled, throwing a venomous glance at Yates when they arrived back there.

Lauren looked at him, her expression steely. 'You should have,' she agreed. 'But it's a bit late for that now. Jack Trembath,

I'm arresting you on suspicion of drug trafficking and for the murder of Sophie Yates, Courtney Inwood and—'

'What?' Trembath said, interrupting. 'Murder? No way.'

'You do not have to say anything, but it may harm your defence if you do not mention something which you later rely on in court. Anything you do say may be given in evidence,' Lauren continued, while holding on to him. 'Do you understand?'

'I want a solicitor,' he spat back.

After Trembath and Yates had been taken away, Lauren turned to the team. 'Let's go down to the trawler and interview the crew. We need to find out what they know. But first I want someone to retrieve the envelope of money that went flying during the arrest, and also the whole area needs to be cordoned off.'

TWENTY-NINE

Matt lingered at the edge of the dock, watching as uniformed officers worked to cordon off the area. They were securing the path from the car park down to the slip where Trembath's trawler, *The Siren's Call*, was moored in Newlyn harbour. He could hear faint murmurs coming from onlookers who had gathered nearby. News of the police operation was spreading quickly through the small coastal community and curious residents peered from streets adjacent to the harbour, speculating about the unusual activity.

Matt knew their presence would draw attention which was why securing the scene quickly was vital, even if it meant a disruption to the normally tranquil port. There would be time later to provide an official statement and ease any concerns from Newlyn's tight-knit population. For now, diligent action took priority.

'I want you to check that the whole area is secured,' Lauren said, issuing commands to two uniformed officers who were on the scene. 'I don't want any rubber-necking locals getting close.'

'Understood, ma'am,' the younger of the two officers replied before heading off to do as instructed.

Lauren turned to her team. 'We'll board the boat together. How many crew usually operate a trawler of this size?'

'Typically, around five,' Clem said, his eyes on the boat. 'I can't be certain with this one, but five's the norm.'

'Have a van ready just in case,' Lauren told another of the uniformed officers who was standing close by. 'We may need to detain the crew for questioning.'

The officer hurried off to arrange transportation.

The familiar churn of nerves and excitement pitted in Matt's stomach as they made their way to the trawler. Were they about to close the case and find all the evidence they needed to charge Trembath?

Their shoes clanked loudly on the metal gangway as they approached and George Bray, the man they'd spoken with before, who was standing on the deck, looked up at them, his forehead creased in confusion and worry.

'Good evening, George,' Lauren began, friendly but firm. 'We're here to search the boat. We'd appreciate your cooperation.'

Bray frowned, his shoulders tensing. 'You'll have to ask the skipper. He's not here right now, but he shouldn't be long. He went out on an errand a while ago.'

An errand? Matt studied the man's face closely, searching for any signs of deception. But his bewildered expression seemed genuine enough for the moment.

'We've already spoken with your skipper,' Lauren said, waving a hand dismissively. 'He won't be coming back for now.'

'Oh. Well I suppose it's okay then.' Bray shrugged. 'What's this about?'

'Illegal activities happening on this boat,' Matt clarified, watching the man's reaction closely.

Bray held up his hands defensively. 'Hey, that's got nothing to do with us crew.'

'We'll determine that,' Lauren asserted.

Matt noticed two more crew members approaching.

'It's the police!' Bray called out.

Lauren stepped forward with authority, cutting through the rising murmurs of the crew, 'Yes, and we'll be questioning all of you. So don't try leaving.' She turned back to Bray. 'First things first, how many of you work on the boat?'

'There's five of us, including the skipper,' Bray said.

'Okay, so where's the missing one?' Lauren asked, scanning the area.

'Below deck, checking the engine's okay for us to leave... but... I guess we won't be doing that tonight, will we?' He glanced at Lauren and then Matt.

'No, you won't,' Matt confirmed.

Lauren turned to the team. 'Tamsin and Billy, you interview the duo over there. Clem and Jenna, go below deck and find the other crew member. Matt, stay with me. We'll speak to George.'

'Yes, ma'am,' the others said.

Lauren turned back to the man. 'When we were last here, your skipper said you were his second-in-command. Is that correct?'

Bray shifted, looking cornered. 'Yeah, I take care of things when he's not around. Why?'

'We know your skipper's been dealing drugs,' Lauren said bluntly. 'We believe he's been bringing supplies aboard when you're out at sea. Do you have anything to share about that?'

The boat creaked under their feet, the salty air accentuating Lauren's words.

Bray exhaled anxiously. 'Look... we were aware of what he was doing. But it was his operation, not ours. We weren't involved, I swear.'

'So you can confirm the supply is brought on board while you're at sea?' Lauren pressed.

'Yeah,' Bray admitted.

'Have you ever seen who he meets out there?' Matt asked intently, searching the man's face for deception. He seemed truthful, but fear often inspired lies.

'Never.' Bray shook his head. 'It's pitch black. I've only seen torch lights in the distance. No faces, nothing. We all kept well away when anything was going down.'

So they all ignored it. Did that make them innocent? If they knew what was happening, morally shouldn't they have done something about it?

'Are the rest of the crew aware of these night-time *meetings*?' Lauren pressed.

'Yeah, they knew,' Bray admitted, his eyes lowered, avoiding Lauren's unwavering stare. 'But we had a sort of... unspoken agreement: don't ask, don't tell. We all need our jobs. If one skipper blacklists you, word spreads like wildfire. It could end your future in the industry. That's why everyone kept their heads down and did their job.'

Bray's words hung in the air. They were an answer to the question that had been on Matt's mind.

'Please show us around the boat. I want to see where the drugs came aboard,' Lauren requested.

'Okay. If that's what you want,' Bray said, in a reluctant tone.

Their footsteps echoed loudly on the creaking deck. In the distance, seagulls called out, contrasting the beautiful surroundings with the sinister dealings that had occurred there.

Bray led them to a rusty hatch at the stern. 'Most of the exchanges happened here.'

Lauren inspected the hatch, frowning. 'Not an obvious spot unless you know where to look.'

'It's a classic smuggling tactic,' Matt commented. 'Cornwall's coast has a long history of such hidden compartments from its rum-running days.'

'How do you know this?' Lauren asked, quirking an eyebrow.

'I find historical smuggling fascinating,' Matt admitted sheepishly.

'I want you to go through exactly what happened during a drop,' Lauren told Bray, turning back to face him.

'It was always the same,' Bray explained. 'Just before midnight, the skipper would signal with his torch. Another light flashed back from a smaller boat coming alongside. The skipper would open the hatch, and they quickly traded packages. It was over in minutes.'

'You claimed to have kept your distance, yet you've now described it precisely. Why's that? Are you sure you weren't involved?' Lauren's tone was stern.

Bray held up his hands. 'Look, this has been going on for a while. At first I watched from afar, without the skipper knowing. I was curious. That's all. I swear I wasn't part of it.'

'What did the skipper do with the drugs after the exchange?'

'He has his hiding places.'

'Do you know where they are?'

'Yes. I'll show you.'

They continued walking around the boat and Bray revealed a few potential stash locations, but they were all empty.

Climbing above deck, Lauren turned to Matt. 'Do you think they used any markers for the rendezvous point?'

Matt shrugged. 'Possibly a buoy. But that's not my area of expertise.'

She turned to Bray. 'Do you know?'

'Your officer's right. There's a buoy out there.' Bray shifted impatiently. 'Are we done? Can I go?'

'Not yet,' Lauren said sharply. 'Tell me more about Sophie Yates.'

Bray's face clouded. 'We were close. I've already told you that. What else do you want to know?'

'Did she know what Trembath was up to?'

Bray hesitated. 'No... Not really.'

'What does that mean?' Lauren asked.

'She was only on the boat a couple of times when there was a drop-off. One of the times she asked me about it and I brushed her off. Said it was nothing.'

'Did she push to know more?' Matt asked.

'Not to me. I don't think she asked the others, either. She wasn't very close to them.' His brow furrowed with concern. 'You can't believe her death is connected to all this?' Bray wrung his hands anxiously. 'Surely there's no way...' His eyes begged her to reconsider.

'I'm afraid the evidence is suggesting a possible link,' Matt said.

He watched as Lauren scrolled through her phone, likely looking for a particular photo. After a moment she apparently found what she was searching for.

'Have you ever seen this woman?' Lauren asked Bray, tilting the screen to show him an image. 'Courtney Inwood. Does she look familiar?'

Bray leant in, a deep crease forming between his brows as he studied the image intently. 'Can't say I recognise her,' he murmured. Bray's jaw tightened, and he was avoiding eye contact. What wasn't he telling them?

'It's vital that you're honest with us,' Matt urged. 'This woman's also dead. There's a possible link with Sophie's death.'

Bray paled. 'You think the skipper...?'

'We're exploring all connections,' Lauren said.

Bray stared out at the shimmering water. 'Times are hard. There aren't loads of jobs like there used to be. Maybe we ignored it when we shouldn't have. But murder...' He shook his head adamantly. 'I can't see it. Not the skipper.'

'That's what we've got to find out,' Lauren said, her voice stern but not accusing. 'But if he is involved, then it's in your best interest to assist us in our enquiries.'

'Am I going to be arrested?'

'No. Not at present,' Matt said. 'But, as DI Pengelly said, your cooperation is essential. Without concrete evidence, it's hard to rule anyone out as a suspect.'

'I'm telling you, me and the rest of the lads had nothing to do with any of this drugs business. We just worked on the boat.' Bray threw up his hands in frustration. 'How many times do I need to say it before you'll believe me?'

'I hear what you're saying,' Lauren said. 'But for now we're taking you all to the station where we can have more in-depth conversations.'

The next morning, the team assembled at the station to debrief on the investigation's latest developments and plan their next moves.

'I appreciate you all coming in today,' Lauren began, rubbing her eyes. Was the strain of their recent workload getting to her? The fluorescent lights hummed above as all the team looked in her direction. 'We need this case as tight as a drum. Jack Trembath has requested a solicitor, and I've been told that one will be with us in an hour. I've already got the search warrant for his house. Matt, we'll get over there straight away.'

Matt took in the facial expressions around the room. Everyone seemed happy to be there, which was good. It was refreshing to see. The team was as gelled as it ever had been in the six months since he'd joined.

'Shall we take anyone else with us?' Matt asked.

'That's not a bad idea. It would ensure we get the job done faster, in case the solicitor decides to show up ahead of schedule, though I highly doubt it. You know what they're like. Clem, Jenna, Billy – you're with Matt and I to search Trembath's house. We need to move quickly before his solicitor arrives and possibly complicates things. Our priority is finding any evidence linking Trembath to the drug smuggling and/or the murders. Tamsin, while we're at the house, I need you focused on digging deeper into Trembath's history and finances. We're building the case from every angle. Look for connections between Trembath, Yates, and our victims. Also, any link with Mary Kerr or Samuel Finch. Oh, and don't forget the crew. Speaking of which, do we have statements from all of them?'

'Yes, ma'am. They were taken last night and they've all been allowed home, but know they mustn't leave the area,' Clem replied, flipping open his notebook. 'According to the statements, apart from Bray, none of the crew admitted to direct knowledge of Trembath's operation, though several mentioned suspicious activity that in hindsight was indicative of his illegal dealings. Most telling was that no crew member was willing to implicate another, suggesting a code of loyalty despite their misgivings.'

As Clem finished, Matt caught sight of the determination on everyone's faces. The team was fully invested in bringing down Trembath.

'My guess is they were too scared to speak. But that's not good. We'll need to evaluate whether to press charges against them. However, if they're willing to testify against Trembath, that could work in their favour,' Lauren said. 'Right, let's get going.'

The team stood, energised by their purpose. It was time to uncover the next piece of the puzzle at Trembath's home.

The cottage Trembath lived in was on the edge of Newlyn. It was a detached double-fronted building that looked at least several hundred years old and had ivy creeping up the wall. A barn stood to the side of it.

As they approached the entrance, the sound of the team's footsteps echoed on the gravel. Lauren gave a firm rap on the door and eventually it creaked open, revealing a petite woman who didn't look at all well. She was barely five feet tall and her complexion had a pale, almost yellow hue. Wrapped around her head was a scarf, which Matt assumed was because she was going through cancer treatment and had lost her hair.

Straightening her posture, Lauren showed the woman her ID. 'Good morning, Mrs Trembath. I'm DI Pengelly and this is DS Price.'

'Is it about Jack? I haven't heard from him all night, and he usually texts to make sure I'm okay. Has something happened?'

Lauren sighed, compassion glinting in her eyes. 'I'm truly sorry to inform you, Mrs Trembath, but your husband is currently being held at Penzance police station.'

The woman's grasp tightened around the door frame, her knees threatening to buckle. Reacting swiftly, Matt extended an arm. 'Take a moment, ma'am,' he encouraged.

'Why?' the woman asked, her eyes glassy with tears.

'May we come inside?' Lauren asked. 'It's best we discuss this somewhere comfortable. Also, we do have a search warrant, which we'll be executing shortly. Do you have any family or perhaps a friend nearby who you can spend some time with?'

'No close ones,' Mrs Trembath murmured, stepping to one side.

'Mrs Trembath, let me walk you back into the house,' Matt offered, holding out his hand and resting it under her elbow.

'Thank you. We can sit in the kitchen? I was about to make some breakfast when you knocked.'

'Of course,' Lauren agreed.

They stepped into the cosy hallway and walked alongside her as she shuffled towards the back of the cottage and into the kitchen.

'Take a seat, and please call me Beryl,' the woman offered, pulling out a chair and sitting herself.

Lauren and Matt followed suit.

'Beryl, I must inform you that we've arrested your husband on suspicion of being connected to two recent deaths.'

Beryl's eyes widened. 'Deaths? I thought you were going to say it's the drugs...'

Lauren's eyebrow quirked. 'You were aware of what he was doing?'

'I found out by accident when I went into the barn one day looking for a screwdriver so I could change the battery of my bathroom scales. I found Jack in there, with it all laid out on the bench.'

'Did you realise what he was doing straight away, or did he tell you?' Matt asked.

'Yes, I did. He was filling tiny plastic pouches with white powder. I know I'm not very worldly but even I knew what it was.'

'What did he say when he saw you standing there?' Matt asked.

'He told me to go away and forget everything I'd seen. Then if he ever got caught I could plead ignorance and not be charged as an accomplice.'

'Did you try to persuade him to stop?' Matt asked.

'No. Once Jack makes his mind up to do something, there's nothing I can do to change his mind. I learnt that years ago.' She gave a resigned smile.

'Did you ask him why he was doing it?' Matt asked.

'I tried but he refused to talk about it.'

'Did you tell anyone what you'd seen?' Lauren asked.

A tear slid down Beryl's cheek. 'Who could I tell? My kids? They'd never forgive him. The police? And risk losing him? I had no choice but to keep it to myself.' A puzzled expression crossed her face. 'But now you're telling me he's suspected of murder. What did he do?'

'We've yet to find out the exact details,' Lauren replied. 'For now, we'd appreciate it if you could show us where he packaged the drugs. Meanwhile, the rest of my team will conduct a thorough search of your house.'

'Please don't let them leave it in a mess. You hear all these things about houses being totally upended,' the woman said, panic in her eyes.

'They won't. My team are very good,' Lauren reassured her.

'Okay,' Beryl said, drawing in a shaky breath.

Lauren turned to Matt, her expression a mix of concern and determination. 'Brief the team about our next steps while I go with Beryl to the barn. I'll meet you in there.' She then addressed the woman. 'Can we get to the barn via the back door?'

'Yes. I'll take you.'

Matt made his way back to the front of the house, where the others were waiting, an air of expectation settled around them.

'Okay,' he began, clearing his throat. 'We've had a chat with Mrs Trembath and the barn is our primary target as it appears that's where her husband conducted all of his drug-related activities. The DI and I will inspect it, while the rest of you can search the house. But, and I cannot stress this enough –' He paused for emphasis. '– please be respectful of her possessions. Mrs Trembath isn't well, and she's here alone so she can't tidy up after us. We have to be as non-invasive as possible, while at the same time being thorough.'

'Understood, Sarge. We'll handle it. You won't even know we've been there,' Billy said. Clem and Jenna also agreed.

Watching them head towards the cottage and go in through the front door, Matt felt a pang of sympathy for Beryl Trembath. Even if the house appeared untouched, she'd still know that all of her possessions had been scrutinised by strangers.

He headed to the old barn, which looked like it had seen better days.

Inside, the weak sunlight filtered through the gaps in the wood, causing shadows to land on Beryl, who was perched on an old stool, her posture weary, while the DI searched the other side of the barn.

Matt approached the woman. 'Mrs Trembath. Beryl. Are you sure there isn't someone we can call to be with you? Given your condition...'

The woman raised a hand, her lips turning up into a slight smile. 'I do have a friend. But she's not close by. She's upcountry in Bath. I can give her a call. I'd rather not involve the kids just yet. They've got enough on their plates with their own families. I don't want to worry them if this all turns out to be a mistake.'

Matt shook his head. He didn't know how to answer the woman without causing her even more anguish.

'Beryl, is this the spot where your husband packaged the drugs?' Lauren called out from the workbench, which was cluttered with tools, packets, and miscellaneous items.

Beryl nodded, her face pale. 'Yes. That's the place. Although I only saw him there the one time. I assume that's where he always did it. I hated knowing what he was up to. Every time he came in here I worried about him being caught.'

The subtle play of shadows charged the barn with a theatrical atmosphere as Matt walked over to the other side to begin searching. He picked up a wooden box and peered inside. 'I've found some fishing line, ma'am,' he called out. 'I'll bag it.' He pulled out an evidence bag and dropped it inside. They'd send it to forensics to see if it was a match for the line wrapped around the girls' necks.

'He's always been a fisherman at heart, both professionally

on the trawler and during any time off,' Beryl said, sighing softly.

Matt continued his search. As he lifted another box and spotted a small brown bottle, his pulse quickened. Its nondescript label didn't reveal much, but his instinct said otherwise. This could be the break they needed. 'Ma'am, I reckon this might be the ketamine?' he said, holding it up.

'Bag it. We'll have it tested. Have a look at this.'

Matt hurried over and stared at an open folder in Lauren's hand which revealed two typed versions of 'The Three Fishers', both with a line cut out. The line that was placed in the victims' mouths.

'We've got him,' Matt muttered, quietly not wanting Beryl Trembath to hear.

Lauren walked over to the woman. 'These printed pages. Do you recognise them?'

'Yes,' she replied, softly.

'Did Jack print them?' Lauren continued.

'No. He's hopeless with computers. I downloaded the poem onto my laptop and printed two copies for him a while back.'

'Did he tell you why he wanted them?'

'He said he liked the poem and he was going to get one of them framed and put up on the wall. It's like a fisherman's lament.'

'But he didn't do that?'

'Honestly, I forgot all about it,' Beryl said, shaking her head. 'Is it important?'

'All I can tell you is this poem has links to the crime scenes,' Lauren said, keeping a fixed look on Matt. 'It's best if we don't delve into details right now. Since your home, including the barn, is now officially part of our investigation, I'm sorry, but you won't be able to stay here. You mentioned your friend—'

'Yes, she's in Bath.' Beryl's voice wavered.

'Right. Pack a bag and we'll arrange for someone to take you there. Why don't you give her a quick call and let her know you're on your way?' Lauren suggested.

'What if she's not there?'

'Let's give her a call first, and if she's not there we'll make other arrangements.'

Beryl pulled out her phone from her pocket and after pressing a few keys she was connected. 'It's me. Can I come and stay for a few days? I'm not allowed at home because the police are here. I'll tell you later.' She ended the call and looked at Lauren. 'Yes, that's fine...'

'Good. But we'd rather you didn't actually tell her about the investigation because at the moment it's in very early stages.'

'What about Jack? Is he going to be allowed home?'

'Not at the moment; he's in custody. But here's my card. If you want any information, give me a ring and I'll let you know what's happening. Matt, will you please escort Beryl back into the house so she can collect her belongings, and I'll stay here to double-check if there's anything else we want to take.'

'What about my laptop? You don't want that, do you?' Panic shone from Beryl's eyes.

'For now, it's not necessary,' Lauren said. 'From what you've told us, it's exclusively for your use, right?'

'Yes, just for my personal activities. It's my lifeline,' Beryl confirmed, clearly relieved.

'You can keep it with you for now, in that case,' Lauren agreed. 'I suggest that you only pack what you need for a short stay. If that changes, someone can return here to collect more of your things.'

While waiting for Beryl to pack, Matt went over their discoveries in his mind. In particular, the small bottle, the contents of which could seal Trembath's fate if tests matched it to what was found in the victims' bloodstreams.

THIRTY-ONE

'Okay, team,' Lauren said, walking into the office half an hour after they'd returned from searching Trembath's house. 'I've spoken to the DCI and a decision has been made regarding the crew. They won't be charged with aiding and abetting, but they will be required to testify against Trembath regarding what they saw during the times he met the boat out at sea and picked up the drugs.'

'That means they can get off scot-free,' Billy said.

'We don't believe they had anything to do with it,' Matt said. 'It was likely they ignored it because they didn't want to lose their jobs, and it's more important that we stop the import of drugs from this end.'

'Exactly,' Lauren said. 'Someone needs to contact the crew immediately to inform them of the decision. They also need to be told that they can't leave the area without first contacting us for permission.'

'Leave that to me,' Clem said.

'What about Trembath's drug supplier?' Jenna asked.

'When we question him, we'll push him to give up his supplier in exchange for leniency on the drug charges,' Matt said. 'But securing a conviction for the murders is our top priority here.' The phone rang on his desk and he answered. 'Price.'

'Trembath's solicitor's here, Matt,' the desk sergeant said.

'Thanks, mate.' He replaced the handset and looked over at Lauren. 'The solicitor's here.'

'Give me a second. I'll collect my folder,' Lauren said, turning and heading towards her office.

Matt looked back at the team. 'Any other questions before the interview?'

'No,' the rest of the team answered, in unison.

'Okay, we'll catch up with you later.'

He walked over to Lauren's office to collect her and they hurried to the interview room. On entering, they were met with Trembath's palpable defiance. His eyes were cold, his posture challenging. The solicitor, sharp-suited and with an unreadable expression, sat close by, maintaining a professional distance.

Ignoring the suspect, Matt pressed the recording on the equipment. 'Interview on Saturday, June 15, those present: DI Pengelly, DS Price...' He glanced at the other two and indicated for them to speak.

'Dudley Morton, solicitor.'

'Jack Trembath,' the suspect said, tersely.

'Right, Mr Trembath, you've been charged with the murder of Sophie Yates and Courtney Inwood, and also for importing drugs. Let's start with the murder of Sophie Yates. She lost her life because she'd found out about your drug operation, is that correct?' Lauren asked.

'No comment,' Trembath replied.

'She discovered that her brother had started using again and found out that you were his supplier, right?' Lauren continued, appearing undeterred.

'No comment,' Trembath answered, once again being predictably obstinate.

Matt took a sideways glance at Lauren. She was a picture of determination and poise. If Trembath thought he was going to get the better of her, then he had another thing coming.

'How did you discover that Sophie was on to you?'

'No comment,' the man repeated.

'Look, Mr Trembath, you're not doing yourself any favours. We know what you've done. We have evidence from your home. We know you prepared the drugs in the barn and we have the testimony from your wife—'

'Leave my wife out of this.' His eyes flared with what appeared to be a mix of anger and fear.

'I'm afraid we can't do that. Your wife told us that she'd seen you preparing the drugs in your barn, and we have evidence of that. Forensics are there at the moment and you can bet your bottom dollar there will be signs, however hard you tried to clean up after yourself.'

'You don't understand. I didn't have a choice.'

'Are you admitting to dealing drugs?'

'The business was tanking, debts piling up,' Trembath said, his voice strained. 'And my wife's growing sicker each day. I can't lose her. That's why we're trying every treatment we can. Look, I got in with the wrong people out of sheer desperation. Not a day goes by when I don't regret it.'

'Did any member of the crew help?'

'No. They were nothing to do with it.'

'Who sold you the drugs?'

'No way will I tell you that. I wouldn't put my family at risk.'

'We can offer you all protection, Jack, if you cooperate. Give us a name, and we'll ensure the safety of you and your family,' Matt said.

Trembath laughed bitterly. 'You think witness protection is going to save us from these monsters? They have connections everywhere. They're shadows in the dark, always watching.'

'Every second you waste, every moment of defiance, puts more people in danger, Jack. Including your wife. Help us stop it. Tell us who's behind this,' Lauren said, her patience seeming to wear thin.

Trembath's shoulder slumped. 'I can't. I just can't.'

'Okay. Let's return to Sophie,' Lauren began, the flicker of determination in her eyes noticeable. 'We found in your barn what we believe to be ketamine, plus copies of the poems that you used to put those words into her mouth.' She opened the folder revealing damning photos of the evidence and slid the copies over to him.

Trembath's face drained of colour. His fingers drummed nervously on the table. 'My wife knew nothing about this,' he said, desperately.

Matt observed Trembath closely, taking in the subtle changes in his posture, the way his eyes darted around the room, settling briefly on his solicitor. His fear was evident. But that didn't change that the man had ruthlessly taken two innocent lives out of greed and self-interest.

'She knew about the drugs and could possibly be charged as an accessory—' Lauren continued.

Trembath's face contorted with a mix of anger and concern. 'You leave my wife out of it!'

Lauren didn't answer immediately, seeming to consider her next words. 'In that case, I suggest you start telling us the truth.'

Trembath glanced at his solicitor. Was he searching for guidance or perhaps an escape? The solicitor's almost imperceptible shake of the head indicated they were in deep waters.

'Fine.' Trembath's voice broke, giving Matt a glimpse of the man beneath the hardened exterior. 'I'll tell you what you want to know, providing my wife is left alone. She's nothing to do with it. She might've suspected, but that's all. Don't charge her. *Please* don't charge her.'

The room was silent. Matt heard the distant murmur of the

station outside the door, but it felt worlds away. He took a deep breath, preparing for what was to come.

'Okay, let's talk about Sophie,' Lauren said, her tone no longer placatory. 'Do you admit to her murder?'

Trembath seemed to falter. 'I didn't want to. I had no choice. She found out about the drugs, and she threatened to tell the police.'

Matt could sense the escalation, the strain in the room building to an unbearable pitch.

'What did you do?' Lauren probed.

'I asked her to meet me so we could discuss it,' Trembath admitted. 'I told her I needed the money for my wife's treatment. She knew about my wife, and I thought that would persuade her to talk to me.'

Lauren, ever the professional, remained impassive. 'But your intention all the time was to kill her.'

He nodded, defeated. 'Yes. I had no choice.'

Matt shifted uncomfortably as Trembath continued. Each word, each confession, was another brick in the wall of the case they'd been building.

'There's always a choice,' Lauren said, her tone icy. 'When you met, you'd already drugged her fish and chips.'

Trembath looked up, appearing surprised at Lauren's mention of the food.

'Yes, how did you know?' Trembath whispered, looking cornered.

'We know that was the last meal she ate,' Lauren replied with certainty. 'You drugged it with the ketamine.'

'Yes, we agreed to meet, had something to eat and then once she was out of it, I took her to a boatshed I own. I then strangled her. Knowing the tide times, I placed her body on the rocks with that piece of poem in her mouth. I wanted to make it look as if she was killed for being a female fisherman.'

Matt's jaw clenched. The sheer audacity, the cold-blooded

nature of the act, made his blood boil. He had to remind himself to stay professional, but deep down, he hoped Trembath would face the full force of the law.

'Why not just kill her and dump the body at sea?' Lauren asked.

'To make sure the focus wasn't on me. I figured you'd question me because she worked on the boat, but I also knew that Mary Kerr had been terrorising Tanya Chenoweth and that gave me the idea.'

'How did you know what Mary was doing?'

'Mary and I go way back. I knew Reg well. She told me one night over a beer.'

'Hang on a minute,' Matt said, interjecting. 'Mary's your friend yet you decided to frame her for murder?' Matt's eyes bored into Trembath, looking for any glimpse of remorse.

The sterile environment of the interview room was lit by a single overhead light, casting shadows amplifying the tension.

'I had no choice,' Trembath said.

'Yeah... So you keep saying,' Matt snapped.

'To confirm,' Lauren asked, her tone calm but relentless, 'before you'd even met Sophie that evening, you'd already decided to kill her?'

Trembath's eyes darted around, avoiding contact. 'You don't understand. Beryl's life depended on it.'

Matt frowned. 'That's not an excuse,' he said. 'What about Courtney Inwood?'

Trembath gave a defeated sigh. 'I wanted you to think that Mary was the murderer because of her hatred of females in the industry, so I had to find another woman to kill. I knew Courtney from the market. As a ploy, I contacted her to see if she'd be interested in setting up a business together and she could sell the fish I caught. We went out for fish and chips, and I did the same again. Look, I'm not proud of what I did, but I was desperate. I needed the money. I had to do something. The business was failing, my wife's dying, there's been some new treatments available in America that I wanted her to have which we don't have over here. I'm not a murderer like others you read about in the papers.'

Matt stared directly at Trembath. 'Well, actually, yes, you are. You murdered two women in cold blood. Desperation doesn't change that. Try to make amends and help yourself at the same time. Tell us who supplied the drugs.'

'I can't!' Trembath said, panicking. 'They'll hurt my family.'

'Sophie had a family. So did Courtney. Think about their pain,' Lauren said, her voice softer, but the words hard-hitting nonetheless.

Trembath looked defeated. 'I'm sorry, but I'll never reveal my supplier.'

'Maybe your crew will,' Matt countered.

He shook his head vehemently. 'They know nothing. No one else does.'

'Okay, we're done for now. We'll pick this up later,' Lauren said.

Matt ended the recording and then called for two officers to collect Trembath. After handcuffing the man, they escorted him out of the interview room with the solicitor following.

Matt exhaled slowly, massaging his temples. 'This is a messy one.'

Lauren closed the file. 'Two lives, just for money. I can't fathom it.'

'The desperation of a dying loved one can drive people to unthinkable lengths,' Matt whispered, his thoughts drifting to his own family.

'But not to murder,' Lauren said. 'He's going to pay for what he's done. And we'll get to the bottom of the drug chain. We always do.'

Matt found solace in Lauren's conviction. They had a long road ahead, but together, they would ensure justice was served.

'What about Mary Kerr? Are we going to charge her?'

'She shouldn't have threatened us with a gun, but she's been through a lot. When it comes out in court that her supposed friend was planning to frame her for murder... well, that's going to hurt a lot. I'll suggest to the DCI that we let her off with a warning, and take away her gun.'

'Good decision, ma'am. Good decision.'

THIRTY-TWO

The gentle hum of conversation surrounded Lauren as she entered the pub, the familiar warmth wrapping around her like a well-worn coat. The weight of the day's events pressed heavily on her, and for a moment, she wished for the comforting solitude of her office.

'Ma'am, over here!' Billy's voice pierced her thoughts, a buoyant note in his tone.

Glancing towards the sound, she spotted her team huddled together at their regular table, their post-case haven. She had meant to arrive with them, but the DCI had required a last-minute debrief. She felt a pang of regret at that – she now knew that being part of these informal gatherings was essential for team camaraderie.

'Alright, everyone? I hope nobody started any wild celebrations without me?' Lauren quipped as she approached the table.

Billy raised his eyebrows, feigning innocence. 'Would we ever, ma'am? Though Clem did try to order a round of the most colourful cocktails on the menu.'

Clem rolled his eyes. 'You mean *you* did, Billy.'

'Okay, I admit it was me,' Billy said, laughing. 'I wanted to celebrate the end of our technicolour case.'

Jenna giggled. 'By that logic, we'd have been sipping on a mix of mud and murky seawater.'

'You always know how to paint a glamorous picture, Jenna.' Matt laughed.

Lauren shook her head in amusement. 'And here I was hoping for a glass of wine to toast the case's end.'

'Oh, don't you worry, ma'am. We've reserved the poshest bottle of wine this establishment has to offer,' Billy said with exaggerated grandeur. 'Which – between us – might be the house red, knowing what this place is like.'

'Are you saying our favourite pub doesn't stock fine wines from the sun-kissed vineyards of Italy? Next, you'll tell me they don't have caviar!' Clem said, feigning shock.

Jenna winked at Lauren. 'We've got peanuts, though. That's luxury enough, right?'

Matt chuckled. 'I'd toast with peanuts any day. Especially if it's to celebrate a job well done with such a fantastic team.'

'Well, looking at your empty glasses, I'd better get another round in. What does everyone want?' she asked.

As orders were rattled off, she felt a touch on her arm and turned to find Billy standing next to her. 'I'll come with you, ma'am,' he offered, smiling.

She had to force her jaw not to drop. Out of all the members of the team, Billy would have been the last one she'd have thought would offer to help. He'd always been the one to moan about her behind her back, or roll his eyes when he thought she wasn't looking. She was ninety-nine percent certain that it was him who had come up with her nickname of the Ice Queen. Not that she'd ever ask him. Some things were best left unsaid.

Lauren couldn't help but let her eyes flit towards Matt. He wore a knowing grin, evidently pleased with what was going on. She'd bet he was thinking that their recent conversations about team dynamics and how she should change her management style so it wasn't focused on micro-managing was now paying off.

Had Matt been right all along?

Was this gesture from Billy evidence of that shift?

She couldn't believe how much everything had changed in the six months since her sergeant had joined the team. She had to admit that being less fixated on managing them meant she was actually enjoying her job more. Because she wasn't forever getting annoyed when everything didn't go the exact way she intended.

None of this change meant that she intended to stay at Penzance. It was still a stepping stone, as far as she was concerned.

'Thanks, Billy,' she said, genuinely meaning it.

The two navigated the crowded pub, elbowing their way to the bar. The warm wood and soft lighting cast a gentle glow over the array of colourful bottles that lined the back.

While they were waiting to be served, Billy's posture shifted subtly, his broad shoulders leaning into the bar, closing the distance between them. 'What did the DCI say in your debrief?' he asked, quietly.

Usually Lauren would keep that to herself, but it wasn't as if they'd discussed anything the team couldn't know. 'He commended me on the team's performance,' she began, carefully choosing her words. 'Despite Trembath not giving up his contacts, what we've discovered has added to police intelligence on drug suppliers, who are suspected of operating out of France. But that won't concern us. There are other teams better equipped than us to take that forward and make any necessary arrests.'

Surprisingly, Billy frowned. 'That's a shame,' he mused, letting out a sigh.

'Were you hoping for more late nights and adrenaline

rushes? Wouldn't that play havoc with your social life? I'd have thought you'd welcome a return to the more routine caseload.'

He chuckled softly, rubbing the back of his neck in thought. 'You mean back to graffiti at the train station. How could I not prefer that to the cases we've been undertaking recently? You know... since Sarge joined, it's like we've been tossed into a whirlwind. Missing children, cold case murders, the chilling pursuit of a serial killer, and now drugs and murders combined. It's crazy, but also really exciting. Of course I don't want to be working twenty-four-seven; I value my free time too much. But you have to admit the job's been a lot more fun recently.'

Lauren couldn't agree more. She, too, loved the excitement of the chase. And having cases like they'd had to work on had improved the skillset of every member of her team. But she needed to manage the team's expectations. Yes, they'd been busy recently. But the odds of that continuing were miniscule.

'I get what you're saying, Billy, but we can't sustain working on cases like this. Not without the whole team burning out. Luckily we won't need to because this is Penzance. It's the bigger teams in the cities that are built for highly charged, complex cases. We don't have the person power, or the facilities. If you really want to work in that type of environment, you could consider putting in for a transfer?'

'You know I can't do that, ma'am... not now I'm seeing some-one,' he said, turning pink. 'But you can't deny that these cases have been good experience for the team?'

She slowly took in his words. 'You're right about that. It's done us all good.'

The bartender came over and she gave their order. Then, between them, they carried the drinks back to the table. After handing them out, Lauren slid into the seat next to Matt. She sat back for a moment, listening as the rest of the team were engrossed in their own conversations, which of course included jokes at one another's expense.

Taking a sip from her wine, she leant in closer to Matt, ensuring their conversation would remain private. 'I've been thinking about driving out to Bodmin tomorrow to have a word with the Frame brothers, as it's my day off. Hopefully they'll be around as it's a Sunday.'

'Okay, tell me what time and I'll go with you.'

She raised an eyebrow. 'You need some downtime, Matt. Spend it with Dani and your parents.'

'Meeting the Frame brothers isn't exactly risk free. Besides, it won't take the entire day. No way am I going to let you do this alone, *ma'am.*' He locked eyes with her, his expression determined.

She exhaled, knowing arguing with him would be futile. 'Okay. If you insist. But remember we're not going to be doing much. I just want to send them a clear message. Make sure they understand that I mean business.'

Matt took a slow drink, keeping eye contact with her the whole time. 'Whatever you decide, I'm with you. But the priority is keeping them away from your cousins. From what you've told me, those boys don't need any more trouble.'

'You can say that again.' A smile tugged at the corners of Lauren's lips, a reflection of her gratitude. 'I appreciate you coming with me, Matt. I'll pick you up in the morning, around ten, if that's okay?'

'Yes, that's fine.' He paused for a moment. 'I've had an idea. Why don't you bring the dogs? Let them spend some time with my parents and Dani. We've got a fenced garden for them to play in. Dani would love it.'

Lauren's brow furrowed in uncertainty. 'Are you sure it wouldn't be too much of an imposition?'

'Absolutely certain. It might stop Dani nagging me every day about it.'

Lauren laughed softly. 'Well, in that case, thank you. I'm sure the dogs would love it.'

Matt waited for a beat. 'And... maybe if you like, you could stay and have some lunch with us once we get back? If I'm not overstepping the mark by asking.'

As he extended the invitation, Lauren noticed the subtle tension in Matt's shoulders, the way he rubbed at the back of his neck – small signs of uncertainty about making himself vulnerable by asking her to his family home. 'Of course not, Matt. I'd love to join you. If you're sure your mum won't mind.'

'She'll love it, trust me.'

'Well, thanks for the invitation. I look forward to it.'

Lauren let her gaze drift around the pub briefly, taking in the familiar faces of their colleagues and then back to Matt. There was an unspoken understanding between them, a camaraderie that went beyond professional respect. She appreciated him – not just as her sergeant, but more and more as a friend. Yet, a small voice at the back of her mind prompted her to question the increasing closeness. She had to remind herself that their bond was platonic, and while it was good to have a friend, boundaries were still essential.

THIRTY-THREE

SUNDAY JUNE 16

The doorbell rang, just as Matt had started coming down the stairs. He glanced at his watch. Ten o'clock on the dot. It had to be Lauren.

He quickly made his way to the bottom, the patter of little feet along the hall signalling Dani hurrying to see who it was. She loved visitors.

Matt opened the door, revealing Lauren with her two energetic dogs, Ben and Tia, both of their tails wagging in sync. Dani's face instantly brightened, a wide grin replacing her earlier inquisitiveness.

'Hello, Lauren. Hello, Ben. Hello, Tia,' Dani said, excitedly, as she rushed forward and gave both dogs a hug.

Lauren chuckled, the sound echoing warmth. 'Good morning, Dani.'

'Move out the way and let Lauren in.' A teasing smile played on Matt's lips as he gestured towards the inside of the house. 'Why don't you take Tia and Ben to the kitchen? I think Grandma has some treats for them.' He looked down at the two dogs, who seemed very eager to explore.

Dani's eyes lit up, her sense of purpose clear. 'Okay. Come

on, Ben. Come on, Tia. Let's go and see Grandma.' She ran towards the kitchen, the dogs bounding after her.

'Are you sure about this? The dogs can be a handful if you're not used to them,' Lauren said, brushing off some imaginary dust from her jacket.

Matt shrugged and smiled. 'Don't worry about it. They'll be fine. This house is in a constant state of chaos, as you can imagine with a young child around. Plus, Dani adores them. Just give me a minute. I'll go and let everyone know that we're leaving.'

Lauren's attention momentarily drifted towards the kitchen where laughter erupted, no doubt courtesy of Dani's antics with the dogs.

'Thanks, Matt. I appreciate you coming with me.'

The scent of freshly chopped vegetables filled the air as Matt entered the kitchen. His mother was making preparations for their Sunday lunch. It had always been a staple when growing up and it was no different now.

He glanced at Ben and Tia, who had clearly made themselves comfortable. They sat by the back door, tails wagging, with crumbs on the floor, evidence of the treats they had just received. Dani, with an exaggerated seriousness only a child can master, was instructing them to 'stay' and 'sit', her little hand gesturing emphatically.

Matt smiled, watching the scene for a moment. 'I'm impressed with your dog training, Dani. I'll have to tell Lauren how good you are and that they listen to what you tell them.'

Dani beamed with pride. 'That's because I'm their best friend.'

His mum looked up from the chopping board, pushing a loose strand of hair behind her ear. 'Are you off now?'

'Yes,' Matt replied, moving closer to where she stood. 'I'm not sure what time we'll be back, but we'll definitely be here for lunch.'

'I was thinking around one-thirty. Does that work?'

'Yes, that's perfect. Thanks, Mum.'

'Are you both going on an adventure? Can I go with you?' Dani asked, leaving the dogs for a second and running over to Matt.

'Sorry, sweetheart, it's work,' Matt replied, ruffling her hair affectionately. 'And no, it's not much of an adventure. But don't worry, we'll be back before you know it.'

'Okay, Daddy. I'm going to play with Ben and Tia now.' She turned her back on him and returned her attention to the dogs.

He left the warm embrace of the kitchen, retracing his steps to the hallway where Lauren was waiting. She looked a tad sheepish. 'I was thinking that maybe I should have popped in to say hello to your parents? They'll think I'm bad mannered if I don't.'

'Don't worry, it was only Mum in there and she'll under-stand. She knows we must get going. You can speak to them when we return. Lunch is at one-thirty, which gives us a good three and a half hours to make our way to Bodmin, discuss things with the Frame brothers, and head back. Though, I doubt we'll need that much time.'

Lauren smiled, her confident posture returning. 'No we don't, you're right. I thought we'd try Bernie Frame first. He lives in the country between Bodmin and St Austell.'

The journey to Frame's house was scenic, with hedgerows and undulating fields giving way to the occasional large country house as they approached their destination. Lauren's car twisted and turned deftly through winding country lanes, ulti-mately leaving the road and heading up a private drive.

Matt sucked in a breath when the house came into view. It must have cost millions. A long gravel driveway snaked its way to the grand entrance that was flanked by meticulously manicured lawns on either side. Tall, ancient trees framed the property, which itself was built from grey stone and looked to date back several hundred years. It had towering chimneys and appeared to have been extended in several places. To the left was a triple garage next to which were some stables.

Lauren stopped close to the front entrance next to two Range Rovers.

'Here goes nothing,' Lauren said, her face tense.

'Don't worry, it will be fine,' Matt said, hoping to reassure her, even if he wasn't totally sure of that himself.

Before they could knock on the door, it was opened by a stern-looking woman, who looked to be in her early sixties. Her eyes were sharp with suspicion.

Without missing a beat, Lauren held out her warrant card, her demeanour firm yet non-confrontational. 'Good morning, I'm here to speak to Bernie Frame.'

'He's not here,' the woman replied curtly.

'We're not here to arrest him. We just want a conversation,' Lauren said, standing her ground. 'Bernie would benefit from talking to me now rather than facing other officers under less friendly circumstances later.'

The woman seemed to weigh Lauren's words, her stern facade softening a touch. 'Okay,' she finally conceded. With a curt nod, she retreated into the vastness of the house, closing the door slightly so they couldn't see inside.

'He's clearly here, then,' Matt said. 'Is that the standard response to anyone who comes to the door, or just because we're the police?'

'I was wondering that, too,' Lauren said.

After only a couple of minutes the door reopened to reveal Bernie Frame himself. He was a mountain of a man, broad-shouldered with a barrel chest. His balding head gleamed under the mid-morning sun, and his piercing blue eyes studied them intently. Despite the expensive clothes he was wearing, there was an undeniable coarseness about him.

'What's this about then?' he asked in a broad Cornish accent, his imposing figure filling the doorway.

His demeanour was that of a man who was used to throwing his weight around, both figuratively and literally. He leant slightly against the ornate doorframe, his intense stare fixed squarely on Lauren.

Lauren met his eyes, her posture erect and confident. 'Where's your brother?' she demanded.

Frame's eyes briefly flickered, giving away a momentary hint of surprise. 'Not here. He's likely at his own place.'

Lauren raised an eyebrow, taking a moment to glance at the sprawling mansion behind him before returning her attention to Frame. 'You'll do for now, then. We understand that you've been intimidating Connor and Clint Cave because they inadvertently disrupted an art heist you had planned.'

Frame smirked, crossing his beefy arms across his chest, a move that only emphasised his sheer size. 'I don't know what fairy tale you've heard, Officer, but you're barking up the wrong tree.'

'You might feign ignorance, Frame, but I'm here to make it crystal clear: steer clear of the Caves.' Lauren took a step closer, still remaining outside of his personal space yet close enough for him to realise that she was serious.

Matt was impressed.

Frame leant down slightly, bringing his face closer to hers, his expression mocking. 'Is that a threat, Detective? Should I be ringing my solicitor?'

Matt tensed, his muscles coiling tightly. His weight shifted forward ever so slightly, ready to spring into action at the first sign of real threat. Though he kept his posture casual, his eyes tracked Frame's every minute movement. Fingers flexing, Matt prepared to react, hoping it wouldn't come to that. Lauren could handle herself, but if this ox of a man so much as lifted a hand in her direction, Matt would put him in his place without a second thought.

But Lauren didn't even flinch. Instead she offered a tight-lipped smile. 'Consider it a friendly warning. We're watching.'

Frame laughed, though it lacked warmth. 'Or what? Say I did know these men, hypothetical-like. You've got nothing connecting me to them. Because if you had, you'd have done something about it.'

Lauren tilted her head slightly. 'There are many ways to apply pressure, Mr Frame. I have a rather extensive network, including some very diligent people at the tax office. Don't you agree that an in-depth audit of your accounts might be intriguing? And I'm not just talking about the finances of your construction company – which, by the way, I've heard serves as a perfect front for your other, less legitimate, ventures.'

Frame's sturdy exterior cracked for a brief second, his jaw clenching. 'Where are you getting this information?' he growled, barely concealing his rage.

Lauren shrugged nonchalantly. 'My sources aren't important. But my message is: stay away from the Caves. Are we on the same page?'

Frame's stare intensified, his lips drawing into a thin line. 'We'll see about that.'

'"We'll see" won't cut it,' Lauren said, coming across like she couldn't care less about his threat. 'Frame, I expect you to do as I say. And ensure your brother gets the message as well.' She took a deep breath. 'Speaking of family, I've heard your son is planning on applying to Oxford. That's really impressive. You must be very proud.'

Caught off guard, Frame's hardened facade faltered. 'What's that got to do with anything?'

'Oh, nothing specific,' Lauren said, her voice dripping with faux sweetness. 'I was thinking how detrimental it might be to his prospects if it came out that his studies are being funded *illegally*.' She did quote marks with her fingers. 'Universities do have their reputation to consider.'

Matt doubted that it would affect Frame's son's chances, but the man himself might not know that.

Frame's face contorted with rage. 'Fuck off,' he spat venomously, slamming the door with such force that the echo reverberated around them for a few seconds.

'I think he got the message,' Lauren said, turning to face Matt, a mixture of relief and trepidation plastered across her face.

Matt ran his fingers through his hair. 'He definitely did. But you know he might now think your cousins are police informants, which could complicate matters.'

The lines tightened around Lauren's eyes. 'You're right. But it had to be done this way. I had no choice.'

They started walking back towards the car, the gravel crunching beneath their feet. 'Frame might decide it's best to leave your cousins alone anyway. I think the tax thing really got to him. And the threat to his son, even though I doubt Oxford would care. But Frame wasn't to know that.'

'Exactly. I have to believe that my cousins are so inconsequential in the grand scheme of things for the Frames, that picking a fight with them, when considering today's conversation, might be seen as more trouble than it's worth.'

Matt took his time answering. 'I want to believe that too, Lauren. I really do. But the Frames are unpredictable, and that worries me.'

She gave him a half-smile. 'I know. But sometimes, you have to play the hand you're dealt. For now I think it's worked out in our favour. I'll contact my aunt and tell her that she doesn't need to pay anything to the Frames and that it's all sorted. I'll also make sure to stress that she's not to let on to the family that I was involved in any way. One thing I don't want is for my cousins to make an appearance in Penzance.'

'Looking on the brighter side,' Matt said as they reached the car, in an attempt to lighten the mood. 'Let's shift our focus to more pleasant things. Like our Sunday lunch. I bet you're going to love my mum's cooking. Everyone does. It never ceases to amaze me that I'm not twice the size I am.'

Lauren's face broke into a full smile. 'I could use a proper meal, for sure. And I can't even remember the last time it was a Sunday roast.' Her stomach rumbled and she giggled. 'As you can tell, I'm hungry. There was no time for breakfast this morning.'

'Well, trust me, you're in for a treat. Mum's Yorkshire puddings are legendary. They're fluffier than clouds.'

Lauren laughed. 'I'll hold you to that promise.'

A LETTER FROM THE AUTHOR

Dear reader,

Huge thanks for reading *Murder at Land's End*, I hope you enjoyed returning to Lauren and Matt's world once again for this new case. If you want to join other readers in hearing all about my new books, you can sign up here:

www.stormpublishing.co/sally-rigby

If you enjoyed the book and could spare a few moments to leave a review that would be hugely appreciated. Even a short review can make all the difference in encouraging a reader to discover my books for the first time. Thank you so much!

I enjoyed writing a book featuring female fishermen in Cornwall because I found the setting of a fishing village on the rugged Cornish coast atmospheric and evocative. Crafting a whodunnit involving females in a male-dominated industry allowed me to challenge stereotypes and create dynamic, empowered women characters

If you'd like to learn more about my writing, receive a free novella and exclusive bonus content, click here:

www.sallyrigby.com

Thanks again for being part of this amazing journey with

me and I hope you'll stay in touch – I have so many more stories and ideas to entertain you with!

Sally Rigby

facebook.com/Sally-Rigby-131414630527848
instagram.com/sally.rigby.author

THE THREE FISHERS

BY CHARLES KINGSLEY

Three fishers went sailing away to the West,
Away to the West as the sun went down;
Each thought on the woman who loved him the best,
And the children stood watching them out of the town;
For men must work, and women must weep,
And there's little to earn, and many to keep,
Though the harbour bar be moaning.

Three wives sat up in the lighthouse tower,
And they trimmed the lamps as the sun went down;
They looked at the squall, and they looked at the shower,
And the night-rack came rolling up ragged and brown.
But men must work, and women must weep,
Though storms be sudden, and waters deep,
And the harbour bar be moaning.

Three corpses lay out on the shining sands
In the morning gleam as the tide went down,
And the women are weeping and wringing their hands

For those who will never come home to the town;
For men must work, and women must weep,
And the sooner it's over, the sooner to sleep;
And good-bye to the bar and its moaning.

ACKNOWLEDGEMENTS

First and foremost, I want to thank my incredibly insightful editor at Storm, Kathryn Taussig, for her invaluable feedback and for pushing me to sharpen all aspects of the plot. I'm also grateful to the whole team at Storm, from editing, marketing and cover design, for their input.

A very special thanks goes out to my advance reader team who gave up their precious free time to provide such thoughtful notes on early drafts – your insights truly shaped and improved the story.

Thank you to my sister-in-law Jacqui and brother-in-law Peter for spending time with me at Land's End and Sennen Cove, working out the best places for bodies to turn up.

Thanks to my daughter Alicia who gave me the initial inspiration for this book.

Finally, thanks to the rest of my family, whose support is always gratefully received.

Printed in Great Britain
by Amazon